The Apothecary

G. P. PUTNAM'S SONS

An Imprint of Penguin Group (USA) Inc.

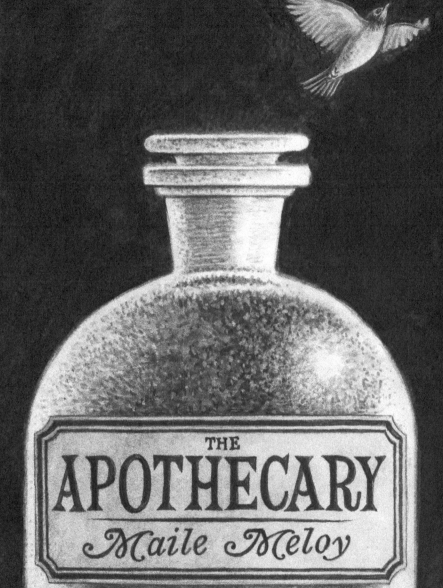

THE
APOTHECARY
Maile Meloy

with illustrations by
IAN SCHOENHERR

G. P. PUTNAM'S SONS
A division of Penguin Young Readers Group.

Published by The Penguin Group. Penguin Group (USA) Inc., 375 Hudson Street, New York, NY 10014, U.S.A. Penguin Group (Canada), 90 Eglinton Avenue East, Suite 700, Toronto, Ontario M4P 2Y3, Canada (a division of Pearson Penguin Canada Inc.). Penguin Books Ltd, 80 Strand, London WC2R 0RL, England. Penguin Ireland, 25 St. Stephen's Green, Dublin 2, Ireland (a division of Penguin Books Ltd.). Penguin Group (Australia), 250 Camberwell Road, Camberwell, Victoria 3124, Australia (a division of Pearson Australia Group Pty Ltd). Penguin Books India Pvt Ltd, 11 Community Centre, Panchsheel Park, New Delhi—110 017, India. Penguin Group (NZ), 67 Apollo Drive, Rosedale, Auckland 0632, New Zealand (a division of Pearson New Zealand Ltd). Penguin Books (South Africa) (Pty) Ltd, 24 Sturdee Avenue, Rosebank, Johannesburg 2196, South Africa. Penguin Books Ltd, Registered Offices: 80 Strand, London WC2R 0RL, England.

BERT THE TURTLE (THE DUCK AND COVER SONG)
By Leon Carr and Leo Corday
Copyright © 1979 by Music Sales Group and Songwriters Guild of America.
International Copyright Secured. All Rights Reserved. Used by Permission.

Published simultaneously in Canada. Printed in the United States of America.
Design by Ryan Thomann. Text set in Adobe Caslon.
The art was done in ink and acrylic paint on Strathmore Aquarius II paper.

Library of Congress Cataloging-in-Publication Data
Meloy, Maile. The Apothecary / Maile Meloy. p. cm. Summary: Follows a fourteen-year-old American girl whose life unexpectedly transforms when she moves to London in 1952 and gets swept up in a race to save the world from nuclear war. 1. Cold War—Juvenile fiction. [1. Cold War—Fiction. 2. Alchemy—Fiction. 3. Adventure and adventurers—Fiction. 4. London (England)—History—20th century—Fiction. 5. Great Britain—History—Elizabeth II, 1952—Fiction.] I. Title. PZ7.M516354Ap 2011 [Fic]—dc22 2010045003
ISBN 978-0-399-25627-1
5 7 9 10 8 6

For Franny

A note to the reader:

My memories of what happened to me in 1952, when I moved to London from Los Angeles with my parents and met Benjamin Burrows for the first time, aren't perfect, for reasons I'll explain in this book. I didn't "forget" those months the way I sometimes forget where I left my glasses, or what was happening in the novel I put down last week, or the name of the woman who sells oranges at the farmers' market. I lost what happened to me in the spring of 1952 in a much deeper, more profound way than that.

But I kept a diary that year, when I was fourteen and my life changed in such unforeseeable ways. The diary was taken from me, but later it was returned. When I read the entries, they were in my own handwriting, but they were as strange to me as if I had written them while asleep, about a dream that had vanished.

People describe their childhoods as magical, but mine—it really was. While I was complaining to my parents about having to leave Los Angeles, a chemist in China was narrowly escaping arrest, and a Hungarian physicist was perfecting the ability to freeze time. I was drawn, through Benjamin and his father, into the web of what they had created.

But if I tell you all this now, you won't believe me. I'll tell it in order, as I reconstructed the events after meeting Benjamin again. For a long time the memories seemed—however fantastic—to be important only to me personally. But lately it has seemed more and more urgent to tell this story now.

Jane Scott
LOS ANGELES, 2011

CHAPTER 1

Followed

I was seven and living in Los Angeles when Japan surrendered at the end of World War II, and my first vivid memories are of how happy and excited everyone was. My parents took me to a parade on Fairfax Avenue, where my father hoisted me onto his shoulders and sailors kissed girls in the streets. In school we made little paper flags to wave and learned that an evil force—*two* evil forces—had been defeated. We weren't going to have wars anymore.

Some of my parents' friends said it wasn't true that we had ended war for all time.

"People said that about the *last* war," they said, sitting on our back patio, surrounded by tall green hedges, drinking wine or lemonade, which is how I remember all of my parents' friends from that time: the women with their hair up in French twists, the men with their ties undone, on the back patio with a drink in hand. "And look where we are."

Others said that such terrible things had happened that the world would never be the same again. But my parents gave those friends hard looks when they knew I was listening.

My father said gasoline wasn't going to be rationed anymore, and we could drive to Kings Canyon, which I imagined was populated with kings, to see the giant trees. My second-grade teacher said we would get real butter again, not white oleomargarine with the yellow color capsule you could add to it. I didn't remember real butter, and I liked the white oleo on toast with sprinkled sugar (my mother never added the yellow coloring because she hated fakery of all kinds), but I did believe that life was going to be better. We would have real butter, whatever that was like, and I might get a baby sister out of the deal. I would name her Lulu. The war was over and the bad guys had lost. A golden era had begun.

For a while, it actually seemed true. I never got a baby sister, but I had the smartest, funniest parents I knew, and they had friends who were almost as smart and funny. They were a writing team, Marjorie and Davis Scott, and they had started in radio and worked together on television shows, first on *Fireside Theater*, then on *I Love Lucy*. They had story retreats in Santa Barbara, and the other writers' kids and I would run through the avocado fields, playing elaborate games of tag and kick-the-can. We would gather avocados that fell from the trees, and eat fat, green slices with salt right out of the shell. We swam in the ocean and played in the waves, and lay in the sand with the sun on our skin.

In my parents' front yard, there was an orange tree, with blossoms that made people on the street stop and look around to see what smelled so sweet. I used to pick myself an orange when I came home from school and eat it over the sink to catch the juice. In school we read a poem with the line "Bliss was it in that dawn to be alive, / But to be young was very heaven!" It was supposed to be about the French Revolution, but I thought it was about my life.

But that was before I started being followed.

First the whole world changed. Another war started in Korea, against the Chinese, who had been our allies in the last war. The Russians, who had also been our allies, had the atomic bomb and seemed inclined to use it against us. The Communist threat was supposed to be everywhere, though my parents thought it was exaggerated.

In school, at Hollywood High, we watched a safety film in which a cheerful cartoon turtle named Bert explained that when a nuclear bomb came, we should get under our desks and put our heads between our knees. It had a little song that went like this:

There was a turtle by the name of Bert
And Bert the turtle was very alert

When danger threatened him, he never got hurt
He knew just what to do!
He'd duck—and cover
Duck—and cover!
He did what we all must learn to do
You—and you—and you—and you—
Duck—and cover!

Our teacher, Miss Stevens, who had been born deep in the last century and wore her white hair coiled up like a ghost's pastry on the back of her head, would lead us in a bomb drill. "Here goes the flash," she'd say. "Everyone under the desks!" And under we'd go—as if our wooden school desks full of books and pencils were going to protect us from an atomic bomb.

The important thing, the films emphasized, was not to panic. So instead, everyone maintained a constant low-grade anxiety. I was only in the ninth grade and I might have managed to shrug off the worry, except that I'd started to think that someone was watching me.

At first, it was just a feeling. I'd get it walking home: that weird sensation that comes when someone's eyes are on you. It was February in Los Angeles, and it was brisk and cool but not cold. The tall palm trees by the school steps were as green as ever.

On the way home I practiced walking like Katharine Hepburn, striding along with my shoulders back. I wore trousers whenever I could, and my favorites were bright green sailor pants, with four big buttons and flared legs. They were worthy of Hepburn as the cuffs swished along. She was my favorite movie star, and I thought if I could walk like her, then I could feel and *be* like her, so sure and confident, tossing her head and snapping out a witty retort. But I didn't want anyone to see me practicing my Hepburn walk, so at first the sensation of being watched only made me embarrassed. When I looked over my shoulder and saw nothing but the ordinary traffic on Highland Avenue, I hugged my books, rounded my shoulders, and walked home like an ordinary fourteen-year-old girl.

Then there was a day when I had the watched feeling, and looked back and saw a black sedan cruising more slowly than the rest of the traffic. I could have sworn it was driving at exactly the speed I was walking. I sped up, thinking that Kate Hepburn wouldn't be afraid, and the car seemed to speed up, too. Panic rose in my chest. I turned down an alley, and the car didn't follow, so I hurried along the side of the buildings, past the trash cans. When I got onto Selma Avenue, which was quiet and tree-lined, there was a man outside a house pruning his roses, but no cars.

My heart was pounding and I made myself breathe slowly. I nodded to the man with the roses and kept walking down Selma. I told myself it was silly to be afraid: No one was following me. They had no reason to follow me. I tossed my hair, wishing it would move in one glossy, curvy mass, and then the black sedan came around the corner ahead and cruised slowly toward me. I felt a cold flush, as if ice water had been pumped through my veins.

I looked back to the rose man, but he had gone inside his house. I gripped my books to keep my hands from shaking, and I kept walking as the black car drove toward me, ridiculously slowly. As it passed, I kept my chin very high and slid a glance sideways. In the car were two men in dark suits. The one closest to me, in the passenger seat, had hair so short he looked like a soldier, and he was watching me. There were two dark, brimmed hats on the backseat. I didn't know any man who wore a hat.

I kept walking, and the black car stopped and idled at the curb. I turned on Vista, my own street, and when I thought I was out of sight, I ran for the house, fumbling for my key. My parents were at work and wouldn't be home yet. I dropped the key and picked it up off the sidewalk as the black sedan turned onto Vista, and then I got inside and slammed the door and slid the chain.

"Hello?" I called to the empty house, just in case. No one answered.

I dropped my books and ran to the back door, which led out to the patio, and I made sure the door was locked. Sometimes we were careless about that door because it led to the hedged-in garden, not to the street, but the bolt was thrown, so the house had been locked all day. I looked out the front window and saw the sedan parked by the curb at the end of the block, waiting. I closed the curtains and turned on the lights in the kitchen, my hands still shaking. The kitchen was the room where I felt safest, because it was where I sat every night with my parents, doing homework while they cooked, listening to them talk.

I told myself it was fine, it was probably in my mind. It was my imagination taking over. I made myself a peanut butter and honey sandwich and started doing my algebra homework. Each problem was like a puzzle, and it helped take my mind off the men who might or might not be sitting in their black car on the corner of our street, behind the curtains I was determined not to open.

At six o'clock, I was deep in a hunt for the value of x when I heard the door open and hit the end of the chain hard. My heart started to race again. I'd managed to pretend that the men weren't really after me, but here they were, breaking in.

"What *is* this?" a man's angry voice said.

Then I realized the voice was more annoyed than angry, and then I realized it was my father's. "Janie?" he called, more alarmed now than annoyed. "Are you here? What's going on?"

We walked that night to Musso and Frank's, which was my favorite restaurant, but it didn't feel like a treat. My parents tried to pretend everything was just fine, but we took back alleys, and they watched the corners at every street. My father walked so fast that my mother and I had to walk double-time just to keep up.

We took a booth, and I ordered the thin pancakes called flannel cakes for dinner. I wanted my parents to object and make me order chicken and vegetables—I wanted things to be normal—but they didn't even notice.

"So who *are* those men in the car?" I asked.

My mother sighed. "They're U.S. marshals," she said. "From Washington. The government."

That didn't make any sense. "What do they want?"

"We've been wanting to tell you, Janie," she said. She always got right to the point, but now she was dancing around whatever she was trying to say. "We have news, and we think it's good news. We're—well, we're thinking we'll all move to London."

I stared at her.

"It will be an adventure," she said.

I looked at my father. "What did you do?" I asked.

"Nothing!" he said, too loudly. A woman at another table looked at us.

"Davis," my mother said.

"But I *haven't* done anything! This is all so ridiculous!"

A waiter brought water glasses to the table, and my mother smiled up at him. When he was gone, she said, "I don't know if you remember Katie Lardner."

"Only from birthday parties," I said, slumped in the booth. I was being what my mother called *a real pill*, and I knew it, but I didn't want to move to London. I liked my friends, and I liked my school. I liked junior lifesaving at the beach, and trips to Santa Barbara, and oranges growing in the front yard. I liked everything except being followed by men from Washington for whatever my parents had done.

"The Lardners moved to Mexico," my mother said, "because her father became a target. It became impossible for him to work here."

"No," I said. "They moved because her father was a Communist." Then the floor of Musso and Frank's seemed to open beneath me. "Oh, *no*! Are you *Communists*?"

Both my parents glanced around to see if anyone was listening. Then my father leaned forward and spoke in a low voice that wouldn't carry.

"We believe in the Constitution, Janie," he said. "And we've been put on a list of people they're watching. That's why they're watching you, when it has nothing to do with you. And I will not have them following my *child*." He thumped the table, and his voice had started to rise again.

"Davis," my mother said.

"I won't, Marjorie," he said.

"I don't even understand what Communism *is*," I said.

My father sighed. "The idea," he said, in his low voice, "is that people should share resources, and own everything communally, so there aren't wildly rich people who have everything and desperately poor people who have nothing. That's the idea. It's just hard to get it to work. The trouble right now is that the U.S. government—or at least something called the House Committee on Un-American Activities—has gotten so paranoid about the *idea*, as if it's a contagious disease, that they're going after innocent people who may hold the idea, or have held it in the past. It isn't fair, or rational, or constitutional."

I was determined not to cry, and wiped my nose with my napkin. "Can I at least finish the semester here?"

He sighed. "Those men want to make us appear in court, under oath," he said. "We could answer for ourselves, but they would ask us to testify about our friends, and we can't do that. We've heard they'll confiscate passports soon so people can't leave the country. So we have to go right away."

"When?"

"This week."

"This *week*?"

My mother broke in. "There's someone we've worked with before," she said. "Olivia Wolff. She already moved to London, to produce a television show about Robin Hood. She wants us to work on it, which is—Janie, it's an amazing opportunity. It'll be like living in a Jane Austen novel."

"You mean I'll get married at the end?" I asked. "I'm fourteen."

"Janie."

"And Jane Austen was *from* there, she wasn't American. I'll be so out of place!"

"Janie, please," my mother said. "This is a great chance that Olivia's giving us. We don't have a choice."

"*I* don't have a choice. *You* had a choice, and you got on that list!"

"We didn't choose to be on the list," my father said.

"So how'd you get on it?"

"By believing in freedom of speech. By having faith in the First Amendment!"

The waiter came and slid our plates in front of us. "Flannel cakes for the little lady," he said.

I gave him a weak smile.

My father stared at my stack of pancakes, with the pat of real butter melting on top. "That's what you ordered for *dinner*?"

"She can have whatever she wants," my mother said.

I glared at my father in defiance, but when I took a forkful of my last thin, golden, delicious Musso and Frank's flannel cakes for a long time—maybe forever—they tasted like sawdust, and I made a face. My father couldn't resist the joke.

"You look like you're eating real flannel," he said, smiling. "Pajamas with syrup."

"Very funny," I said.

"Look, kiddo," he said. "If we can't laugh together, we're not going to make it through this thing."

I swallowed the sawdust. "Don't call me kiddo," I said.

CHAPTER 2

The Apothecary

It's safe to say I was not graceful about the move to London. I was no witty, patient, adaptable Jane Austen. And if I was anything like Katharine Hepburn, it was in the scenes where she's being a giant pest. I cried in the taxi all the way to the airport, past the churning oil rigs on La Cienega. I cried on the first airplane I'd ever been on, which should have been exciting, and *was* exciting—all those tiny buildings below—but I wasn't going to give my parents the satisfaction of knowing that I was enjoying it.

At Heathrow Airport in London, there was a framed picture of the brand-new Queen Elizabeth II on the wall.

"She's not that much older than you are," my mother said. "And she's been through a war, and her father's dead, and now she has to be queen, poor thing."

"See?" my father said. "Your life could be worse."

I looked at the picture of the young queen. We had escaped ahead of the U.S. marshals, locking up the house and packing only the things we could carry. My parents were going to be writing for the BBC under fake names—*fake names*, when my mother wouldn't even put yellow food coloring in margarine! We were living like criminals or spies. Although I was angry, standing there looking at the plucky young queen's portrait, I allowed myself to think that my mother was right, and it might be an adventure.

But February in London crushed those hopes. We took a taxi through streets that were still bomb-scarred and desolate, seven years after the war's end, to a tiny third-floor flat on St. George's Street in Primrose Hill. Across the street was a haberdasher—my father said he was like a tailor—standing outside his shop with his hands behind his back and a look on his face as if no one would ever come in.

Our new landlady, Mrs. Parrish, took off her apron and patted a wild cloud of hair to show us around. She said the gas water heater over the kitchen sink was broken, and we would have to heat pots of water on the stove.

The kitchen was along one side of the living room, no bigger than a closet, and could be closed away just like a closet. The rooms were freezing and the walls seemed damp. The brown wallpaper was water-stained near the ceiling.

We must have looked dismayed, because the distracted Mrs. Parrish suddenly focused on us. She was *not* going to let some spoiled Americans fail to appreciate their good fortune. "You're lucky to get the place, you know," she said.

"Of course," my mother said quickly. "We're very grateful."

"People are queuing up for a flat like this, with its own lavatory, and separate bedrooms, and a working telephone line. But the BBC asked to hold it, specially." It was clear that we did not deserve such a bounty, when her countrymen, who had lost so much, were still going without private bathrooms.

"We're very grateful," my mother repeated.

"Do you have your ration cards for the marketing?"

"Not yet," my mother said.

"You'll need those," the landlady said. "And you'll find that the butcher sells out first thing in the morning, ration cards or no." She lowered her voice. "I can sell you some eggs, if you like. They're hard to get, but I know someone with hens."

"That would be very nice."

Mrs. Parrish showed us where to put penny coins into the gas heater in the wall, to make it work. We didn't have any English pennies, but said we would get some.

"Mark you," she said, brushing dust from the heater off

her hands, "it doesn't do much. Apart from eat up pennies. You'll want your hot water bottles for the beds."

"We don't have hot water bottles," my mother said.

"Try the apothecary," the landlady said. "Around the corner, on Regent's Park. He'll have pennies, too."

And she left us alone.

My mother started investigating the closet kitchen, and my father and I put on every warm thing we had, which wasn't much, to go find the apothecary, which my father said was like a pharmacy. The sky over St. George's Street was gray, and the buildings were gray, and people wore gray. It sounds like a cliché, but it was true. Going from Los Angeles to London in 1952 was like leaving a Technicolor movie and walking into a black-and-white one.

Around the corner on Regent's Park Road, just as the landlady said, we came to a storefront with two bay windows full of glass bottles. A painted sign over one window said **APOTHECARY**, and one over the other window said **ESTABLISHED 1871**. My father pushed the paned glass door open and held it for me. The shop had a strange smell, musty and herbal and metallic all at once. Behind the counter was a wall of jars. A balding man on a wheeled ladder, halfway up the wall, pulled a jar down. He seemed not to have noticed us, but then he spoke. "I'll just be a moment," he said.

He carefully climbed down the ladder with the jar in one hand, set it on the counter, and looked up at us, ready for our needs. He had wire-rimmed glasses and the air of someone who didn't rush things, who paid close attention to each particular task before moving on to the next.

"We're looking for three hot water bottles," my father told him.

"Of course."

"And how about some chocolate bars?"

The apothecary shook his head. "We have them sometimes. Not often, since the war."

"Since the *war*?" my father said, and I could see him calculating: twelve years without a steady supply of chocolate. He looked a little faint. I wondered if he could get a prescription for chocolate from a doctor. Then I could have some, too.

"Come back again," the apothecary said, seeing his dismay. "We may have some soon."

"Okay," my father said. "We'd better get some aspirin, too." I could tell he was embarrassed by his undisguised need for candy, and he always made jokes when he was embarrassed. I could feel one coming. "And how about something for my daughter, to cure homesickness?"

"*Dad,*" I said.

The apothecary looked at me. "You're American?"

I nodded.

"And you've moved here to a cold flat with cold bedrooms that need hot water bottles?"

I nodded again, and the apothecary guided the ladder along the back wall on its metal wheels.

"I was joking," my father said.

"But you *are* homesick?" the apothecary asked, over his shoulder.

"Well—yes," I said.

He climbed the ladder and chose two jars, tucking one beneath his arm to climb down. At the counter, he unscrewed the lids and measured two different powders, one yellow and one brown, into a small glass jar. "The brown is aspen, the yellow is honeysuckle," he said. To my father, he said, "Neither will hurt her." To me, he said, "Put about a dram of each—do you know how much a dram is? About a teaspoon of each in a glass of water. It won't take effect right away, but it might make you feel better. And it might not. People have different constitutions."

"We really don't—" my father said.

"It's free of charge," the apothecary said. "It's for the young lady." Then he rang up the hot water bottles and the bottle of aspirin.

"Thank you," I said.

"You'll want some pennies, too, for the wall heater," he said, handing me our change in a fistful of big brown coins that clinked, rather than jingled, into my hand.

Decipimur specie rectie

CHAPTER 3

St. Beden's School

The next morning, I swallowed my aspen and honey-suckle, over my mother's halfhearted objections, to prepare myself for my first day at St. Beden's School. Showing up at a new school is never easy, especially in the middle of the year, when friendships are already established, and hierarchies understood. In England, all of that was heightened to a terrifying degree. St. Beden's was a grammar school, and to get in you had to pass a test. Most kids failed the test and went to something called a "secondary modern school," which wasn't as good, and where the kids were just biding their time before they could get jobs. So the students who got in to the grammar schools thought—rightly—that they were on top of the pile.

The school was in a stone building with arches and turrets that seemed very old to me but wasn't old at all, in English terms. It was built in 1880, so it was practically brand-new. It had dark-paneled walls inside, and paintings of old men in elaborate neckties, and somehow it had escaped bomb damage. Two teachers walking down the hall wore black academic gowns, and they looked ominous and forbidding, like giant bats. The students all wore dark blue uniforms with white shirts—jackets and ties for the boys, and pleated skirts for the girls. I didn't have a uniform yet, and wore my bright green Hepburn trousers and a yellow sweater, which looked normal in LA, but here looked clownishly out of place. I might as well have carried a giant sign saying I DON'T BELONG.

The school secretary, whose tight gray curls reminded me of a sheep, gave me my class schedule. As a ninth-grader, I was to be in what they called the third form, but it wasn't anything like freshman year at Hollywood High. My first class was Latin.

"But I don't know any Latin," I said. "I can't join the class in the middle of the term."

"Everyone in third form takes Latin here," the secretary said. "You'll be fine."

Then she called to a startlingly beautiful girl walking past in the hall.

"Miss Pennington," she said. "Please show Miss Jane Scott to your Latin class. She's new, from California."

The beautiful girl stopped in the door of the office and looked down at my green trousers, then lingered on my scuffed canvas shoes. She looked up at my face with a bright smile in which I could detect mockery, but I was sure the secretary couldn't.

There are Sarah Penningtons in the United States—you probably know one. I'm sure they exist in France and Thailand and Venezuela. My Sarah Pennington, at St. Beden's, was a near-perfect specimen of her kind. She had no adolescent awkwardness or shyness about her. She had clear, rosy skin, and wide blue eyes, and a long blond braid down her back. She seemed to glow with the perfect health that money can sometimes bestow. She certainly hadn't been subject to wartime rationing. That she was rich, and that her money had survived the war, was clear even in a uniform. The fabric of her skirt seemed to move with her, while the other girls' skirts hung stiffly against their legs. It's possible that no one had ever denied Sarah Pennington anything: that her wealth and loveliness had ensured that she never needed to ask, or aspire, or even hope, before the thing she wanted was there. The look on her face was one of calm assurance that the world would always be so.

I walked with her down the hall, feeling hopelessly inadequate.

"Our Latin teacher is Mr. Danby," she said. "He's terribly demanding, but he's so dreamy. He was a hero in the war."

"What did he do?"

"He was a pilot in the RAF, and shot down all sorts of planes before he was captured in Germany. He was a prisoner of war for two years. After the war, he became a teacher, and he teaches as if he's still flying missions. If his students don't learn Latin, he thinks he's failed. Some people hate it, but I think it's lovely."

I sneaked a sideways look at her. She spoke in a strange, artificial, grown-up way, and I wondered if she was imitating some English actress. She didn't talk like a fourteen-year-old.

Mr. Danby's class had already started when we got there. I was prepared not to like him, just because Sarah Pennington did, but he was undeniably appealing. He was young, with green eyes and long lashes and soft brown hair that curled at his temples. He wore an academic gown that was disarmingly rumpled, as if he had left it in a heap on a chair and sat on it. He was talking to the class, and he seemed exasperated.

"The city we live in was once *Londinium*," he was saying. "The capital of the Roman Province of Britannia. Latin was spoken here in the street, in the fish market. It is the language of Virgil, of Seneca, of Horace. I don't think it's too much to ask that you be able to recite a little!"

The students—some amused, some frightened—glanced to us in the doorway, as a possible distraction. Mr. Danby turned, too.

"Ah, Miss Pennington," he said. "You're just in time for my rant."

"We have a new student," Sarah said. "This is Jane Scott. From California." It was startling, in front of all those faces, to hear my name announced so formally. No one ever called me Jane. And she made the state sound faintly ridiculous, as if perhaps I had made it up.

"Janie," I muttered, feeling the heat in my face.

Mr. Danby said, "Thank you, Miss Pennington."

Sarah beamed at him and sashayed in to take her seat.

The class was seated in alphabetical order, which meant that I was seated right behind Sarah Pennington. A large boy named Sergei Shiskin, with dark hair flopping across his eyes, had to move back one desk to make room for me.

"Sorry," I whispered.

"It's all right," the boy whispered back. "I don't get called on, in the back." He spoke with a Russian accent, and I imagined that a Russian kid would have an even worse time at the school than an American.

Mr. Danby called up students one at a time to recite long passages in Latin, and I felt as if I were standing on a beach in heavy surf: Each student's recitation crashed over me like a wave of words, then withdrew again, leaving nothing I could understand.

Finally the bell rang and the class was over, and the students sprang to their feet.

"Remember to do these translations of Horace," Mr. Danby called, over the noise of books and papers and talk. "For tomorrow!"

I looked at the two Latin sentences he had written on the chalkboard, one long and one short, both incomprehensible. I gathered my things slowly, putting off my next trial.

"Miss Scott," Mr. Danby said as the last students filed out. "I take it you don't feel comfortable with Latin."

"I've never studied it before," I said, clutching my books as a shield.

Mr. Danby looked at the chalkboard and read, *"Vivendi recte qui prorogat horam, Rusticus exspectat, dum defluat amnis.* 'He who delays the hour of living rightly is like the rustic who waits for the river to run out.'"

I tried to sort the Latin words into anything like that meaning. I was nervous, but Mr. Danby reminded me of some of my parents' friends, the ones who talked to me as if I was a full-fledged person and not just a child. Somehow I summoned the courage to ask him, "What's a rustic?"

"In this case it's a fool, who won't cross the river until the water is gone."

"And the second one?"

"Decipimur specie rectie," he said. "'We are deceived by the appearance of right.' You see why I put the two together."

I hazarded a guess, encouraged by his assumption that I *did* see. "Because you can't always know what it means to live rightly?"

"Exactly," he said, smiling. "They taught you something in the wilds of California. How are you finding St. Beden's?"

I tried to think of something nice, or at least neutral, to

say. "My mother said moving here would be like living in a Jane Austen novel, but it isn't really."

"But your story couldn't be Austen, with an American heroine," he said.

I couldn't help smiling at him. "That's what *I* said!"

"More of a Henry James novel," he said. "The American girl abroad. Are you an Isabel Archer or a Daisy Miller?"

I blushed, but told the truth. "I don't know. I haven't read any Henry James novels."

"You will soon enough," he said. "But you wouldn't want to be Isabel or Daisy. They come to bad ends, those girls. *Confide tibi*, Miss Scott. Far better to be who you are."

℞

That conversation with Mr. Danby was the high point of the morning. I was lost in history—they were studying medieval battles and kings I'd never heard of—and in math, which was a confusing sort of geometry and which they bafflingly called "maths." At lunch, I stood with my tray full of unappetizing food, surveying the lunchroom. It wasn't easy to be who you were, if you were the awkward new girl at a strange school. At the end of one of the long, old-fashioned tables, Sergei Shiskin was sitting alone. He was the only student I knew by name who'd been somewhat nice, so I sat at the other end of his empty table and we nodded to each other with the recognition of outcasts. I wondered why I hadn't just sat right *across* from him, but it was too late for that.

Sarah Pennington sashayed past, and I tried to come up with a smile for her.

"At the Bolshevik table, are we?" she asked. Her gang of girls—none as pretty as she was, of course—followed her, giggling.

I knew Bolsheviks were Russian Communists, and I looked at my tray to keep my composure, but that was no help. The meat looked like it had been boiled. There was a small piece of rationed gray bread, with no butter, and not even any oleomargarine. I was pushing the potatoes around with my fork when a startlingly loud, long alarm went off.

"Bomb drill!" one of the lunch ladies called, coming along the long tables. "Under the tables, please!"

It was *Duck and Cover*, English-style. Sergei and I both got under the long table, and everyone in the lunchroom pushed back their benches and did the same.

Everyone, that is, except one boy. He was at the next table over, and he sat calmly where he was, eating his lunch. From my place on the floor, I could see the lunch lady in her white uniform approach.

"Mr. Burrows," she said. "Get under the table, please."

"No," he said. "I won't."

His eyes were serious and intent, and his hair didn't flop limply over his eyes like so many of the boys' hair did, but grew back from his forehead in sandy waves, leaving his face exposed and defiant. The knot of his tie was pushed off to the side, as if it got in his way.

"Do you want an engraved invitation?" the lunch lady asked, with her hands on her hips.

"It's idiotic," he said. "I won't do it."

"I'm sure you were wetting your nappies out in the country during the Blitz," the woman said. "But some of us were in London, and a bomb drill is *not* a time to play at rebellion."

The sandy-haired boy leaned toward her, across the lunch table. "I wasn't in the country," he said. "I was here. And we both know that these tables would have done *nothing* against those bombs—not the V-1, not the V-2, not even the smaller ones dropped by planes."

The lunch lady frowned. "I'll be forced to give you a demerit, Benjamin."

"But this isn't even a V-2 we're talking about," he said. "This is an atom bomb. When it comes, not even the basement shelters will save us. We'll all be incinerated, the whole city. Our flesh will burn, then we'll turn to ash."

The woman had lost the color in her face, but her voice still had its commanding ring. "Two demerits!"

But the boy, Benjamin Burrows, was making a speech now, for the benefit of the whole lunchroom. He had a thrilling, defiant voice to go with his thrilling, defiant face. "That is, of course," he said, "assuming we're lucky enough to be near the point of impact. For the children in the country, it will be slower. And much, much more painful."

"Stop!" she said.

A short bell rang to signal the end of the drill, and people climbed out from under the tables, but I stayed where I was. I wanted to watch Benjamin Burrows a little longer without being seen. I was terrified by what he'd said, but moved by his defiance. I tried to sort out whether it was the terror or the excitement that was making my heart beat inside my rib cage at such an unexpected pace.

CHAPTER 4

Spies

I was supposed to take the Underground to Riverton Studios in Hammersmith after school, to see my parents at work. *Robin Hood* wasn't on the air yet, but they had built a whole Sherwood Forest in a cavernous, warehouselike soundstage, and they wanted me to see it. I was walking home to drop my books off, in an ambivalent drizzle, thinking about orange trees and avocados, when I passed the apothecary's shop on Regent's Park. Through the window, I saw a familiar sandy head of hair. I stopped to watch through the glare on the glass. Benjamin Burrows was shaking his head angrily and saying something to the kind apothecary.

I pushed the door open just enough to slip in, and stepped behind a row of shelves as if browsing for toothpaste. There was no bell on the door, and Benjamin and the apothecary were too occupied with their argument to notice me. Benjamin wore a leather satchel, like a messenger bag, slung on a long strap across his chest. He didn't wear a wool cap like most of the other St. Beden's boys did.

"I don't see why it matters," he was saying. "Mrs. Pratt's just a nutter who likes being sick."

"The delivery is still late," the apothecary said.

"I had *things* to do."

"You had things to do here."

"Poxy things," Benjamin muttered.

"We still have this shop," the apothecary said, "through war and through difficult times, because we take care of our customers. Your great-grandfather did it, and your grand-father did it, and people trust us to do it now."

"But you *wanted* to be an apothecary, like them," Benjamin said. "I don't want to!"

The apothecary paused. "When I was your age, I didn't want to be one, either."

"Well, you should've got out while you could!" Benjamin said. His anger, which had seemed so fitting against the lunch lady, seemed petulant against his father. If I'd had to guess, in the lunchroom, what Benjamin Burrows's father might be like, I would never have picked the quiet, methodical apoth-ecary. Benjamin snatched the paper bag off the counter and stormed out the door without seeing me.

I tried to slip out behind a row of shelves, too, without being noticed, but the apothecary said, "Good afternoon. It's the girl with the homesickness, isn't it? Did the powder help?"

"I don't know," I said. "I was thinking about home on my way here. About orange trees. And blue sky."

The apothecary looked out at the drizzle. "It would be strange not to think about orange trees and blue sky on a day like today," he said. "No matter what powder you took."

"And my new school is pretty awful," I said.

The apothecary laughed. "The man who develops a tincture against the awful new school will win the Nobel Prize. It would be far more useful than the cure for the common cold."

I smiled. "When you have the tincture, will you give me some?"

"You'll be the first."

There was an awkward pause.

"I fear you overheard my argument with my son," he said.

"A little bit."

"He's a very bright, very talented young man, and he would be a fine apothecary, but he has no interest in it."

"Maybe he'll change his mind."

The apothecary nodded. His mind seemed to be elsewhere, so I said good-bye and slipped out the door.

I dropped my books at the flat and set out for Riverton. My father had left elaborate directions to the studio. But as soon as I was in the street, I had the feeling, once again, of being watched. I knew it couldn't be the marshals—they had no jurisdiction in England. I turned and saw nothing, just the cabs and cars and people walking home.

I ran down the steps of the bomb-battered Underground, weaving around the slow old people with their bags, and hid behind a pillar to see who came down after me. There were housewives and students, and men leaving work early, and then there was Benjamin Burrows, with his incorrigible hair and his bright, curious eyes. I stepped back behind the pillar.

I watched Benjamin look around. He stood on the platform, facing away from me, as if disappointed and unsure what to do next, so I left my hiding place and tapped him on the shoulder.

He turned, startled. Then he smiled as if I'd won a game we'd been playing. "Very good," he said.

"Why are you following me?"

"Because you interest me."

That wasn't the answer I'd expected. I'd never interested a boy before, at least not that I knew of. There were boys in Los Angeles who had been my friends, or the children of my parents' friends, but I'd never crossed into the land of *interest*.

"I saw you at school," he said. "Why'd you come to London in the middle of the term?"

"None of your business."

"Are your parents in the CIA?"

"What?"

"It's a simple question," he said. "Are they spies?"

"No! They're writers. They're working for the BBC."

"That's a good cover for spying. Are they journalists?"

"They're television writers."

He looked puzzled. "Why'd they come to England to do that? There's much more television in America."

"Because," I said, "well—because they believe in the First Amendment."

Benjamin screwed up his face. "Which one is that again?"

"Freedom of speech." I was glad to know the answer. "And the press. And, um—religion, I think."

"But they aren't journalists," he said. "So what's the thing they want to be free to say?"

I realized I didn't know.

He narrowed his eyes merrily at me. "They aren't Communists, are they?" he said, teasing.

"No!"

"Then what?"

"I don't *know*," I said, trying to say it like Katharine Hepburn would, as if she didn't give a fig about anything so ridiculous and petty.

"I don't care if they are," he said. "For mind control, Communism has nothing on television. People can listen to *The Archers* on the wireless and still have a conversation with their families, but once they've got a television set, it's all over."

I didn't know what *The Archers* was, and Benjamin's confidence made me feel inarticulate and naïve. So I struck out in the only way I could, and said, "Why don't you want to be an apothecary?"

His manner changed abruptly: He became guarded and annoyed. "How do you know that?"

"Maybe I'm a better spy than you are."

A train pulled up to the platform, and people spilled out.

I checked the destination. "This is my train," I said, and I stepped through the open doors.

To my surprise, Benjamin boarded after me. We found two seats facing forward. My heart started pounding.

"Don't tell me you're going to Riverton, too," I said coolly, to hide my confusion.

"You shouldn't ride the train alone."

"Why? Because strange boys might follow me?"

"How d'you know I'm supposed to be an apothecary?"

"I was in your father's shop when you were talking to him," I said. "But I don't understand why you have to be one, just because your father is. That seems very—I don't know. Nineteenth-century."

Benjamin slumped back in his seat. "It's not nineteenth-century, it's just *English*," he said. "There's an *expectation*."

"That you become what your father is?"

"In some cases. In my case. The Society of Apothecaries pays my school fees, and I wouldn't be at St. Beden's without them. I'd be at some grim secondary modern, getting mullered every day."

"Mullered?"

"Pounded on. But the Society assumes that if they pay for my school, I'll become one of them."

"So why don't you want to?"

"Because it's bloody boring! My father's just a pill-counter!"

"He gave me a powder for homesickness."

Benjamin looked interested. "Did it work?"

"I don't know," I said. "Maybe. The hot water bottles did."

Benjamin's interest vanished, replaced by contempt. "You see? He sells hot water bottles. And ointments for babies' nappy rash. It's so pedestrian. There's nothing less interesting."

"So what do you want to be?"

He paused. "I want to live a life of travel and adventure and service to my country."

"You want to be a soldier?"

He seemed embarrassed to have said so much. "No."

Then I realized. He had tailed me unseen, and thought my parents were spies. "You want to be a spy!"

He frowned. "If that was true, I couldn't tell you."

"I think you just did tell me."

"Well—I'd like to work for the Secret Intelligence Service," he admitted. "In some way. But don't tell anyone."

I nodded. I guessed the Secret Intelligence Service must be England's spies. I glanced across the aisle and whispered, "I think that man in the bowler hat heard you."

He looked quickly to see, but the man was so buried in his book that he wouldn't have noticed if the train ran off the tracks. Benjamin smiled, relieved. He looked down at his shoes. "It's just that I've never told anyone," he said.

A garbled voice came over the loudspeakers, announcing Hammersmith Station, and the train started to slow.

"This is my stop," I said, getting up. I hated to do it. It was the first time in England that I'd felt so happy and comfortable, and I didn't want to get off the train. Benjamin followed, and we stood facing each other on the platform as people streamed around us. Benjamin's dark eyes were actually a warm brown, with bright flecks of copper in them, like the scattering of freckles across his nose.

I glanced away, unsettled, and tried to think what to say. It didn't seem right to invite him to the studio, and my parents would tease me if I showed up with a boy. Across the platform, the train going the other direction pulled in.

"I should go," Benjamin said. "I still have deliveries to make."

"Thanks for keeping me company."

"Listen," he said. "What are you doing Saturday?"

"I'm not sure."

"Meet me on the steps of the school at two and I'll show you Hyde Park."

"I'll have to ask."

"Look, if your parents let you take the Underground alone, they'll let you go to Hyde Park." His return train was about to leave.

"Okay," I said.

"Terrific!" He started across the platform.

I walked away, thinking dizzily that I had a *date*, when I heard Benjamin's voice say, "Janie, wait!"

I turned, wondering what I would do if he tried to kiss me.

"I forgot to ask," he said. "Do you play chess?"

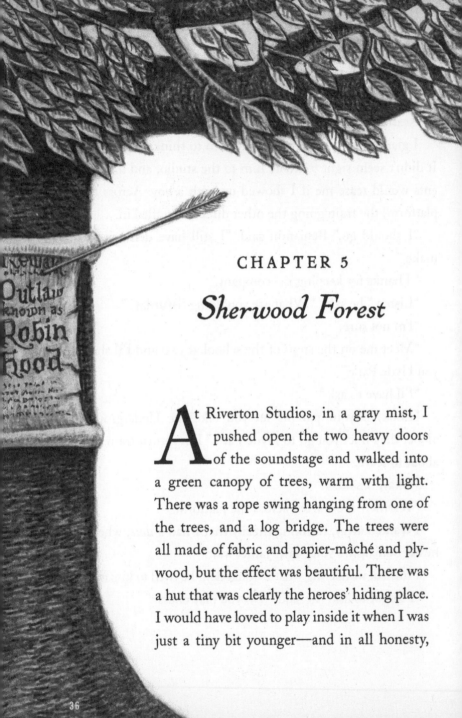

CHAPTER 5

Sherwood Forest

At Riverton Studios, in a gray mist, I pushed open the two heavy doors of the soundstage and walked into a green canopy of trees, warm with light. There was a rope swing hanging from one of the trees, and a log bridge. The trees were all made of fabric and papier-mâché and plywood, but the effect was beautiful. There was a hut that was clearly the heroes' hiding place. I would have loved to play inside it when I was just a tiny bit younger—and in all honesty,

I still wanted to. I didn't see any actors, and thought they must not be filming yet. No one noticed me, and I stood for a moment taking it in.

My parents were across the soundstage, talking to a tall woman with piled-up red hair, and I could tell that my father was acting out a scene. He did that all the time—he couldn't just suggest a story idea, he had to act it out. My mother stood with her arms crossed and watched him with her full attention, and with an expression that could be adoring one second and skeptical the next, depending on what she thought of his idea. It always made me feel that she knew him perfectly, and loved him, but couldn't be fooled.

Then my father saw me and threw up his hands. "Ah, but here is Maid Marian!" he cried in a full Robin Hood voice. "To tell us if we should attack the knight!"

I knew, from years of scenes being acted out in our kitchen, that the thing to do was to join in, and try to move the scene forward. "Does he come to fight?" I asked.

My father looked to the others. "Why, no," he said. "He has no horse, no men-at-arms."

"Then you may approach," I said. "But you mustn't attack."

"What wisdom," he said, "in one so young." Then he broke the Robin Hood character and hugged me. "You found us! Come meet Olivia!"

The redheaded woman, their new boss, didn't shake my hand but pulled me in and hugged me warmly, too. "Thank you for loaning me your parents, Janie," she said. "They're saving my life!"

"How was school?" my father asked. "How were the teachers?"

"They're making me take Latin," I complained. "But I don't know any Latin!"

"Wait—you might actually *learn* something?" my mother said, pretending to be aghast.

I rolled my eyes. *"Mom."*

Olivia Wolff led us into her office, pushed coats off a chair for me, and perched on the edge of her cluttered desk. "Sit down," she said. "How was it, really?"

I made a face. I couldn't help it. "Not *everything* is bad."

"Did you make friends?"

"Maybe one."

"What's her name?"

I felt myself blushing. "His name."

Olivia clapped her hands. *"His* name! That's a good start."

"He invited me to play chess in Hyde Park."

"Chess means he's smart!" my father said. "He's smart, right?"

"Is he nice?" my mother asked.

"Is he cute?" Olivia asked.

"Is this an interrogation?" I asked. "I thought we moved here to get away from those."

"Touché," my father said.

Olivia laughed. "No question—she's your daughter."

"So what's your boyfriend's name?" my mother asked.

"He's not a boyfriend," I said.

"That's what my daughter always says," Olivia said. "Any time I think she has a boyfriend, she says it's a figment of my imagination."

"Ah, he's a Figment!" my father said, putting on an exaggerated English accent. "Young Master Figment, of the London Figments."

"Fourteenth cousins to the queen!" Olivia trilled.

"I can never remember," my mother said, "if the elder Figment son is *An*drew or *Al*istair."

Normally I loved my parents' quickness with jokes, and would wish for them a boss like Olivia who was just as quick, but occasionally it could be really annoying. "His name is Benjamin," I said. "And he's not my boyfriend."

"Benjamin Figment!" my father said. "I like him already. Let's brush up your chess tonight. I don't want my daughter shown up by a chap called Ben Figment."

"I have homework."

"Just let me give you a good opening."

"*Dad*," I said. "Seriously."

"So what's so bad about the school?" Olivia asked. "It sounds glorious to me—Latin and chess dates and all."

"It's just scary," I said. "I don't know anyone. At lunch I sat near a Russian kid, and a girl called me a Bolshevik."

"Ah," Olivia said, growing serious. "Well, imagine being the Russian kid."

"And the food is terrible."

"Welcome to England."

Just then, a girl in her twenties with big eyes and a wide, lipsticked smile put her head into Olivia's office. I knew she was going to be their Maid Marian because I'd seen a photograph, but it was still startling to see her up close. I'd lived in Los Angeles long enough, at fourteen, to know that actress beauty isn't like ordinary beauty and always seems kind of otherworldly. Her hair was set in soft curls and she had eyelashes that you could sweep the floor with. She wore a black dress with an impossibly tiny waist and a full skirt.

"They took my measurements and I'm off," she said. "I have a date!"

"To play chess?" Olivia asked.

The girl looked confused. "No . . . we're going dancing."

"Of course you are," Olivia said. "This is Janie, who just moved here from Hollywood."

"Oh, that's so tragically sad," Maid Marian said. "Do you miss it terribly?"

"Yes," I said. "But it's just a neighborhood."

"Just a neighborhood! Will you beg your parents to write some good scenes for me so *I* can go there, and be famous?"

I looked at my parents. "Uh—sure."

"Thank you!" Maid Marian said. "Now I have to run."

"Knock him dead," Olivia said.

Maid Marian beamed, and the skirt disappeared out the door with a flounce. My parents and Olivia looked at one another.

"She's beautiful," I said.

"Yes, well, she's giving me a pain," Olivia said. "She seems to think the program is about Maid Marian and her Merry Men."

My father said, "What if we do a story where she has to flirt with the Sheriff of Nottingham, to—I don't know, steal the keys to the jail or something, to spring Robin. And the sheriff thinks she's really in love with him."

Olivia shrugged. "Maybe—then what?"

The three of them started spinning the idea out. They were happy and comfortable with one another, and good at what they did, and they didn't treat me like a child. They treated me like one of them. I thought about the apothecary's powder and realized I wasn't homesick anymore.

I kept thinking, as the adults talked, about Benjamin taking a train to Hammersmith that he didn't need to take, just because I *interested* him, and I couldn't keep a dopey smile off my face. I had a date, I was pretty sure. It wasn't dancing, and I didn't have perfect curled hair and a bell-like skirt, but I had a date to play chess.

CHAPTER 6

His Excellency

I got through the Friday at school by keeping my head down, and I stayed in study hall at noon because I couldn't face the lunchroom. I would have loved to sit with Benjamin, but what if he didn't want to sit with me? I couldn't take the chance.

That night, my mother made a dinner of scrambled black-market eggs from the landlady. She had brought home, as a hand-me-down from Olivia Wolff's daughter, a warm flannel nightgown that was so long it touched the floor. It was old-fashioned and shapeless, but I was grateful—the apothecary's honeysuckle and aspen might work, but the hot water bottles only lasted so long in a chilly bed.

On Saturday afternoon, Benjamin met me on the steps of St. Beden's with his satchel slung across his chest. I hoped my face didn't show my relief that he'd actually turned up. On the walk to Hyde Park, we talked about school. He laughed when I said the secretary reminded me of a sheep, and I wished I'd been brave enough to sit with him at lunch. It was so easy to talk to him, especially when we were both walking and looking around at the London streets and I didn't have to stare at him across a lunch tray.

In the park, Benjamin chose a table and set up the chessboard swiftly, giving me the white pieces and lining them up without having to think. I always had to think about where they went. I wished I'd let my dad give me some advice.

"I'm not very good at this," I said.

"Terrific," Benjamin said. "Then we'll play for money."

"Seriously, I'm not going to be a match for you."

"Never mind," Benjamin said. "I want you to watch the park bench over my left shoulder. There's a man sitting there with a wooden leg."

I looked up. A broad-shouldered man in a gray overcoat was seated facing away from us, reading a newspaper. Beneath the bench I could see two feet in black boots. They looked like ordinary feet. Maybe one was a little smaller than the other. "How can you tell?"

"I've been watching him," Benjamin said. "Do you know the Russian boy at school, Sergei Shiskin?"

"He sits behind me in Latin," I said. "He's nice."

"That's his father, Leonid Shiskin, who works for the Soviet embassy. He comes here every weekend. Tell me when someone else sits down."

The chess date suddenly seemed less like a date, and I felt myself deflate a little. "Is that why we're here? I'm helping you *spy* on him?"

"We're just playing chess. It's your move."

I slid a white pawn toward his king, and Benjamin pushed out the black pawn in front of his queen's bishop.

I slid out my own bishop, and Benjamin frowned at it. "Are you sure about that?"

"What does it matter, if the game is just a cover?"

Benjamin sighed. "You have to make your cover convincing," he said. He moved a knight out. "You have to *believe* in it. For example, Leonid Shiskin is an accountant for the embassy. He acts like an accountant and lives like an accountant."

"Maybe because he *is* an accountant."

"But he's an accountant who passes secret messages to people in this park. By leaving part of his newspaper on that bench. It's your move."

I saw a chance at his king, and moved my queen out two spaces.

Benjamin shook his head. *"Janie."*

"I'm threatening checkmate!"

"No, you're not." He moved his knight so it blocked the checkmate and could take my queen *or* my bishop.

"Oh," I said. I studied the board. "I told you I wasn't any good."

"When English people say that, they don't *mean* it," Benjamin said.

"Well, Americans do!"

"What's Shiskin doing?"

I looked. "A man just sat down on his bench," I said, and then I stared. "Oh, Benjamin, he took the newspaper!"

"What does he look like?"

"Plump. Nice coat. He has a black walking stick. How did you know that would happen?"

Benjamin peeked over his shoulder at the man, who moved lightly away, like a much smaller man, sauntering as if out for a Sunday stroll. He didn't seem to need the walking stick, and swung it once in a circle. "I've never seen that man before," Benjamin said.

"Do we follow him?"

Benjamin seemed unsure. "What's Shiskin doing now?"

"Still reading the rest of his paper."

Benjamin swept the chess pieces into his bag. "Let's follow."

We set out in the direction the man with the walking stick had gone, and I cast a glance back at Mr. Shiskin, who looked up at me over his newspaper. I quickly turned around. Benjamin was ahead of me, and beyond him our target was waiting to cross a street.

We followed at a distance, down side streets to a handsome brick building with white trim, where the man went inside. A sign over the door said CONNAUGHT HOTEL. I thought the doorman gave us a suspicious look as we hesitated outside.

"Act rich," Benjamin said. "Pretend we belong." And he

strode with a burst of apparent confidence and entitlement toward the hotel door.

I followed, having to take a few quick, not-so-confident steps to catch up to him. He nodded curtly to the doorman, who opened the door for us. I tried to think what Sarah Pennington would do: smile at the doorman? Flirt? Condescend? In my sudden shyness, I stared straight ahead, as if the doorman wasn't there, which I knew wasn't right at all.

There was a hush in the lobby. Plush carpet absorbed sound, the voices were muted and polite, and there were high notes of clinking glass from a bar somewhere. A carpeted staircase led up to the right of the dark, polished wood reception desk, and the man from the park bench was nowhere to be seen. Benjamin went to the desk.

"I'm meeting my uncle here," he said. "He's a bit fat, I'm always telling him, and uses this silly walking stick. Have you seen him?"

The long-nosed clerk at the desk gave Benjamin a level stare. "Many people use walking sticks," he said. "May I ask your uncle's name?"

"Oh, I just call him Uncle."

There was a pause. "I'm sure you do. But that wouldn't be what *we* call him, would it?"

"I suppose not."

The clerk gave him a tight smile. "It's not my place to determine which of our guests is more corpulent than others."

"Well, I didn't mean that—" Benjamin said.

"Good day, young man."

"Oh!" a voice from behind me said. "It's Jane from California."

I turned to see Sarah Pennington standing in the lobby. It was as if, by trying to imitate her rich girl's entitlement, I had summoned her into being. She wore a blue raincoat the color of her eyes, and she stood with an older version of herself, a blond woman with a dove-gray hat perched on one side of her elegant head.

"This is my mother," Sarah said. "Jane is a new student at St. Beden's."

"How do you do?" Sarah's mother said.

"It's really Janie," I stammered. "I'm fine. And—this is Benjamin."

"I know Benjamin," Sarah said, smiling at him and then meaningfully at me. "Quick work, Janie."

"Sarah!" her mother said.

I was shocked, too. I could feel myself blushing up into the roots of my hair. And Benjamin wasn't acting rich anymore, in the presence of actual rich people. He seemed very interested in the buckle on his satchel.

"Are you staying here?" I managed to ask.

"Oh, no, we were only shopping," Sarah said. "And we stopped for tea."

"Thank you, your excellency," the clerk said behind us.

All four of us turned to see who was so grand. I noticed that Sarah and her mother turned more subtly than Benjamin and I did, and then my heart skipped. The man at the desk, who'd been called "your excellency," was the one we'd been following! He nodded to us and walked in his effortless way to the front door, swinging his black walking stick.

"Do you know that man?" Benjamin asked Sarah's mother, when the door had closed after him.

"I don't," Mrs. Pennington said.

"What does it mean that the clerk called him 'your excellency'?" I asked.

"I suppose he might be an earl or a viscount."

It was the first time I had heard the word, and it sounded like "vye-count." I know now that it's a level of aristocracy above a baron and below an earl.

"Maybe he could marry Aunt Cecilia," Sarah said.

Mrs. Pennington pressed her lips together and it was her turn to blush, behind her face powder. "It's time we went home," she said. "Perhaps next time the two of you could join us for tea."

"Aunt Cecilia's an old maid," Sarah said confidentially, in a way I knew was meant to torment her mother. "We're *desperate* to find her a lonely viscount."

"Sarah!" her mother said.

"Bye!" Sarah said, waving over her shoulder as she was hustled out the door.

Benjamin turned to the desk clerk. "Is that man who just left an earl or a viscount?"

"I thought he was your uncle," the clerk said.

"He will be if he marries Aunt Cecilia," Benjamin said. "And she's a treat. Looks like Lana Turner."

The desk clerk smirked and looked very interested in his paperwork.

"I bet he's an exiled Russian prince," Benjamin said.

"We protect the privacy of all our guests, titled or not. Now I'm afraid I must ask you children to leave."

When I got home, my father looked up from a script he was reading. "Who won the great chess match?"

"Benjamin."

"Well, you'll take him next time."

"I hope so. I'm going tomorrow."

My parents glanced at each other. "Already?" my mother asked.

"For a rematch," I said. "I have some pride."

The truth was that Leonid Shiskin, of the Soviet embassy, went to the park on Sundays, too, and Benjamin wanted to watch him again.

"Huh," my father said, closing his script to look carefully at me.

"Huh," my mother echoed.

"Do we get to meet young Master Figment?" my father asked.

"Only if you stop calling him that," I said. "And not tomorrow. I'm meeting him at the park."

I was already planning the things I would write in my diary, but first I got the chessboard out. Benjamin's spying might be crazy, but he was dashing and brave, a real Robin Hood, not a fake one. I thought some of his boldness must be rubbing off on me, and I wasn't sure that was a bad thing.

"I'll take that chess lesson now," I said.

CHAPTER 7

The Message

When we got to Hyde Park on Sunday, Mr. Shiskin was already on his bench with his back to us, in his gray overcoat. Benjamin set up the chess pieces, giving me the white ones again, while I kept an eye on Mr. Shiskin over his shoulder.

I moved my king's pawn out, and Benjamin, as I knew he would, slid out the pawn in front of his bishop. I brought out my king's knight, as my father had told me to, and was rewarded by one of Benjamin's approving smiles.

"Very good!" he said. He brought out his queen's pawn.

I brought out my queen's pawn and Benjamin took it, and I took his pawn with my knight. Benjamin nodded with pleasure and moved his king's knight out. I looked over his shoulder at Mr. Shiskin. Another man was sitting next to him. I'd completely missed his arrival.

"Someone's there!" I said. "A man."

"What kind of man?"

"I can only see the back of his head. He's wearing a hat."

Benjamin watched my face, as if to read there what I was seeing. "What's he doing?"

"Nothing. Just sitting there." The newcomer, even from behind, seemed oddly familiar.

Benjamin glanced over his shoulder to look at the man, then put his head in his hands. "Oh, *no*," he said.

Then I realized. I hadn't recognized him, out of context. "It's the apothecary!" I said. "It's your father!"

Benjamin pretended to study the chessboard. "He's going to muck it up," he moaned. "Why'd he have to choose that bench? If he's there, Shiskin can't make his drop."

"Maybe he *is* the drop."

"He's *not* the drop."

But as I watched, Benjamin's father took a section of the newspaper from the bench, without looking at Shiskin. I felt goose bumps rise on my arms. "Your father just picked up the newspaper," I said.

Benjamin stared at me. "No he didn't."

"He did! He's walking away now. You can look."

Benjamin turned, and we watched his father pause to unfold the newspaper and read whatever was there. Then the apothecary's whole manner changed. He tore up a small piece of paper, threw it with the newspaper into a trash bin, and hurried off down the street. Shiskin had already disappeared in the other direction, walking unevenly on his wooden leg.

"Come on," Benjamin said. "We need that message."

We ran to the trash bin his father had used.

"Watch where he goes," Benjamin said, and he reached into the trash and came up with the folded newspaper and some shreds of paper. He pieced the scraps together on the ground as I looked over his shoulder. The note was in scrawled capitals:

I felt dizzy and wondered if someone was playing a game with us—or if Benjamin and his father were playing a game with me. "Is this real?" I demanded. "Are you making this up?"

The desperate look on Benjamin's face told me he wasn't. "Which way did he go?" he asked.

"Across that street. Who's Jin Lo?"

"I don't know."

As we followed his father, I looked to my left, instead of to my right where the cars were coming, and heard the blare of a horn. Benjamin pulled me back and kept me from being run over by a taxi. The driver leaned out the window and swore at me. Benjamin's father ducked into a red phone booth on the other side of the street.

"Did you know your father knew Shiskin?" I asked.

"How would I know that?"

We crossed the intersection at an angle and stood in line with people waiting for a bus, trying to blend in. I had never felt so conspicuous. The apothecary came out of the phone booth without seeing us.

"Give him fifty paces," Benjamin said.

"Is he working for the Russians?"

"I don't know."

"Do you think he knows that viscount? Or earl?"

"Stop asking me questions!"

We trailed his father through the streets. The apothecary moved surprisingly quickly, and seemed to be headed for his shop. By the time we'd reached Regent's Park Road, we'd lost sight of him. We stood in a recessed doorway, watching, but no one went in or out of the shop.

"Let's go in," I said. "Just ask him what's going on."

"I can't," Benjamin said. He was pale and had lost all his courage.

"You have to."

"What if he's a spy for the Soviets?"

"Then at least you'll know." I stepped out into the street, looking to my right this time.

Benjamin gave in and we moved uncertainly toward the shop. He looked over his shoulder to see if we'd been followed. The door was locked, and he opened it with his key.

The shop was silent, but smelled oddly of smoke. Benjamin locked the door behind us, and we moved through the silent aisles toward a light in a back room. I tried walking on tiptoe, but that made my legs shake. I had to put my heels down to stop the trembling.

In the back office, the apothecary was burning papers in a small metal wastepaper basket, feeding them into the fire.

"Benjamin!" he said. "You can't be here! They're coming!"

"Who's coming?"

"I'm not certain. But you mustn't be here!"

"Are you a spy for the Russians?"

His father peered at him through his spectacles. "Of course not!"

"But I saw you in the park! Shiskin passed you a message. He works for the Soviet embassy."

The apothecary shook his head. "I don't have time to explain, Benjamin. I have to hide the book."

"What book?"

The apothecary answered by pulling a large leather-bound volume from a cupboard. Then we heard the locked door rattling in the front of the shop. "They're here!" he said. "You both have to hide." He set down the book to lift an iron grate in the floor, revealing stairs leading down to a cellar.

"I'm not going down there!" Benjamin said.

"You'll go *now*," his father said, with a sharpness I hadn't imagined he was capable of. As if he had just had the desperate thought, he thrust the book into Benjamin's hands.

"We can stay and help you fight them!" Benjamin said.

"Go!" his father said.

"We'll go get the police," I said.

"No police! I need you to protect the Pharmacopoeia and keep it safe. *Please* do this thing for me."

"Protect it from what?" Benjamin asked.

"Anyone who comes looking for it."

"What about you?"

"I'll be all right. Just take care of the book. It's been in our family for seven hundred years."

"Dad, wait!"

"I have a plan. I'll be fine. Just go." The apothecary lowered the grate after us. Someone was pounding at the front door.

The cellar smelled like damp earth, and we found ourselves at the bottom of the stairs in a concrete-floored room. Enough light came down through the iron grate that we could see a little of what was around us. There were shelves lined with dusty jars, and there was a heavy iron door in one of the walls. Benjamin tried the door handle, but it was locked.

I heard a violent explosion upstairs, and it made us both crouch behind the shelves. There were footsteps and voices, speaking what sounded like German.

"Do you understand them?" I asked.

Benjamin shook his head.

We listened while the men searched the office. I could hear Benjamin's breathing in the dark, and my own, which was unsteady. He looked at the heavy book on his knees, and I knew he was wondering if it was worth more than his father's life. I could tell he wanted to go upstairs and fight.

"There are too many of them," I whispered. "Your father said to keep the book safe."

We waited what seemed a long time, then heard a scraping of metal above us, and Benjamin pulled me back farther into the dusty shadows behind the shelves. The grate was pulled away, and a man's head peered into the cellar. He had a long scar across one cheek, and the hideousness of a face hanging upside down. He seemed to be grinning, or gritting his teeth: They were bared in the dim light as he looked around. Then we heard the clang of a police car's bell on the street, and someone shouted in German. It was clear that the voice was urging the others to leave. The horrible upside-down face disappeared, and the grate was lowered again.

Benjamin and I crouched in the darkness, barely daring to breathe. As the immediate terror faded, I realized that his

arm was across my shoulders,
and the side of my body against
his. He seemed to become aware of it, too,
and he relaxed his grip on my arm. We moved an inch
apart and my arm tingled where his fingers had been. The
police bell had faded into the distance: They must have been
after someone else.

When the shop was silent above us, Benjamin and I crept
back out, pushing the heavy grate open. The place had been
ransacked. Papers were thrown on the floor, drawers opened,
chairs toppled. Broken jars of herbs filled the air with sharp,
strange smells. Things had been pulled off the shelves in the
front of the shop: bottles of pills, boxes of bandages, bags of
cotton wool.

The apothecary was gone.

CHAPTER 8

The Pharmacopoeia

Benjamin and his father lived in a flat above the shop, and we decided that it would surely be watched. So we went to my flat, where my parents were sitting at the card table we'd set up near the tiny kitchen. I could tell I was interrupting some serious conversation, but I didn't have time to wonder what it was. We had decided not to tell them what had happened, because they would want to call the police, and the apothecary had told us not to.

My father turned in his chair and smiled. "How was the rematch?" he asked.

"It was . . . fine," I said. I'd forgotten all about chess.

"Who won?"

Benjamin and I glanced at each other. "The game got interrupted," I said. "His father had to go to Scotland to visit his aunt. She's sick."

"I'm so sorry," my mother said, all concern. "I hope she's all right."

I felt suddenly and sadly grown up—not because I had brought a boy to meet my parents, but because I had told them a lie. "I wondered if he could stay here tonight," I said. "I mean, his father asked if he could."

My parents glanced at each other. "I don't see why not," my father said, after a pause that suggested that he *did* see why not.

My mother made scrambled eggs again for dinner, and we ate at the little card table, where we all had to sit too close together. Benjamin was formal and polite, and everyone seemed uncomfortable.

"We haven't really figured out shopping yet," my mother said. "So we're relying heavily on our landlady's eggs."

"They're delicious," Benjamin said. "It's hard to get eggs."

There was an awkward silence.

"So what do your parents do, Benjamin?" my father asked.

"My father is the apothecary down the street."

My father pushed back his chair with a screech of wood. "No kidding!" he said. "The source of all our heat. And your mother?"

Because my mother worked, my parents always made a

point of inquiring about other kids' mothers. Nowadays it seems a perfectly normal thing to ask, but in 1952, most kids' mothers stayed home, and the question was sometimes embarrassing.

"She died when I was little," Benjamin said.

I stared at him. I'd never thought to ask about his mother, but he hadn't said anything about her *dying*.

"I'm so sorry," my mother said. "How did it happen?"

"In a bombing raid," he said. "In the war."

"Oh, Benjamin, how terrible."

"I was just a baby," he said. "I don't really remember her."

There was another long silence. My parents, who were usually so warm and friendly, had no idea what to do with this tragic news and this stiff, formal boy. I wished they could have seen him during the bomb drill, defiant and strong, when they would have admired him. I saw now why he couldn't take the drill seriously—or why he took it *so* seriously that he wouldn't take part in it, if it wouldn't do any good.

Benjamin's leather satchel was leaning against our little couch, with the Pharmacopoeia sticking out of it because the buckle wouldn't close over the big book. My father nodded toward it, to change the subject.

"What's the great tome?" he asked. "Is that for chemistry?"

"Sort of," Benjamin said.

"Can I see it? I'd like to see what they teach in England."

"I'm very tired, sir," Benjamin said, too quickly. "And have an essay to finish. Do you mind if I just work on that?"

"Of course not," my father said. He gave Benjamin the wide smile he used in friendly arguments, or when he knew someone was lying to him. "If you'll stop calling me 'sir.'"

When I was sure my parents were asleep, I crept out to the living room, where my mother had made a bed for Benjamin on the couch. He had the Pharmacopoeia open on his lap.

"You didn't tell me your mother was dead!" I whispered.

"Where'd you think she was?" he asked. "Timbuktu?"

"I didn't have time to think about it."

"Well, I don't have time to talk about it," he said. "I've been looking at the book. It's mostly in Latin."

He made room for me on the couch. I felt shaken by his father's disappearance, and curious about the book, but none of that dispelled my nervousness about sitting with him in the middle of the night on my parents' couch. It was impossible to imagine any boy from Hollywood High sleeping in my parents' living room in Los Angeles, and there was no one back home who had made me feel so unsettled and strange.

I looked at the book—in the excitement, I hadn't really taken it in before. Pages were slipped in between the bound pages, which seemed to be hand-lettered, in an old calligraphic style. The paper was ivory inside, brown around the edges, and scarred with burn marks. It looked like a very old, important version of my mother's overstuffed *Joy of Cooking*.

"I think the Latin's really old," Benjamin said. "Or some

of it is, anyway. I'm supposed to be able to read Latin, to be an apothecary, but I'm no good at it."

"What language is that?" I asked, pointing to some words made up of letters I didn't recognize.

"I think it's Greek."

He flipped another page. There were symbols and little drawings interspersed with the text. One looked like a snake inside a circle. "Maybe that one's a cure for snakebite," I said.

"Why would he need to hide *that* from those Germans?"

"Because the book's valuable?"

"They weren't ordinary thieves."

"I guess not." I shuddered, remembering the man with the scar. "Where do you think they took him?"

"I don't know. I wish I understood German."

"And Latin."

"And Latin."

"Or Greek."

He closed the book and we studied the embossed symbol on the cover. It had a circle at its center, with an upside-down triangle in it. Around that circle was a star with seven points, inside another larger circle, with smaller circles between the points of the star.

I ran my hand over it, feeling the ridges and indentations in the smooth, worn leather.

"That symbol looks familiar," Benjamin said. "But I don't know why."

"We could ask Mr. Danby to translate some of the Latin."

"We can't just go showing it to people."

"Mr. Danby's a war hero."

"I don't recall my father saying we could show it to war heroes. He said we had to keep it from anyone who wanted to see it."

"Well, Mr. Danby *doesn't* want to see it," I said. My eyes were starting to itch with tiredness, and my eyelids threatened to close. "It's too bad your father had to get kidnapped for you to start doing what he asks you to do."

"You're not taking the seriousness of this, Janie."

"I really am," I said. "I'm just so tired."

I laid my head against the arm of the couch, just to rest it for a minute, and the next thing I knew, Benjamin was shaking me awake. It was still dark in the room, and I wasn't sure where I was. I fought my way out of sleep.

"The symbol on the book!" Benjamin whispered. "I know where I've seen it before!"

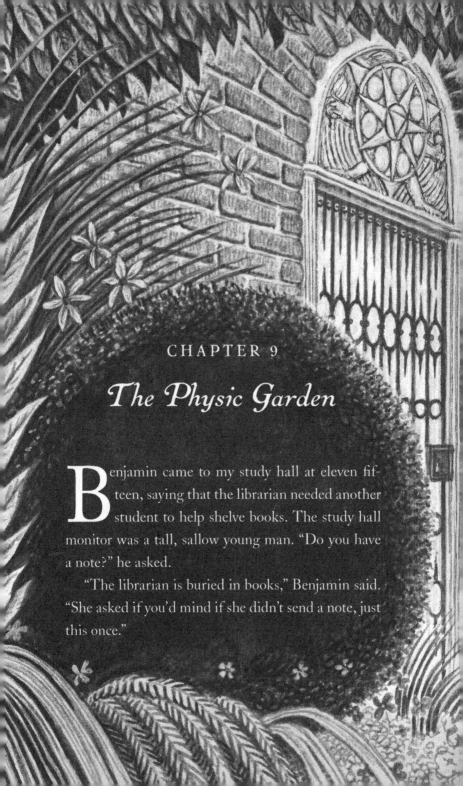

CHAPTER 9

The Physic Garden

Benjamin came to my study hall at eleven fifteen, saying that the librarian needed another student to help shelve books. The study hall monitor was a tall, sallow young man. "Do you have a note?" he asked.

"The librarian is buried in books," Benjamin said. "She asked if you'd mind if she didn't send a note, just this once."

I raised my hand. "Can I go?" I asked. "I want to be a librarian someday."

This drew a ripple of laughter from the other students, which got them a frown from the monitor. I knew he felt sorry for me, as the pathetic new girl who stayed in at lunch.

"All right," he said. "But tell her to send a note next time."

I gathered my things, and when we were sure the hall was empty, we slipped out the main door and down the steps. Benjamin didn't remember exactly where the Chelsea Physic Garden was, but he knew it was near the Thames, so we walked along the river.

I know now that the Physic Garden was started in the seventeenth century, as a kind of museum and nursery for medicinal plants. Botanists and ships' physicians brought specimens back from all over the world, as England expanded its empire, and the specimens were planted in Chelsea. The garden is still there, if you visit. The British Empire may be gone, but the Physic Garden is its green ghost, growing a little bit of India, China, Africa, Australia, New Zealand, and the Pacific islands, right in the middle of London.

"I used to go with my father all the time," Benjamin said. "He would collect cuttings, and I would skip stones on the little pond, which was really too small for skipping stones, until a gardener would tell me to stop or I'd break a window."

"Why'd you stop going?"

"I turned ten and thought I was too old for it. I didn't need to be watched anymore, and I thought I didn't need to tag along to the stupid garden."

We found the high iron gate on the embankment and pushed it open. There was a little stone guardhouse, but no one was in it. The garden was lush and thriving and made the phony Sherwood Forest in Riverton look like the papier-mâché that it was. It was almost magically green, and silent, as if the plants somehow absorbed all the city's sounds. The paths were lined with leafy stalks that grew as high as my head, and trees from which yellow flowers hung, and something that looked like rhubarb, with enormous spreading leaves.

"If *my* father came here for work," I said, "I'd go with him all the time."

We walked down a path where the trees on either side grew together in a canopy, so we were almost in darkness in the middle of the day. Every few feet, a vine hung down, with a single pink flower at the end. There were rustling noises in the undergrowth—birds or little animals. At the end of the path, there was another gate.

"There it is!" Benjamin said, and I followed his eyes to the top of the wrought iron. There was the symbol embossed on the cover of the Pharmacopoeia, with the circles and the star. We peered inside, to a walled inner garden. Across some paths and beds was a small brick house with white trim. Benjamin tried to open the iron gate, but it was locked.

"Should we climb it?" I asked.

But just as I spoke, a figure emerged from the little brick house. It was a man, and he looked as if he had once been tall and imposing, but now he walked with a stoop. He had a gray beard and a wrinkled, kind face. He wore a long brown oilcloth coat and Wellington boots, and carried a basket and a pair of pruning shears.

"Hullo!" Benjamin called. "Sir?"

The figure looked up, surprised in his solitude.

"I'm sorry to bother you," Benjamin said. "My father's a member of the Society of Apothecaries. I have a Society scholarship, actually. And I . . ."

The man in the oilcloth peered at him. "Is that Benjamin Burrows?"

It was Benjamin's turn to be surprised. "Yes!"

The man hurried over and opened the gate with an ancient key. "Come in, come in," he said, and he looked behind us, down the green tunnel. Then he relocked the gate.

Inside his tidy brick house, the gardener took off his oil-cloth coat and hung it on a peg, then gestured to the chairs at his table. "Who is the young lady?" he asked suspiciously.

"My friend Janie," Benjamin said. "She's American." He said it as if it made me somehow—innocent.

"I see," the gardener said. Then he turned to Benjamin. "I remember you as a little boy, running around the garden. I knew your grandfather well. Your father always comes looking for the most unusual plants. Is he well?"

"I don't know," Benjamin said, and he looked to me for encouragement. I nodded—the gardener seemed entirely trustworthy—so Benjamin sat at the table, and I did, too. He told the story of the men who had come for his father, and also of the message passed in a newspaper on the park bench.

The gardener looked alarmed. "They've taken Jin Lo, too?"

"Who's Jin Lo?"

"A Chinese chemist," the gardener said. "A correspondent of your father's. You saw the men who came to your father's shop?"

"Only one," Benjamin said. "He had a scar on his face. They spoke German."

"And did your father—tell you anything? Or show you anything?"

I could see Benjamin struggling not to mention the book. "Well . . . ," he said.

The gardener sighed. "I understand that merely to ask will make you suspicious, but we may have limited time. Do you know where the Pharmacopoeia is?"

Benjamin glanced at me once more for reassurance, then pulled the book out of his satchel and slid it onto the wooden table.

The gardener's eyes widened. "Ah," he said. He seemed deeply affected, as if the book were a sacred object. He touched it slowly, in awe. "I haven't seen it in a very long time."

"We came here because the symbol on the front is on the gate of your garden," Benjamin said.

"Yes," the gardener said, running his gnarled hand over the weathered cover. "It's the Azoth of the Philosophers. The triangle in the center is Water, the source of all life. The seven smaller circles are the operations of alchemy: calcination, separation, dissolution—why are you making that face?"

"Because alchemists were crackpots," Benjamin said. "Fools trying to make gold."

"*Some* were trying to make gold," the gardener said. "There will always be those who are driven by greed. They've given the rest a bad name. But Sir Isaac Newton was an alchemist. Have you not studied calcination and separation and dissolution?"

"No," Benjamin said, a little embarrassed.

"What on earth are you learning in school?"

"Maths," Benjamin said. "English."

The gardener frowned. "Reading *novels*," he said, with disdain. "And now you've been entrusted with the Pharmacopoeia, wholly uneducated."

"I just need to know about the book," Benjamin said. "I don't read Latin or Greek."

The gardener shook his head. "There are hundreds of years of secrets in it, learned through lifetimes of research and practice. And we have so little time."

"Can you tell us *some* of it?" I asked.

The gardener considered the two of us, taking our measure, then opened the book with great reverence, careful not to crack the old pages. "Well—I don't know how to begin. There are simple infusions, like this one, the Smell of Truth. It makes it impossible for a person to tell a lie. This symbol here, with the sun at its zenith, means that you have to harvest the *Artemisia veritas* herb for the infusion at solar noon, which is quite different from noon on the clock." He turned a page. "Then there are masking tinctures, which change the appearance of things without changing the thing itself. This one, for example, the *Aidos Kyneê*, confers a kind of invisibility. It's named for the mythological cap of the Greek gods. *Aidos* means modesty, so it's a covering of extreme modesty, which is ironic, because of course—"

"What does that say?" I asked, pointing to a note written in the margins, up the side of the page, in a different handwriting.

The gardener tilted his head and read silently in Latin. "It says . . . that if more than one person uses the masking tincture, it's best to leave one small part of the body out, to avoid—well, knocking into each other, I suppose. This must be advice from someone who's used it. The book is a living document, you see. New knowledge is always being added."

"How about the knowledge that it's all rubbish?" Benjamin asked. "Can we write that in? It's not possible for people to be invisible!"

The gardener ignored him and turned another page. His eyes brightened as he read the Latin instructions there. "Here we are," he said. "The most difficult of all are the transformative elixirs, which actually change the substance at hand. This one, the avian elixir, turns a human being into a bird."

"Of course it does," Benjamin muttered.

The gardener raised his bushy gray eyebrows at him. "You must allow for the possibilities, Benjamin. I've never seen it, but I hear it's a very beautiful process."

"And when you transform—you can fly?" I asked.

"Of course."

"Why does my father have a book of phony magic spells?" Benjamin asked.

"They aren't *spells*," the gardener said. "It's a Pharmacopoeia, a book of medicines, or it was originally. Many of the processes in the book began as methods of healing, many generations ago: How to close a wound? How to combat sickness in the human body? Those were the original questions, but in certain minds they took unexpected directions, having to do with the fundamentals of matter. Just as cave drawings led to the ceiling of the Sistine Chapel, early medicine led to the Pharmacopoeia. The world is made up of atoms, which can be influenced and masked and even rearranged, by someone with the necessary skills. I'm surprised your father hasn't begun to train you."

Benjamin looked down. "He's asked me, sometimes, to help him," he said, "but I always had something else to do. I thought he just wanted me to take over his shop. You know—selling bath salts and hot water bottles."

The gardener gave a dismissive wave of his hand. "The Society of Apothecaries wouldn't give you a scholarship for that. They expect you to carry on your father's real work."

"Which is *what*, exactly?" Benjamin asked. "Why did those men take him?"

"I don't know," the gardener said. "That's what you must discover. As soon as possible."

"We could ask Mr. Shiskin," I said tentatively. "He's the one who delivered the message."

"But we don't know if we can trust him," Benjamin said. "And why would he tell anything to a couple of kids?"

"We could use the Smell of Truth," I said. "From the book."

Benjamin and the gardener looked at me. I waited for their scorn.

"You know, that's not such a terrible idea," the gardener said finally. "Can you safely come in close contact with this man?"

"We know his son, from school," I said.

"Then it's worth a try." The gardener squinted at the light outside the window. "Let me check my charts. We can't do much with a sextant inside the garden, since we can't see the horizon."

He took a book off his shelf and ran his finger down a list. "Solar noon will be at . . . twelve fourteen and nine seconds," he said. "We can come close to that." Then he led us outside to a sundial, a triangular pointer of oxidized green copper mounted on a squat stone base. The sun wasn't bright, but the shadow of the pointer was visible, and it fell just after noon.

"Why does it matter when you harvest the herb?" I asked.

"The book says it's because the fullest light of day eliminates all shadow and deceit," the gardener said. "Very poetic. But it may in fact have something to do with photosynthesis, and the molecular structure of the *veritas* plant. The early alchemists knew that it was necessary to harvest it at noon, but perhaps not exactly why. The herb has always been planted beside the sundial, here." He pointed to some bunched green leaves in careful rows.

We waited, watching the barely moving shadow.

"None of this makes any sense," Benjamin said.

The gardener looked at him appraisingly, as if gauging his ability to do the job at hand. "We all feel strange, even apprehensive, when confronted with our own destiny," he said. "You have to find your father. Whatever his plan is, he's going to need you."

"Can you come help us?" I asked.

"Oh, no," the gardener said. "I'm old and arthritic and rarely leave this garden—I would only slow you down and raise suspicion. And now it's time."

He reached down to snip the leaves with his shears.

"There we are," he said. "You crush the leaves and boil them in water to release the smell. But you'll have to be careful. It can be an insidious little herb if you aren't prepared for the truth."

CHAPTER 10

The Smell of Truth

W e left the Physic Garden and walked back down the Chelsea Embankment with the *veritas* herb and something like a plan—or at least I thought we had a plan. But Benjamin was having none of it.

"It's all rubbish!" he said. "Invisibility spells. Herbs that make you tell the truth if you cut them at noon. If the gardener told you he was king of the fairies, would you believe him?"

"No," I said. "But it's possible that the herb affects the brain somehow, like alcohol does, or coffee."

"So you want to just *waltz* into Shiskin's house and get him to smell a pot of leaves. Do you know how a Soviet agent is trained?"

"Do you?" I asked.

"I know we're no match for it."

I wasn't sure what had made me so brave—possibly being in another country that was so different from my own, possibly trying to match what I thought was Benjamin's courage. But I felt determined to move forward in the only way we could. "You said you wanted to live a life of adventure," I said. "Let's just test the herb and see if it works."

Benjamin rolled his eyes but had no argument, so we went to my flat, which was eerily quiet with my parents at work. I filled a pot with water, according to the gardener's instructions, and boiled the crushed herb on the tiny kitchen-closet stove. Benjamin sat stubbornly at the card table with his arms crossed. The leaves turned dark green in the hot water, and the steam from the pot was sharp and minty. I stood over the pot, breathing it in for a few long seconds, then turned to him.

"Now you do it," I said, feeling strange and a little giddy.

Benjamin eyed me. "D'you feel all right?"

"A little strange," I admitted. "But go ahead. You're the one who thinks nothing will happen."

"And how do you propose to test it, Madame Curie?"

"We have to think of a question that we wouldn't otherwise want to answer."

He stood over the pot, looking down at the leaves. "Something like, 'Who do you fancy?'"

"That might work," I said, even though it was the last question I wanted to answer. But it was impossible, suddenly, to tell a lie.

Benjamin took a deep sniff over the steam and turned to me. "All right," he said. "So who do you fancy?"

I hesitated. "Fancy means *like*, right?" I asked, stalling.

"Of course."

I gritted my teeth against the answer coming out, but I couldn't stop myself. "You," I said helplessly.

"Me?" Benjamin flushed crimson. I was sure I was doing the same. His freckles darkened when he blushed.

"*Oh*, that's embarrassing," I said. "I hate this. Quick, before it wears off, who do you fancy?"

"I don't want to answer."

"You'll have to."

I could see him struggling with the effort. "Aargh," he said. "I hate this, too! All right! I like Sarah Pennington!"

I was too shocked, briefly, to be mortified that it wasn't me. *"Sarah Pennington?"* I said. "She's awful! She's mean and pretentious!"

"I know." He seemed genuinely sorry about it. "But she's also beautiful. I don't *want* to like her. But I can't help it! She sits in front of me in maths, and the curve of her neck, under that braid, drives me completely mad."

"*Stop!*" I said. "Enough! It works."

We glared at each other in silence.

"Anyway, she has a crush on Mr. Danby," I said before I could stop myself.

Benjamin was aghast. "Mr. Danby?"

"She thinks he's dreamy. And she's right! He's also smart, and nice!"

Benjamin looked pained, and there was another long, sullen silence. I didn't know if I was happy to have hurt him or not, so I crossed my arms and looked out the window at St. George's Street below. The sad haberdasher across the street was standing in his doorway as usual, waiting for customers who never came.

"How do we tell when this thing wears off?" Benjamin asked.

"*I don't like you,*" I said, experimentally. "But that's not a good test. At the moment it's kind of true. Say you don't fancy Sarah Pennington."

"I don't fancy Sarah Pennington."

"There we go," I said, with a pang in my heart. "You can lie. It's worn off."

"Let's pretend that never happened," he said.

"Do you still think it's rubbish?"

He shook his head. "No," he said. "It works."

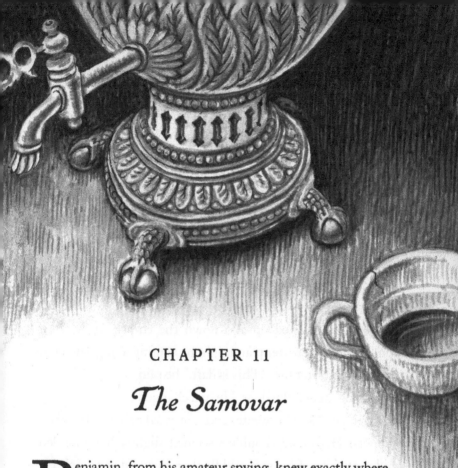

CHAPTER 11

The Samovar

Benjamin, from his amateur spying, knew exactly where the Shiskins lived, in a flat near the Soviet embassy. The afternoon had grown cold, and we walked in silence, nursing our regrets about the Smell of Truth, scarves wrapped around our faces and hands shoved in our pockets.

The Shiskins' front door was in a row of narrow brick houses, all attached to each other. There were steps leading up to it. Benjamin said, "So now what?"

"Well," I said. "We'll say we're here to see Sergei. Maybe I have a Latin question."

"You don't know enough Latin to have a question!"

"So it's a social visit. We want to show him this wonderful tea we've discovered."

"As if *that* doesn't sound suspicious."

"You have a better idea, Mr. Super-spy?"

"No."

"All right," I said, and I strode up the steps and rang the bell, thinking he would rather be with Sarah Pennington anyway, so why was I doing this?

"Janie, wait!" he said.

"Are you coming or not?"

Benjamin looked up and down the empty street, as if someone with a better plan might be coming along, then ran up the steps after me. "This is daft," he said.

Sergei opened the door. He had changed out of his school uniform, and wore a sweater and gray wool pants, with house slippers. His broad shoulders seemed slightly less rounded and protective of his soft middle than they did at school. He was surprised to see us, and tossed his hair out of his eyes. Loneliness came off him like steam rising, so I tried to summon some confidence that whatever crazy thing I proposed, he would want to join in.

"Hi, Sergei!" I said. "We wondered if you were busy."

"For what?" he asked.

"We're thinking of entering the science competition at school," I said. "But we need a third person on our team."

"Science competition?" Sergei said. "There is a science competition?"

"We want to do botany as our subject," I said, willing myself not to blush. "Right now we're exploring the properties of this one particular herb."

"A remarkable herb," Benjamin put in, pronouncing the *h*, as if to clarify. "May we please come in?"

Sergei stood back from the door, and we walked into a small anteroom hung with coats, with a staircase that led up to a second floor. I wondered if his father was up there, the Soviet agent.

"We have to brew it, like tea," I said. "Can we use your kitchen?"

"You want the samovar?"

We must have looked at him blankly.

"It's a Russian teapot."

"Perfect!" Benjamin said.

I heard uneven footsteps upstairs as Sergei led us into the kitchen. I remembered Mr. Shiskin's wooden leg. So he was home, and we could try the herb on him. The kitchen clearly belonged to two men living alone: It was full of unwashed dishes and smelled of onions.

"My mother is in Russia with my sister," Sergei said, in apology. "Here is the samovar."

It was a large silver urn, elaborately decorated in relief with leaves and vines, with a teapot on top. It looked out of place in the shabby kitchen.

"It was my grandmother's," he said. "We just had tea, so it's hot."

"Terrific," Benjamin said.

I heard a thump upstairs, and then another, and then the careful sound of Mr. Shiskin's wooden leg coming all the way down the stairs. I tried to act natural, bustling around in the kitchen, but my heart felt like it would leap out of my chest.

Then Mr. Shiskin was standing in the kitchen doorway. "What are you doing with the samovar?" he asked. His accent was more Russian than Sergei's, less British, and he was even bigger up close. His body filled the door frame and his hands looked the size of baseball mitts.

"Making tea, sir," Benjamin said. "Sorry to intrude."

"You are Sergei's friends?"

"Yes," I said.

He gazed past us to the dirty dishes in the sink. "My wife is in Russia," he explained. "I am not a good housekeeper."

"We don't mind, sir," Benjamin said. "If you and Sergei want to sit in the parlor, we're about to do an experiment."

Mr. Shiskin's eyes narrowed in suspicion. "What experiment?"

"We'll show you," Benjamin said, with the air of a magician about to do a trick. "It's *science*. Please, have a seat in there."

The two Shiskins removed themselves reluctantly to the little front parlor, and Benjamin and I stuffed the crushed leaves into the samovar's teapot and filled it with boiling water from the urn. We could hear the Shiskins talking together, and I heard the words "science competition" mixed in with the Russian.

"You think it'll work in the samovar?" I asked.

"I don't know," Benjamin said. "We'll have to pour it into something else."

I handed him the only clean teacup from a row of hooks, and we filled it with the pale greenish brew. "Just don't smell it yourself," I said. "Or we'll start confessing everything."

Benjamin took the cup in one hand, held a tea towel over his face with the other, and headed into the parlor. I followed.

"The very *fascinating* thing about this herb," Benjamin told the Shiskins, through the towel, "is the way the smell changes, over time. It starts out very sharp and exhilarating. Here, please try." He held the cup out.

Mr. Shiskin leaned away. "Why do you cover your face?"

"I'm getting a cold, sir. Please, smell the tea before it changes."

"You smell it first. It might be dangerous."

"Oh, I've already smelled it," Benjamin said.

"And you are sick!"

"An unrelated winter cold. I don't want to infect you."

Mr. Shiskin crossed his thick arms over his chest. "We are Russian. We don't get colds."

Sergei said something imploring to his father and the older man finally sighed, uncrossed his arms, and leaned over the diminishing steam from the cup. He seemed startled by the smell, and looked up sharply at Benjamin.

"Where did you get this plant?" he asked.

"In—in the park."

Mr. Shiskin lunged from his chair toward Benjamin, surprisingly agile in spite of his size and his wooden leg. "*Chush sobach'ya!"* he said. *"You* smell it, and then tell me again where you found it!"

I backed into the kitchen, and Benjamin backed up after me, holding the teacup in front of him like a weapon. Mr. Shiskin seemed even bigger and more powerful now that he was angry.

Sergei was mortified. "Leave them alone, Papa!" he said. "They're going to let me on their science team!"

"They are *not* your science team!" Mr. Shiskin said.

Sergei ducked in front of his father, arms spread wide, and stood protecting us. "Three years we have lived here," he said, "and this is the first time my friends *ever* came to visit, and now you chase them out!"

"They are not your friends," his father said, pushing him aside. "They invent this to get to me."

I stumbled backward in a panic, and my sleeve caught the silver faucet of the samovar. I tried to steady the urn, but it crashed to the floor. The hot water spilled out of the teapot, and the whole kitchen was filled with the bracing, minty smell of the leaves. There was no avoiding breathing it in.

"Where did you get this plant?" Mr. Shiskin asked again.

The giddy feeling came over me: the compulsion to blurt out the answer. I bit my tongue until it hurt, but I couldn't stop myself. "At the Chelsea Physic Garden," I said. "From the gardener."

He turned to Benjamin, who still had the towel over his face. "This is true?"

"No!" Benjamin said, his voice muffled. "I don't know what she's talking about! *She* doesn't know what she's talking about!"

"It's true," I said. "On Sunday, you passed a message to Benjamin's father. Then those men came for him. Who are they?"

Mr. Shiskin stared at me. His face turned an ashen gray as the blood drained from it. Then he switched on a radio on the kitchen counter and turned up the volume. "Stupid children!" he hissed, under the sound of cheery dance music. "You think no one is listening?"

I knew about houses being bugged, but it hadn't occurred to me that this one might be. Shiskin was right: We were stupid children. How had I thought we were equipped to conduct an interrogation?

Under cover of the music, Shiskin whispered, "This is where I have seen you—in the park. Is Marcus Burrows your father? Take down this ridiculous towel."

Benjamin lowered the towel. "He is."

"Who else knows you have connected him to me?"

"Only the gardener."

"Did you see your father taken?"

"We were hiding in the cellar. We heard German voices."

"Did you see a man with a scar?"

"*We're* supposed to ask the questions here!" Benjamin said.

"You have *no idea* the danger you are in!" Shiskin whispered hoarsely.

"The man with the scar was there," I said. "Who is he?"

"He is a member of the Stasi," Mr. Shiskin said. "The East

German secret police. But he is working under the command of Soviet security, the MGB. They must have discovered the apothecary." He slumped into a chair and put his head in his hands. His eye fell on the dented samovar on the floor.

"You know what other thing 'samovar' means, in Russia?" he asked. "It is a word for the soldiers who lost their arms and their legs in the war, from shells and exploding mines. Because they look like teapot with no arms and legs, you see? The Soviets sent them to Siberia so people would not see them and know how terrible is the war. My brother was one of these, until he died there. They took his body and then they punished him for it. Losing my own leg, I could accept. But I could not forgive what they did to my brother, a war hero. When he died, I decided to help your father."

There was a silence while we absorbed the horror of this confession. The dance music jangled along.

"Help my father with *what*?" Benjamin finally asked. "Why did the Soviets want him?"

Mr. Shiskin fought the urge to answer; I could see the muscles in his neck distend. There was a loud trumpet solo on the radio. "There are two other scientists working with your father," he said. "They have come to London to take part in his plan."

"Is Jin Lo one of them?"

Mr. Shiskin was purple with the effort not to speak. "Please stop asking questions. I don't wish to compromise your father. If he and Jin Lo have been captured, I am in grave danger from both the British and the Soviets. So is your gardener. And so are you. I beg you to stay away from my son."

"But Papa, they can't!" Sergei said. "We're on the science team together!"

"There *is* no science team!" Mr. Shiskin barked. "They lie to you!"

Sergei cowered for a moment, then said meekly, "Then they could join chess club instead."

"Mr. Shiskin, I need to find my father," Benjamin said. "Tell us how to do that, or we don't leave Sergei's side. It'll be science team practice all day long. *And* we'll join chess club."

Shiskin hesitated, but the combination of truth serum and blackmail must have been too much for him. "I don't know where he is," he said. "We are to meet in two days, at the Port of London. If your father is not there, we will be finished."

"Finished *how*? And what's the plan?"

Shiskin shook his head, reached into his pocket and produced a tiny capsule.

"Cyanide!" Benjamin said, diving to stop him. "No!"

Shiskin knocked Benjamin to the floor with one powerful arm. Then he put the capsule between his teeth and crushed it. "It is not cyanide," he said. "You have read too many stories. It will only make me mute, for a time. I thought I would use it against the MGB and torture—not a boy and a pot of tea."

"Just tell me why Soviet security would be interested!"

"I only want peace," Shiskin said. "Just leave my boy al—" Then his voice vanished. There wasn't even a whisper left. He couldn't make a sound.

"Wait! I need to know!" Benjamin said.

The jitterbug ended, and silence fell briefly over the radio. I heard a whimper from the corner. Sergei was sitting on the wet kitchen floor with his grandmother's dented samovar in his lap and a devastated look on his face. His father was in danger, he was not a member of a science team, and still no one had come to his house, in three long years, as a friend. Another song started up.

Mr. Shiskin all but picked up Benjamin and me by the scruff of our necks, propelling us into the hall, past the stairs and the hanging coats. He could be eloquent in silence: There was nothing mute about the way he deposited us outside like two bags of trash and slammed the door.

CHAPTER 12

The Return to the Garden

The one urgent thing we knew, from Mr. Shiskin, was that the gardener was in danger and we had to warn him. The Physic Garden was closed for the night by the time we got to Chelsea, and the gate was padlocked. Benjamin made his hands into a sling for my foot so I could climb up onto the brick wall. I pulled him up after me, and we dropped down onto the grass below.

It was fully dark, and we walked straight for the corridor of green with the hanging flowers that led to the inner

garden. The lushness of the plants seemed sinister in the dark, instead of verdant and springlike.

Under the carved Azoth of the Philosophers, we peered through the gate. A light was on in the gardener's little house.

"Hullo!" Benjamin called.

"If he's inside, he can't hear us," I said.

We climbed that gate, too, dropped over, and made our way toward the house. As we passed the sundial in the shadows, I thought it looked strange. The metal triangle that indicated the time was missing. It had been snapped off at the base. I touched the rough edge of un-oxidized copper. "How could that happen?"

We both looked at the house. It seemed innocuous, a light burning somewhere inside. We crept quietly toward the door, which stood ajar, leaving a vertical line of light.

"Should we knock?" I asked.

Benjamin pushed at the door and it creaked, making both of us jump back. The house was silent. "Hullo?" he called again.

He pushed the door open, and we stepped inside.

"I don't like this," I whispered. "We should leave."

A lantern with a glass shield sat lit on a chair by the door, as if someone had planned to take it outside. The gardener's oilcloth coat was hanging on its peg. The table was set meticulously for one, with a place mat, a folded cloth napkin, and a white bowl, none of which had been used.

There was a woodstove at the other end of the room, with a pot on it. Benjamin picked up the lantern and held it over the pot. Some kind of soup had been simmering there, but the fire had gone out in the woodstove and the soup was congealed around the edges.

As I moved away from the stove, my foot hit something on the floor and I bumped into Benjamin, rattling the lantern's glass shield.

The spill of light caught the sole of a rubber boot, which I had tripped over. Then a second boot. I held my breath as Benjamin raised the lantern to reveal two legs in wool trousers, stretched out on the floor, suspenders over a wool shirt, and then the gardener's gray beard.

A scream caught in my throat. The gardener's shirt was dark with something wet. I started to see spots around the edges of my eyes, breaking up the room, until I could only see straight ahead. In that small circle of vision, I could see the jagged, broken pointer of the sundial sticking out of the gardener's chest. I didn't faint, but fell to my knees beside him.

"Janie!" Benjamin said.

I had learned in First Aid, for junior lifesaving, that you were never supposed to remove an impaled object, because the person might bleed to death, but it seemed unthinkable to leave the horrible thing there, and anyway he was already dead. I reached for the sundial to pull it out, but a hard and callused hand caught my wrist and gripped it.

I screamed.

"Shh," the gardener whispered, still holding my wrist. His palm felt like it was made of rough bark, as if he had become one of the trees he planted.

"You're alive!" I said.

"You must run," he said. His voice was faint and hoarse, and his eyes were fixed on me cloudily.

Benjamin had crouched beside me on the floor. "We have to call for help."

"*No*," the gardener said, rousing himself to make the effort. "Can't . . . trust police."

"Why not?"

He shook his head.

I thought of the Physic Garden outside, all those medicines, brought back from all over the world. "Isn't there some herb that can make you better?" I asked. "We can go get it!"

He squeezed my hand, but I could tell he was weakening. "*Veritas*," he managed to say. The Smell of Truth. We had come to tell him about it, and to tell him he was in danger— but we were too late.

"We used it!" I said. "And it worked. Could it help you now?"

The gardener shook his head again. "No." He was having trouble breathing, and his white eyebrows knitted together in an exhausted frown. "Remember," he said, "you must . . . *allow* for the possibilities."

Then his grip on my hand relaxed, and his body grew eerily still.

"Wait!" I said, fumbling under his scratchy beard for a pulse. The skin of his throat was loose and still, and I felt no pulse, only my own heart pounding.

"Is he dead?" Benjamin asked.

"I think so."

"We have to get out of here."

"I don't think I can move."

"You *have* to. Whoever killed him might come back."

He pulled me by the hand, past the waiting table where the gardener would never eat dinner again, and out the open door. We passed the ruined sundial and the *Artemisia veritas* planted in neat green rows.

"Wait!" I said, tugging Benjamin back. I knew the gardener hadn't given up his last breath just to ask if the Smell of Truth worked. "He was trying to tell us something about the herbs."

I knelt by the rows of leafy plants, but saw nothing, so I felt blindly between them and under them, and then my hand touched something smooth and hard. It was a small bottle, hidden under the leaves, with a piece of paper tied around it with string.

"He left us something," I said.

"Take it," Benjamin said. "Let's go!"

I put the bottle in my pocket, and we climbed the fence to the outer garden. The trees seemed to loom and reach for us as we ran toward the outer gate, where we clambered over again.

On the other side, in the street, I got a stitch in my side from running. I slumped down against the stone wall and felt tears welling up. "They killed him because of us," I said. "For helping us."

"Get up," Benjamin said. "We don't know that."

"It's true! Shiskin's house was bugged, and I talked about the gardener there. It was so stupid!"

"We have to go."

"We have to tell the police."

"We can't trust them."

"We have to tell my parents, then."

"Absolutely not," Benjamin said. "There was a murder. They'll have to call the police. And we can't do that."

"But maybe we should! A *murder*. Oh, Benjamin, it's all my fault!"

"Here," he said, fishing a handkerchief out of his coat pocket. "Take this."

The handkerchief was white, perfectly pressed and folded into a square. His father must have ironed it: the kind, methodical apothecary. Benjamin was right that we needed to find him. He'd know what to do.

I wiped my nose and put the handkerchief in my pocket, where I felt the hard glass. "What about the bottle?" I asked.

"First let's get somewhere safe," Benjamin said.

CHAPTER 13

The Gardener's Letter

I wouldn't, under the circumstances, have described my parents' flat as *safe*, but I had to get home. My parents were furious. "So you just waltz in here at ten o'clock at night?" my father demanded.

"Is it ten?" I asked. I would have guessed much later.

"Do you know how *terrified* we were?" my mother asked.

"I think so."

"Where *were* you this late?"

Benjamin and I had agreed, after much debate as we made our way through the streets, not to tell them about the murder. Both the gardener and the apothecary had told us not to trust the police. But my parents could tell I was upset and had been crying, so we had to tell them something.

"It's a really long story," I said.

"So start at the beginning," my father said. "And I want the truth!" He pointed at Benjamin. "Did your mother really die in the war?"

"Yes," Benjamin said.

"Okay, that sounds true. Let's go from there. Did your father go visit a sick aunt?"

"No."

"I knew it! Where is he?"

"I don't know."

"Then we should call the police," my mother said.

"No!" Benjamin said. "We can't trust the police."

"Have you done something wrong?"

"No," he said.

"So why can't you trust them?"

"I just can't."

"*You* don't trust the federal marshals," I reminded my father. "And *you* didn't do anything wrong."

"That's different."

"How do you know?" My father hated it when people jumped to conclusions about other people's situations, and I wasn't going to let him do the same.

He relented. "I don't," he said. "So tell me. Where were you?"

"At a friend's house, working on a science project,"

Benjamin said. "We made . . . a bit of a mess, and our friend's father was angry with us."

That was pretty much true.

"So you cleaned up the mess, and you didn't think to *call* us, and then what?" my father asked.

"That's it," Benjamin said. "It took a long time."

"What's the name of the friend?"

Benjamin hesitated. "Stephen Smith."

"You're lying, Figment," my father said. "I've worked in show business a long time, and I know what lying sounds like."

"I can't tell you his name," Benjamin said, with stubborn dignity. We had promised Mr. Shiskin we would leave him and Sergei out of it, and Benjamin wouldn't budge on that.

"Then I want you out of my house."

"He doesn't have anywhere to go!" I said. "Let him stay one more night."

"If he tells me the truth, I'll consider it."

"He can't! He promised!"

"Promised who?" my father said. "I'm waiting."

Benjamin was silent, his head stubbornly bent forward.

"Out, Figment," my father said. "Now. And Janie, you're going to bed."

I begged my parents to reconsider, but it did no good, and I got into bed feeling helpless and trapped. The gardener was dead and Benjamin was out in the streets, in mortal danger, and there was nothing I could do. I was writing furiously in my diary about how my parents didn't—couldn't—understand *anything*, when I heard a tap at the window. I slid the window open, and Benjamin climbed in off the ledge, with his satchel slung across his chest, taking off his shoes before his feet silently touched the floor.

"How'd you get up here?" I whispered. I was too amazed to worry about the fact that I was only in my nightgown. Anyway, it was the long flannel hand-me-down nightgown from Olivia Wolff's daughter, and it was about as revealing as a nun's habit.

"I climbed that tree to the window ledge."

"If my parents catch you—"

"They won't. I'll leave early in the morning."

I tried to think about the options, and the consequences, but I had no argument. He really didn't have anywhere else to go.

Benjamin set his satchel down carefully and spotted the diary open on my bed. "You keep a diary?"

I closed it and slid it beneath my pillow. "Sometimes."

"It doesn't say anything about the Pharmacopoeia or the gardener, does it?"

"No." That was a partial truth. "Not so anyone else could understand it."

"It would be bad if someone found it, and could understand."

"They won't," I said. My eyes filled. "Benjamin—the gardener."

"We have to be strong," he said. "Don't cry."

I brushed away the tears. "Where will you sleep?" My bed was very narrow, and even if it hadn't been, the question of sharing it was too embarrassing to think about.

"On the floor."

So I gave him one of my wool blankets, and he lay down on the floor with his satchel for a pillow. He stretched out on his back with his hands behind his head.

"Why did your father call me Figment?" he asked.

I climbed into bed, under the one remaining blanket, and tried to push the gardener from my head. "Because he thinks he's funny."

"But *Figment*?"

"When I told them I was going to play chess with you, my mother was teasing me about having a boyfriend. Someone said, as a joke, that it was a figment of her imagination. That's all it took—they were off."

Benjamin was silent, looking at the ceiling. "It's nice that they tease you," he finally said. "My dad's always so serious. I wonder what he'd have been like if my mother hadn't died. If he would have been more—I don't know. Like your parents. Able to joke about things."

I couldn't imagine *not* having parents who joked: It was part of every day. I was silent because I didn't know what to say.

"What does your diary say about me?" Benjamin asked.

"That I can't believe my parents sent you out in the cold."

"That's all?"

"That you're kind of a bully when you play chess."

"A bully! That's slander!"

"The truth is a defense," I said. I wasn't sure what that meant, but it was something my father liked to say, before the U.S. marshals started looking for him.

Benjamin smiled. Then there was a knock at my bedroom door, and we both froze.

"Under the bed!" I whispered, and he rolled silently beneath, pulling his satchel and the blanket after him. I got my diary back out and posed with it on my knee.

"Yes?" I said, in a sullen voice.

My father pushed the door open and looked in. "Lights out."

"I'm still writing."

"You need your sleep."

"So does Benjamin, and you sent him out in the cold."

I was trying to act as I would have acted if Benjamin weren't in the room, but without drawing my father into the room to discuss it. It was a gamble, and I lost it: My father sighed, and crossed to the bed and sat down. The metal springs squeaked. I held my breath, hoping he wasn't crushing Benjamin.

"Janie," my father said. "I know you're upset. Your mother and I just want you to be safe. Benjamin seems like a resourceful boy. He's probably safe at home right now."

I was going to say that Benjamin's home wasn't safe, but I didn't want to start narrowing down the options for where he might actually be. "Maybe," I said.

"You really like him, don't you?"

"*Dad,*" I said, imagining Benjamin under the bed. Even though I'd already told him I fancied him, I thought we could set that aside, in the category of Things the Smell of Truth Made Us Do. I wasn't going to say it again.

"It's okay, you can tell me," my father prodded.

I said nothing.

"He's a nice kid, Figment," my father said. "A little arrogant, though."

I thought I heard a noise under the bed. I shifted, squeaking the metal springs, to cover it.

"And not as responsible as I'd like. Your mother and I were scared today. We thought something terrible had happened to you."

"I know," I said. "But it didn't." I thought of the gardener bleeding on his worn floor and wondered if we had left footprints, or fingerprints.

"The funny thing is that we'd been waiting for you to get home, to tell you that Olivia wants us to go on location for a few days, to film at a castle. The speech we'd prepared started with how responsible we think you are. But then you didn't come home to hear it. It got later, and *later*, and we got pretty worked up. And now I think we have to take you with us."

I stared at him. "But I have school."

"It's just a few days."

"I'm so far behind already." I couldn't leave Benjamin to look for his father alone, and I cast around frantically for ideas.

"Janie, it's a *castle*," my father said.

"I know!" Once I would have loved to skip school to go on location to a castle, but it was unthinkable now. "What was your plan before, when you were going to say how responsible I am?"

My father frowned. "That Mrs. Parrish, the landlady downstairs, would look after you."

"Perfect!" I nearly shouted.

"But Janie, you came home at ten o'clock tonight. You can't do that with Mrs. Parrish."

"I won't! I promise!" I didn't know, at the time, how true that would be.

My father shook his head. "We thought about telling Olivia we couldn't go, but we've just started working for her." He paused, looking at his hands. "We haven't wanted to make you afraid or upset, Janie, but we really need this job."

"I know," I said. "I'm sorry I was a pill about leaving LA. And I'm sorry I was late tonight. But I'll check in constantly with Mrs. Parrish and I'll be fine. Really. You can go."

My father sat on the bed thinking. Then he shook his head. "I don't know what else to do," he said. "You really did scare us. We got so mad because we love you and want you to be safe. You understand that?"

"I do. I love you, too."

"Now lights out, okay?"

When the door clicked closed, Benjamin rolled out from under the bed. *"Arrogant?"* he whispered.

"But nice," I whispered back.

"And irresponsible!"

"We were home really late," I said. "And you wouldn't tell him anything!"

"Oh, right, so I should have told him that someone kidnapped my father and stabbed the gardener with a sundial?"

"No," I said.

We sat in silence. Then Benjamin said, "So you get to stay in London."

I looked at him—was he glad? Had I done right to campaign to stay? "Yes," I said warily.

He didn't catch my eye, or give any indication of feeling. "What did the gardener leave us?" he asked.

The note! I'd forgotten to read it. My coat was hanging on the bedpost, and I drew out the little brown glass bottle. The note was tied to the neck with a piece of twine.

I unfolded the piece of paper and spread it on the bed. Benjamin sat beside me and his hand brushed mine, which made it hard to concentrate for a second, but then I was caught up in the letter.

Children,
After much reflection, I begin to think
that my life may be in danger. The
man with the scarred face is walking
in the garden as I write. I will hide

this letter among the only plants you know to be useful. If you return to the garden in my absence, perhaps that's where you'll go. I know of no other way to contact you safely.

It is clearly of the utmost importance that you find Benjamin's father. I'm convinced that what he wants is for the good. I have tried to think what I could offer to help you find him, when I may have little time.

There was a transformative elixir you doubted could exist, and I have taken the liberty of making some for you, from the directions in your remarkable book.

I have contemplated using it myself, to escape, but I am old, and have nowhere to go. I would be lost outside the garden. Please give the elixir the respect it deserves—use it not as a frivolous plaything, but approach the transformation with the seriousness that your father has always brought to his work. That will be the best way to find him.

I pray that you will not find this letter under dreadful circumstances. I would prefer to pass the bottle directly into your hands. But I am not hopeful. I wish you all luck.

Your friend

I picked up the bottle when I finished reading the letter. "A transformative elixir," I said. "It's the bird spell."

"Oh, great," Benjamin said. "The nuttiest one."

"Don't you think it works?"

"No," Benjamin said. "If it did, he would have used it to escape."

"To go *where*? He had nowhere to go, like he said."

"It just isn't possible, Janie. It isn't like smelling some

truth serum. There are physical laws—the conservation of mass, for one thing. A human being can't just become a tiny bird-sized thing. We'd have to become something the size of *us*. Like a baby ostrich. And a lot of good that would do."

"A giant condor?" I suggested.

"A bit conspicuous in central London." He reached toward the bottle. "Here, let's try it now and see."

I pulled the bottle back. "The gardener said not to use it as a plaything," I said. "Think how *amazing* it would be, if it worked, to become a bird and fly!"

"Uh-huh," Benjamin said.

It did seem fairly unlikely. The exhaustion of the day swept over me and a yawn seemed to take over my whole body. "How are you going to get out of here in the morning?"

"Same way I came in." He turned over on his side with his head on the satchel, pulling the blanket up.

I reached over and turned out the light and we lay in silence for a while. My brain was spinning through everything that had happened, stopping first on the upside-down face of the man with the scar, then on Shiskin's angry switching on of the radio. Then on the cold stillness of the gardener's throat as I felt for his pulse, then on my parents' fury and the fact that they were going away, and my conflicted feelings about not telling them everything. Then on Benjamin Burrows lying on my bedroom floor. I could tell from his breathing that he wasn't asleep either.

"Benjamin?" I whispered.

"Yes?"

"What are we going to do tomorrow?"

"I don't know."

"I'm not used to someone sleeping on my floor."

"You don't have girly sleepovers back in Hollywood?"

"Sure, but no one *sleeps* at them," I said. "And anyway, you're not very girly."

"I'll take that as a compliment. It's a step up from 'arrogant.'"

"He said 'resourceful,' too."

"I like 'resourceful.' Hey, Janie?"

"Yes?"

"I'm glad you're staying in London."

"Thanks," I said. "Me too."

I smiled idiotically at the ceiling for a while, and then lay listening to Benjamin's even breathing in the dark, trying to concentrate on our problems so that my brain could solve them while I slept. It was a trick my mother had taught me, but I had never been thinking about problems this big before. Eventually exhaustion won out, and I fell asleep.

CHAPTER 14

Scotland Yard

When I woke, Benjamin was already gone. A note on the windowsill said he'd meet me at school. While I was eating breakfast, the postman brought my school uniform, wrapped in brown paper. I put it on and surveyed myself in the bathroom mirror in a stiff pleated skirt, a white button-down shirt, and a navy blue blazer. They all had tiny tags on them that said UTILITY.

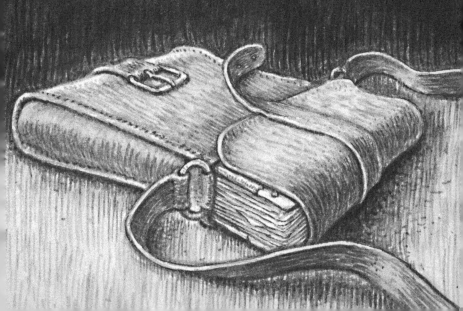

"What does that mean?" I asked my father, showing him the tag.

"Must have something to do with rationing," he said. "Government-issue clothes, no frills, no extra fabric."

The skirt was too big, and my mother brought me a safety pin to make it tighter. "If they really wanted to save fabric," she said, "they'd send the right size. And leave out all these pleats."

"You can't have a uniform skirt without pleats," my father said.

My mother smiled at him. "Is that in the Magna Carta?"

"Sure," he said. *"No schoolgirl of the realm shall be caused to attend her place of instruction in the absence of—"* He stopped, thinking.

"Of sufficient folds of lambswool about her lower limbs," my mother said.

"By the law of the land," he said.

My mother laughed, and I did too. Things felt normal with them again, and I was grateful. Then my mother caught my hand and grew serious. "Janie," she said. "You'll check in with Mrs. Parrish every morning and afternoon? And be safe?"

"Of course!" I said. "I have sufficient folds of lambswool now. I'll be fine."

We went down to talk to Mrs. Parrish, who agreed cheerily to the arrangement and gave me a hug before I left her apartment. I smelled something that at first I thought was pine needles—maybe some unfamiliar English cleaning product. But then she straightened uncertainly, and I realized that the smell was gin. It was eight o'clock in the morning. I didn't want to worry my parents, who were waiting in the hall, so I said nothing and gently closed her door.

At school, I didn't see Benjamin outside, so I walked in alone. No one stared at me in the halls, in my uniform. It was the perfect disguise, and I thought that if I could look like an ordinary schoolgirl, maybe I could be one.

In Mr. Danby's Latin class, I slid unnoticed into my chair. Sarah Pennington swanned in and took her seat in front of me. The boy next to me, I noticed, had his jacket sleeves rolled up, and he had inked an *F* on the little tag so it said *F*UTILITY.

Sergei Shiskin wasn't at his desk, but I told myself he was probably just late. I tried not to think about the man with the scar slinking into the Shiskins' kitchen and reaching for a knife. I realized we should have told them what had happened to the gardener, to warn them.

There were new quotations from Horace on the chalkboard. A pimply boy with a squeaky, breaking voice recited a passage, and my mortification for him almost made me forget we were in danger. While he stammered, I studied the nape of Sarah Pennington's neck beneath her braid. Her skin was smooth and creamy, I had to admit. And the fine blond hair that escaped her braid curled silkily behind her small, round ears. But still it was just a neck—it didn't seem very earth-shattering to me.

Finally the bell rang, and people started to file out. Sarah

Pennington gave Mr. Danby a thousand-watt smile as she passed his desk. "Thank you, Mr. Danby," she said.

He nodded vaguely. "You're welcome, Miss Pennington." Then he turned to me. "Miss Scott, I brought you these."

He handed me paperback copies of *The Portrait of a Lady* and *Daisy Miller*, both by Henry James. The girls in white dresses on the covers seemed very far from anything that mattered, at the moment. But I appreciated the gesture.

"Thank you," I said, and I felt myself blushing. Sarah Pennington shot me an unforgiving look as she left.

Mr. Danby had the sort of eyes that can't help looking *kind*. They had wounded depths in them. If he hadn't been a war hero, he could have been a movie star. In Hollywood, he would have been both. He'd have been discovered at a lunch counter as soon as he got demobilized, and a studio would have engaged him to marry some starlet for the publicity. It seemed very English of him to be a plain old Latin teacher. I realized that we were alone.

"Are you finding London less painful yet?" he asked, erasing the chalkboard.

Images of the dead gardener and the terrified apothecary flashed through my mind, but I pushed them down. "School's okay," I said.

"And everything else?"

"It's . . . fine."

"I don't suppose I can do anything to help."

It occurred to me that if I hadn't told Benjamin about

Sarah Pennington's crush, he might agree that it was worth asking Mr. Danby for help. And Sarah Pennington's crush had nothing to do with anything. Mr. Danby was kind and wise, like the gardener, but he was also worldly. Obviously he knew what it was to be in danger, if he'd been shot down over Germany. And he knew the system, in England, in a way my parents couldn't. I took a deep breath.

"Well," I said, "there's this book."

Mr. Danby stood with the eraser, looking puzzled, then said, "Yes?"

"It's a very rare book, and some people are after it."

"Which people?"

"I'm not sure."

"And to whom does it belong?"

"My friend's father. But he gave it to my friend to protect."

"And where is his father?"

"We think he might have been kidnapped."

Mr. Danby looked alarmed. "Kidnapped? You've spoken to Scotland Yard?"

"No." I was in too deep here. "We—my friend isn't sure the police would understand."

"Miss Scott, that's . . . you have to tell the police. Has he done something wrong?"

"No!" I said. "It seems like maybe someone was after the book."

Mr. Danby said, "What kind of book?"

"It's written mostly in Latin. And some Greek. So I

thought maybe you could help us understand it better. But my friend doesn't want to show it to anyone."

"I see."

"But maybe I can convince him. If you're willing."

"If you like, of course," he said. "But I really think you should go to the police. Goodness, Miss Scott, I thought you were only having difficulty with the labyrinthine St. Beden's social codes. This seems—well, rather worse."

⚕

When I told Benjamin at lunch about our new ally, he was furious. "You did *what*?" he said.

"I didn't tell him anything specific," I said, flustered by his anger. "But I think he can help us." We were alone at the empty table where I had watched him stare down the lunch lady.

"We aren't supposed to tell anyone!"

"Your father never said that. He said you had to keep the Pharmacopoeia safe from people who want it. And we need help to do that. We're in over our heads."

Benjamin scowled at the food on his tray and said nothing. Then a familiar, loud, long bell rang.

"Bomb drill!" called the lunch lady. "Everyone under the tables!"

"Again?" I said, looking around. People started to push back their benches.

"It's so stupid," Benjamin said, his shoulders set in opposition to the noise.

"It is," I said. "But I don't think this is the time to make a scene and get kept after school. Or have them try to call your father."

"It's ridiculous."

"I'm getting under the table."

"We'd be incinerated in an atomic bomb blast," Benjamin said. "Instantly. We'd be ash by now."

"I know," I said. "Ash. Here I go." I slid underneath.

Benjamin stayed in his seat, and I saw the lunch lady's ankles in white cotton tights approach. "Benjamin?" she said. "Do I have to send you to the headmaster?"

I heard him sigh, and then he pushed back his bench and climbed under.

"Thank you, Mr. Burrows," she said, and her white-encased ankles moved on.

Benjamin crouched inches away from me under the table. "Happy?" he asked.

"Yes," I said. "That was smart."

When the drill ended, we climbed out again. Sarah Pennington was giggling about something with her friends. The other students climbed out from under their tables, laughing and talking.

Then I noticed a uniformed police officer and a man in a brown suit standing by the door, speaking to the lunch lady. She turned and pointed to us, and they crossed to our table.

"Benjamin Burrows and Jane Scott?" the man in the suit asked, standing behind me. He was tall, with his hat in his hand, and he had the wispy fair hair of a child or an old man. "I'm Detective Montclair, of the Metropolitan Police. This is Officer O'Nan. You'll have to come with us, please."

"Why?" Benjamin asked.

"Please," the detective said.

"Are we under arrest?"

The detective glanced at Officer O'Nan, who was short and stocky, with bristly hair like a hedgehog. In that moment, Benjamin lunged toward the door.

"Run, Janie!" he said.

I scrambled up, taken by surprise, but the men were right behind me, and the detective grabbed my shoulders.

"Let go!" I cried.

Everyone in the lunchroom was staring at us now.

Benjamin reached the door at a run, but the lunch lady in her white uniform was standing in front of it with her arms crossed. The uniformed policeman tackled Benjamin, taking him sprawling.

Benjamin's satchel, with the Pharmacopoeia in it, slid across the floor and stopped at Sergei Shiskin's feet. I saw a look pass between Benjamin and Sergei, and Sergei quietly picked the bag up. He shouldered it as if it were his own, and I was impressed with how cool and collected he was.

Benjamin kicked and fought so that all the attention stayed on him, and the policemen didn't seem to notice how he'd passed the satchel off. I tried to twist free, too, but the detective was strong, and they finally wrestled us both out the door, under the disapproving eye of the lunch lady. She looked as if she'd expected as much—as if resisting the bomb drill was bound to lead to police custody sooner or later.

A dark sedan was parked outside the building. "We haven't *done* anything," Benjamin protested as they dragged us to it.

"Then why are you struggling?" O'Nan asked.

"Because we haven't done anything!"

They pushed us into the car. I looked out the window at the students who had spilled out of the school. Sarah Pennington watched with her friends, and Sergei stood quietly with the satchel. Officer O'Nan took the driver's seat.

"Are you arresting us?" I asked as the car pulled away from the school.

"Not yet," Detective Montclair said, turning from the passenger seat to smile at us. His wispy hair was askew from the struggle, and he had crooked teeth. "We just have some questions."

"About what?"

"A man was stabbed to death last night at the Chelsea Physic Garden."

"*What?*" Benjamin said. "We don't know anything about that!"

I was in a panic. Someone must have seen us coming out of the garden. We needed to establish an alibi, but we couldn't with the policemen listening.

We drove in silence through the London streets, away from St. Beden's and into neighborhoods that seemed dirtier and more run-down, the bomb damage from the war more obvious and unrepaired. My mind was racing through possible explanations we could give for being at the garden. Our botany project for the science competition, maybe—except that the science competition didn't really exist.

"Why are we going to the East End?" Benjamin asked.

"Because that's where Turnbull Juvenile Court is," Detective Montclair said.

"I thought we were just being questioned."

"You are," he said. "Nothing to worry about. Just ordinary procedure."

"I want to call my parents," I said, even though they were at a castle in the country.

"Naturally," the detective said.

"You can't question us without them present," I improvised.

He smiled his crooked smile. "Oh, yes, we can, my dear," he said. "This isn't the 'land of the free,' you know. You just sit tight."

CHAPTER 15

Turnbull Hall

We stopped at a three-story brick building with a peaked roof, like an orphanage in a Dickens novel. Turnbull Hall had been built in the nineteenth century as a place where the poor could live and eat and get an education from reform-minded university graduates, and it might once have been a fine, clean, noble place. By 1952, though, it was grubby and cold, with sooty windows and surly guards, and held a juvenile court and a reformatory school.

Officer O'Nan immediately took Benjamin into one room, and Detective Montclair steered me down a hallway, past a classroom full of bored and pasty-looking children. There was a smell of poverty and abandonment and neglect, and of generations of kids who didn't get enough baths or enough love.

We arrived in an empty, run-down classroom, and Detective Montclair told me to take a seat. He sat opposite me, squeezing into a child-sized desk. His fine hair was still disordered from our struggle.

"Now, do you go by Jane or Janie?" he asked.

"Jane," I said flatly. I didn't want him acting like my friend.

"You're American."

I nodded.

"Parents working here, yes?"

The detective's manner was very calm, his voice soothing, and I was reminded of a king cobra I'd once seen in a film, which hypnotized its prey, swaying back and forth, before striking like a bullet. I nodded.

"How do you find London?"

"Are you arresting me?"

"No."

"Then I'd like to go now."

"Why don't you tell me what happened in the garden?"

I bit my lip. Obviously, they had separated me from Benjamin so they could compare our stories. But we hadn't had time to get them straight, and anything I said might be different from what Benjamin said.

"If I'm being arrested, I'd like a lawyer," I said. My parents had told me that you *always* needed to ask for a lawyer if you were accused of something, *especially* if you were innocent.

"But you haven't been arrested."

"Then I'd like to leave."

"Then I might have to arrest you."

"Okay, go ahead. And I'd like a lawyer."

He paused, tilting his head. "Do your parents like their jobs, Janie?" he asked.

"Yes. And it's Jane."

"Well, *Jane*," he said, "I can have you deported for refusing to cooperate with a police investigation, and then your parents would have to take you home. But I get the feeling that they don't *want* to go back to Los Angeles."

"What makes you think that?"

"I've read their file."

"They have a *file*?"

"Of course they have a file," he said. "We don't just let any old Communists in."

"They aren't Communists!"

"And now you have a file, too. So let's fill it with good things, shall we? Things, say, about what a cooperative foreign national you are, and how *helpful* in matters of grave importance."

"I'm fourteen," I said. "I can't have a file."

Detective Montclair looked around the ancient classroom and smiled his crooked smile, as if approving benignly of the shabby desks and dusty chalkboards. "When this building was built," he said, "a child could enter the workforce at six. You might have been at work for eight years by the age of fourteen. Difficult work, too. Physical labor. So I think you're old enough to answer a few questions about a murder, to help the country that has so generously allowed your Communist parents in, and seen fit to employ them."

"Stop calling them Communists. They aren't."

"Where were you last night?"

"At home."

"All evening? If we call your parents and ask them if you came home late, what will they say?"

I bit my lip harder, to keep the tears of frustration back. If only Benjamin and I had figured out our story ahead of time. If only I could have warned my parents to keep their mouths shut. I had a feeling Scotland Yard could track them easily to their castle in the country.

"I see from your face," Detective Montclair said, "that your parents might have a different story."

I said nothing.

"You know, if Benjamin acted alone," the detective said soothingly, "you can tell me that."

I glared at him. I wanted to tell him that a German man with a scar on his face had probably killed the gardener, and that they should be looking for him right now, but I was afraid to contradict what Benjamin might say. And the gardener had told us not to trust the police.

"Why don't you think about it for a bit," the detective said.

He left the room, and I was alone. I guessed he was going to talk to Benjamin. I would go to jail for obstruction of justice at the very least, and maybe even for murder. I wondered again what we had touched, in the gardener's cottage, and left prints on. The lantern, at least. I felt trapped and frightened, which I supposed was exactly what they wanted, but knowing that they wanted it didn't help.

After half an hour, the stocky Officer O'Nan came to move me to a room with a door at each end and two cage-like cells along one side, right next to each other, separated by a thick concrete wall. It seemed improvised, added long after the original building. Benjamin was in the first cell, holding the bars helplessly. There was another boy with him, who looked small and ragged, but then the policeman led me past and put me in the next cell and I couldn't see them anymore. The cell was cold and damp, with a low wooden bench.

O'Nan left, and I went to the bars.

"Benjamin?" I whispered, remembering the Shiskins' bugged kitchen and telling myself not to say anything incriminating, or loud.

"What'd you tell them?" he whispered back, around the concrete wall.

"Nothing! They tried to get me to turn on you and say you did it. I *hate* them."

"They did the same to me."

I put a hand out through the bars to see how far away the other cell was, and met Benjamin's hand reaching toward mine. An electric shock of surprise went through me. Our fingers interlaced and squeezed.

"It's going to be all right, Janie, I promise," he said.

Then the other boy's voice chimed in, from Benjamin's cell. It was high and clear, with an accent you didn't hear at St. Beden's. "So, d'you two have a plan for gettin' us out of here, or do I have to spring us myself?" he demanded.

We unlocked our hands.

"That's Pip," Benjamin said. "He's a pickpocket. And a housebreaker."

"Leastways I never *murdered* no one," the boy's voice said.

My heart started to pound, and I thought of jailhouse movies I'd seen, with snitches planted in the cells. "Benjamin," I whispered. "They put him in there hoping you'd talk to him!"

"I thought of that already," Benjamin said, in a full, loud voice. "Good thing I've got nothing to tell."

"Oh, they'll pin it on you anyways," Pip said cheerfully. "They're right good at that."

I heard a scuttling noise and turned to see a long gray rat moving along the wall of my cell, beneath the low wooden bench. It seemed to be heading for my feet, and I screamed, in spite of myself.

"Janie?" Benjamin called.

"There's a rat in here!"

It froze and crouched along the wall.

"Sounded like you was being murdered," the other boy said.

I felt indignant, because I was *not* some shrinking violet. In the past twenty-four hours, I'd seen a man die, let a boy stay in my room, and been threatened with deportation. I thought I'd handled it all pretty well. But a fat, dirty rat running at your feet was horrible. It watched me with beady, curious eyes, waiting for my next move.

"I want to go home," I said pathetically.

"Then lend me a hair grip," Pip said, from the other side of the wall.

"What's a hair grip?"

"It's, y'know, a little wire folded in half, like. For your hair."

"A bobby pin," I said.

"That's a silly name."

"I don't have one."

"*What?*" Pip said. "You're a girl, ain't you?"

"I don't wear them!" I said, still watching the crouching rat.

"She has American hair," Benjamin's voice explained.

"What's American hair?" I asked.

"It's—you know, there's sort of a lot of it, and it's not all pinned back."

"You're making that up."

"No," Benjamin said. "You can always tell Americans by their hair. And their shoes."

"It's true," Pip's voice agreed.

I looked down at my shoes and remembered my too-big skirt. "Wait!" I said. "I have a safety pin!"

"Well, why din't you *say* so?" Pip said.

I took the pin out of my skirt and handed it around the wall, hoping my skirt would stay up.

"Wish it was a bit longer," he complained.

"It's all I've got, okay?"

By pressing my forehead against the bars, I could just see Pip's dirty hands fiddling experimentally with the safety pin in the lock. It seemed hopeless.

Then the door outside the cells to our right opened, and Pip's hands quickly withdrew. A pink-faced matron in a gray wool dress came in and said, "There's someone here to see you."

"Me?" Pip said.

"No," she said.

There were footsteps in the hall behind her, and then Mr. Danby came into the room. I'd never been so relieved to see anyone in my life.

"Are these the children you mean?" she asked. "Not the little one, the other two."

"These are they!" Mr. Danby said. "Have they treated you all right, Miss Scott?"

I wanted to throw my arms around him, through the bars, but I sensed that would embarrass him. "No!" I said. "They keep saying we're not really arrested, so we can't have a lawyer. And they threatened to deport my parents, and it's freezing, and there's a *rat* in here. And we haven't even done anything!" I added that last part as an afterthought.

"Let's get you out of there, then," he said. "And really, madam, can you do something about the rats? It's unsanitary for the children."

"Certainly, sir," the matron said, though I could tell she intended to do nothing. She unlocked the bars and let me out.

Benjamin said, "What about the police? How do you have the authority to let us out?"

"He's from the Foreign Office," the matron said.

"The *Foreign* Office?" Benjamin said. "As in the *government* Foreign Office?"

"Yes," Mr. Danby said, looking slightly abashed. I didn't know why our Latin teacher was handling matters for the government, but I thought Mr. Danby could handle anything, so I didn't care.

Pip tried to slip out after Benjamin, but the matron closed the door on him with a clank and relocked it. He pressed his face between the bars. "Take me, too!"

I had thought Pip was younger than we were, when I'd

only seen him quickly, because he was so much smaller than Benjamin, but now I guessed he was thirteen or fourteen, like us. His hair was cropped close to his head in the way of the other Turnbull children, to combat lice, and his eyes were enormous, an unsettling bright hazel. He reminded me of a lemur I'd once seen in a zoo. "Don't leave me!" he cried.

"I apologize," Mr. Danby said. "I'm only authorized to take Mr. Burrows and Miss Scott."

"But they're my mates!" Pip said.

Mr. Danby turned to Benjamin. "Is that true?"

Benjamin shook his head. "I think he's a snitch."

"I ain't a snitch!"

Mr. Danby and the matron led us away down the hall.

"Please!" Pip howled after us. "Take me with you!"

Mr. Danby ignored him.

We passed the empty classroom where I'd been questioned, and the one full of ragged-looking students. There was a fight going on, and the matron stopped to break it up. I felt sorry for the kids, stuck in here.

"What a miserable place," Mr. Danby said when we were farther down the hall and out of earshot. "Dickens would recognize it in an instant. We'll go someplace warm for a hot cocoa."

"Where's Detective Montclair?" I asked.

"I sent him away."

"What do you do for the Foreign Office?" Benjamin asked.

"It's difficult to explain, but I'll try."

"Are you a *spy*?"

Mr. Danby smiled. "Would I tell you if I were?"

"You *are*!" Benjamin said, delighted. "But then why do you teach Latin?"

Mr. Danby sighed. "Our country lost many good men in the war," he said. "And now we're in another war, of a different kind. You're clever, so I'm sure you know that we have always stationed people in our best schools to keep an eye out for emerging—*talent*."

Benjamin went silent. I could feel his excitement at the idea that Mr. Danby was a spy, charged with recruiting new spies. Myself, I'd had plenty of excitement already, and was ready for a hot cocoa.

"And the truth is," Mr. Danby said, "that I was assigned to St. Beden's to keep an eye on you, in particular."

"On *me*?" Benjamin asked.

"We'll go to E. Pellicci's, just up the road," Mr. Danby said. "I have a driver waiting, and it's rather a good little café."

The matron joined us again and unlocked the heavy front door with a ring of keys, and Benjamin beamed at her as if they were old friends. "Thank you, madam, for the fine hospitality," he said, imitating Mr. Danby's arch politeness.

The matron scowled at Benjamin, but stood aside and let us out the door.

On the steps of Turnbull, there was sunlight and a fresh breeze, and I realized how sour and unhappy the air inside had been. I breathed deeply, and felt almost safe. Mr. Danby was going to make everything all right. "There's the car," he said.

A shining green sedan idled in the curving drive. The driver turned to look at us, and smiled a welcoming smile. I felt Benjamin catch my arm, and the blood seemed to turn to ice in my veins.

Mr. Danby's driver was the man with the scar.

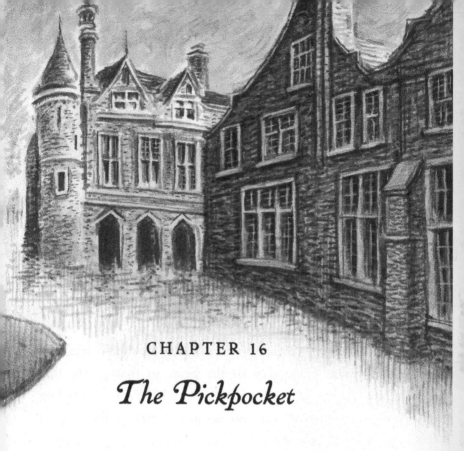

CHAPTER 16

The Pickpocket

It took about a second and a half to register what the smiling, scarred face of the driver meant. It meant that we weren't going to have cocoa, and that Danby was not our friend, and that whatever he did for the Foreign Office— if he did work for the Foreign Office—was not in our interest. Those facts came through in a flood, as if I'd torn off a blindfold in a bright, crowded room. Benjamin and I both had the same response, almost instantly: We ran *back* into the dismal, foul-smelling, cold Turnbull Hall.

The matron must have been watching us through the

cracked door, because we nearly knocked her over as we ran inside. Benjamin slammed the door behind us and leaned his shoulder into it.

"Give me the keys!" he commanded, holding the door-knob so it wouldn't turn. "Arrest us again! Just give me the keys!"

Danby pounded on the other side. "Open this door!" his muffled voice shouted.

The matron hesitated. "But . . . he's from the government."

"No he's not—he's a Soviet spy!"

I hadn't yet put all the information together to get to that point, but I realized that Benjamin was right. Shiskin had told us that the Scar was working for the Soviets, and Danby was working with the Scar, so that meant that Danby was working for the Soviets. If he'd been keeping an eye on Benjamin, it was because of the apothecary, *not* because Benjamin seemed like raw talent for the British Secret Service.

"Stuff and nonsense!" the matron said, regaining her composure. She moved toward the door as if to open it, and I grabbed the ring of keys from her hand. She yanked my hair with surprising strength, pulling my head back. I tossed Benjamin the keys, then turned and shoved her away. She fell heavily to the floor, and I resisted the urge to apologize.

Benjamin locked the front door and we ran back past the tumbled matron, down the hall. He stuck his head into the classroom full of children.

"There's a Russian spy chasing us!" he said. "Where's the back door?"

The children were too surprised to speak, until one small boy piped, "Through the kitchen!"

We ran on, and the children all jumped up from their desks and spilled after us. They filled the hall, blocking the way like a herd of sheep. I heard the matron shouting at them to stand aside.

We ran through the door to the holding cells, and Benjamin found the key to lock it behind us. Pip was still working the lock of his cell with my safety pin, and he looked up at us with surprise. "Where's your mate?" he asked.

"He's not our mate!" I said. "Will you help us escape, if we let you out?"

He shrugged. "I've almost got this picked."

Benjamin pushed his hands away and unlocked the cell with the keys.

"I almost had that!" Pip said, stamping his foot. "An' it's a bloody hard one!"

"There's a way out through the kitchen," I said. "Do you know where the kitchen is?"

"This way," Pip said, and he led us out the far door of the room.

We ran down one whitewashed hallway, and then another, and encountered a strong, sour soup smell. Finally we arrived in a large, steamy room with pots on the stove, and three cooks in stained aprons. Without slowing down, Pip took a bread roll off a tray and bit into it. Beyond the cooks was a door that looked like it led outside.

"There it is!" I said.

But then the door swung open, and Danby stepped in.

"Turn back!" Benjamin cried.

We ran back down the narrow hallway again.

"Upstairs!" Pip said, through a mouthful of bread. We wheeled right, up a flight of wooden stairs, with Danby close behind. At the top of the stairs there was an old trunk, and Benjamin pushed it so it bumped and slid down the stairs with an appalling noise. Mr. Danby dived backward as the trunk slammed into the wall. Pip whipped the remains of his bread roll at his head for good measure, hitting him just above the eye.

We ran down a long, narrow hall and up another flight of stairs, and then up a ladder that led to a trapdoor in the ceiling. Pip pushed open the trapdoor and hoisted himself into the dim attic with the agility of a spider, his legs disappearing into the dark. Benjamin and I followed more clumsily. We were in a dim, dusty space under the eaves, full of broken school desks and stacked mattresses.

"Over here!" Pip called from somewhere in the dark.

Benjamin and I dragged a musty old mattress onto the trapdoor to keep it closed. Then we crawled on our hands and knees to get to Pip, trying not to bump our heads on the low ceiling. He had found a small, filthy window, the pane crosshatched with old tape, and was trying to push it open.

"What's out there?" I asked.

"The roof."

"Then what?"

"I don't *know* yet," he said. "You fancy waiting here?"

The sash wouldn't open, so Pip leaned back on his hands and kicked the glass out with his heels. The tape kept it from shattering easily, and it took several kicks.

"Oh, that's discreet," Benjamin said.

Pip ignored him and picked shards of glass out of the frame.

"Why's it taped?" I asked.

"To keep bombs from breaking the windows in the war," Benjamin said.

Pip leaned out, looked around, and got hold of something above the window on the outside. He was ridiculously graceful and limber, and we watched his skinny legs disappear as he lifted himself up and out.

I stuck my head out the window and looked down at the pieces of glass on the ground, far below. No one seemed to have noticed the broken window yet, but looking down made me terribly dizzy. I heard a bumping noise over by the trapdoor. Someone—probably Danby—was trying to get it open, but the mattress was weighing it down. I looked up at Pip on the roof, but the roof seemed impossibly far above the window.

"I can't climb up there!" I said.

Pip was calm. "Take the top of the sill with your left hand," he said, "and reach for the roof with your right."

I did, sure I was going to fall.

"Now stand on the sill and give me your left hand."

I did, and Pip pulled with surprising strength. I clambered up. The slate roof was steeply pitched, and worn and slippery, and I clung to the peak of it. Something in the pit of my stomach *strongly* objected to the height.

Pip hoisted Benjamin up after me.

"Now what?" I asked.

"We look for a gutter," Pip said. "A pipe. Some way down." He scrambled down to the edge of the roof to look, and just watching him made my stomach seize and flip again. If getting to a gutter meant climbing down that steep pitch, I didn't think I could do it. Benjamin seemed no better off than I was—he was straddling the roof's peak as if it were an unpredictable horse.

A cry went up below. All of the children had spilled out of the back of the house, and they stared up at us from the ground, with the pink-faced matron.

Pip climbed, still more like a spider, back up to join us. "They're right underneath the gutter pipe," he said. "We can't climb down."

"Some plan," Benjamin said.

"Right, you come up with a better one!"

"The elixir!" I plunged my hand into the pocket of my school blazer. The gardener had told us to use it only for a good purpose, and escaping off this roof seemed awfully good. But my pocket was empty. I felt the other one. "It's gone," I wailed. "I was sure I had it."

"What's a lickser?" Pip asked.

"An *elixir*," Benjamin said. "Like a potion."

I was too stunned by the loss to lie. I lowered my voice so the people on the ground couldn't hear. "It was supposed to, well . . . to turn us into birds," I said. "At least we think it would. But I lost it."

"How could you *lose* it?" Benjamin asked.

That made me indignant. "You didn't even think it would work!"

"But you did!" he said. "So you should have kept it!"

Then we heard a grunt of effort, and saw Danby's hand grip the roof where we had climbed up from the broken window. I looked back at Pip in a panic, and he was holding up the little brown bottle, between his thumb and forefinger.

"This it?" he asked.

"How did you get that?"

"From your pocket," he said. "When you left with your mate there." He nodded toward the pale fingers gripping the roof's edge.

I put my hand on my blazer pocket and tried to think when Pip could have reached into it. It seemed impossible. There was another grunt, and a second hand appeared on the roof next to the first. Then Mr. Danby's face appeared, strained with effort. He hadn't yet figured out how to lever himself up onto the roof.

"Benjamin," he called. "Janie. Please. That man you saw in the car is a friend. He's been working for England. I can give you proof."

"You're lying!" I said. I turned back to Pip. "You have to give me the bottle."

Pip backed away, along the peak of the roof. "So you can leave me again?" he said. "What if I just drink it, and leave *you*?"

"We *couldn't* take you with us before," I said, crawling forward. "But now we can. We'll all leave together."

"How long does it last?"

"We don't know."

"Is there enough for all three of us?"

"Probably."

"You don't know!"

Danby got one leg up over the edge of the roof with a thump. Pip stood, right on the peak, and ran effortlessly away. Benjamin and I tried to follow, but my feet kept slipping down the sides.

The gothic roof of Turnbull had two peaks, like a child's drawing of two triangular mountains side by side, and then a round turret beyond. Pip slid easily down into the valley between the two peaks and clambered up the second one. I hesitated behind him.

"Go!" Benjamin said.

So I slid with effort after Pip and started climbing. Benjamin followed.

Danby was still slipping along on the first peak, in slick leather-soled shoes. "Don't be ridiculous, Miss Scott," he called. "We're on the same side!"

Pip slid down the second peak, which dropped off into empty space, except where it attached to the cylindrical turret. The crowd on the ground had moved so they were still just below him. He edged over to the base of the turret and started to climb up it. Benjamin and I followed. The brickwork on the turret wall was uneven, and the bricks created footholds and handholds, so it was possible to scale. I'd even started to get used to the height. The children were cheering, and looked happy and excited, as if they were watching a film.

Once we had climbed into the top of the turret, it was as if we were in a kind of lookout post. There didn't seem to be any way to get back inside the house. Maybe there had once been access, but now there was only a drain to let out the rain. The lookout had walls about three feet high, so the people below couldn't see us unless we stood and looked over the wall, which we did.

The children immediately cheered, and the matron looked stern. "Come *down*," she said. "You have nowhere to go."

"Call the detectives!" Benjamin said. "Tell them to come back!" He pointed at Danby, who had sat down on the nearest peak to rest. "That man is a Russian spy!"

Danby, his striped socks revealed below his trouser cuffs by his bent knees, wiped his handsome forehead with a handkerchief. "Benjamin," he said wearily. "I am no more a Russian spy than you are."

"Jump!" one of the ragged children shouted to us. "We'll catch you!"

"Yes, jump!" some of the others joined in, shouting and laughing and leaping, to demonstrate how we should do it.

Danby started climbing down the roof toward the base of our turret.

I sank down behind the wall and turned to Pip. "Open the bottle," I said. "We'll all take some."

But Pip hesitated, and Benjamin lost patience. He snatched it away, unscrewed the top, and drank.

Right away, a startled look came over his face, and he set the bottle down. For a second, nothing more happened. I looked over the wall and saw Danby trying to scale our turret. His feet slipped, and he swore.

When I looked back at Benjamin, he had started to shrink. His head grew longer in front and sank into his shoulders, and his body tilted forward at the hips. A feathered tail grew out behind him, and he kept rapidly getting smaller. His hands disappeared, and his arms became wings. Then everything I recognized as Benjamin was gone.

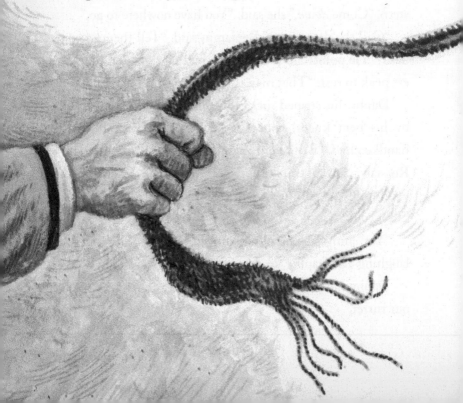

CHAPTER 17

Flight

Where Benjamin had been, on the stone floor of the turret of Turnbull Hall, was a plump-chested, sand-colored bird with a crest of feathers on his head. I've wondered since that day about why I wasn't more astonished, watching Benjamin turn into a bird. But it's very hard *not* to accept your friend turning into a bird when you see it happening in front of you, and could reach out and touch his feathered head if you wanted. I didn't recognize the type of bird he was at the time, but I learned later that it was a skylark, which is a very scruffy, energetic, Benjamin-like bird. "I don't know what exactly you are," I said. "But you're definitely something that flies. And you're not the size of a giant condor."

"That's amazing," Pip said. He grabbed the bottle, drank half of what was left, and handed it off to me. His eyes widened. "Oh, that *is* odd, that is," he said.

After a few seconds, he started to shrink, too, and his head tilted and lengthened into a beak, and then he was a tiny, dark-feathered swallow. He shook out his curving wings as if to test their length.

I had been so preoccupied with their transformations that I hadn't noticed Danby's exasperated face rising over the turret wall. He stared at me, and then at the two birds. He looked down over the side of the turret for the missing boys, and then back at me. "Where did they go?" he asked.

"What is it, sir?" the matron's voice called anxiously from below. "What's happened?"

"Only the girl is here," Danby called back. "And two birds."

"Two what?"

"Two *birds*," Danby said.

He started to push himself up over the turret wall toward us, and I moved away from him.

Pip the swallow gave a little double hop and lifted off, as if casually, into the sky. He didn't look like a child who'd become a bird with no preparation—he flew as if he'd been a bird all his life, dipping and soaring through the air. Benjamin the skylark watched him, too.

A high, piping child's voice came up from the ground, saying, "Perhaps they became the birds!"

An older girl said sharply, "People don't just become *birds*."

I thought of the gardener saying we had to *allow for the possibilities*, and I felt sorry for the older girl, who couldn't make room in her imagination for what the smaller child had guessed.

Danby seemed suddenly to make room for it in his imagination, and he grabbed at the skylark, but Benjamin leaped just out of reach along the turret wall. Then he was in the air. He gave a birdcall of surprise, and swooped and chirped in a way that sounded like laughter. He wasn't as graceful as Pip, but he was flying. There were cheers from the children, who were all allowing for the possibility now.

While Danby watched Benjamin fly away, I drank the rest of the bottle. The elixir was syrupy in texture, and bitter and mossy in taste.

I felt a strange, rushing feeling in my veins, and understood why Benjamin and Pip had looked so surprised. I'd never been aware of each individual blood vessel in my body like that, and of the blood coursing through them. Then I felt my heartbeat speed up, and my bones seemed to lighten. I dropped the bottle and it fell to the ground. The distant sound of glass smashing on the walk below seemed to shake Danby from his reverie, and he lunged toward me.

My skull felt like it was changing shape, and lightening, and I thought: *Allow for the possibilities*. And then I leaped, still human, off the roof. Danby caught the end of my scarf, and it's a good thing it wasn't tied on, or he might have broken my neck. It slipped over my shoulder as I jumped, and I left him with the scarf in his hand.

I plummeted, of course, but I knew from Benjamin and Pip how quickly I would change. My hands became wings in midair, and my legs became tiny bird legs. I stretched my new wings tentatively and rose up just as they finished growing, and just before I would have crashed into the hard ground.

I rose to the second-story windows, and then the third. I looked down at myself and saw a smooth, round red-feathered stomach. I was a robin! But there seemed to be something wrong with my upper wings, just around my bird's shoulders. Then I remembered Danby snatching my scarf away just as I was changing, and realized my wings must be missing feathers.

Benjamin and Pip were circling overhead, calling out to me, and I fluttered clumsily toward them. I started to think about what I should do to get to where they were, but as soon as I started analyzing all the necessary motions, I felt myself fall.

"Catch the robin!" Mr. Danby called.

"I'll get her!" the matron said.

The ground came dizzyingly close, and the children shouted, "Fly! Fly away!"

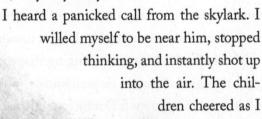

I heard a panicked call from the skylark. I willed myself to be near him, stopped thinking, and instantly shot up into the air. The children cheered as I rose free.

We were
high over Turnbull,
looking down at the dumb-
struck and furious adults and the
laughing, triumphant children. And then
we were sailing away.

I had sometimes, before that day, had dreams about flying, but dreams had *nothing* on the real thing. We soared high over the streets of the East End, and the people looked tiny below. We could see where the bombs had fallen in the war, and where they had left buildings untouched. Pip wheeled and hovered and then dived with rocket speed toward the ground before soaring up again with a gleeful, birdlike laugh.

I couldn't manage the acrobatics with my incomplete wings. I wondered if Danby still had the scarf, or if it had turned to feathers in his hand. I looked back toward Turnbull and saw the green sedan pulling out of the drive. I realized that Danby and the Scar would know where Benjamin's father was, and if we followed them, they might take us there.

Benjamin must have thought the same thing. When I swooped to follow the sedan through the streets, the boys did, too. We passed a few actual birds as we flew, and they all gave us a wide berth, not trusting a skylark, a swallow, and a robin all traveling together. One curious crow flew close to investigate, but it seemed to detect something unnatural about us, and cawed and flapped away.

The green sedan drove south, and west, and then stopped in an ordinary London neighborhood, with rows of terraced houses. The car parked in a side street, and neither of the men got out.

I dropped down to the roof of the parked car, trying to land softly but nearly hurtling off the edge. The passenger window was open, letting out a curl of cigarette smoke, and I perched just above it. Benjamin landed beside me, then Pip. My hearing was better than usual, as a robin, and I could hear the Scar, out of sight in the driver's seat, say in heavily accented English, "Children do not become birds, like this."

"I would concur," Danby said, "except that I saw it happen."

"They cannot shrink so."

"But they did!" Danby said. "It's because of that book. The apothecary's book. That Scott girl, the American, was ready to hand it over to me."

Benjamin turned to me. His shiny bird's eyes were bright, and he held his beak at a significant angle. You wouldn't think that a skylark's face could convey *I told you so*, but I'm here to tell you that it can. I was glad that Danby hadn't discovered that Sergei had the satchel with the Pharmacopoeia in it.

"The children had clearly seen you before," Danby continued. "Which means you've been careless."

The German's voice was icy and clear. "I am never careless."

"They must have seen you at the shop," Danby said. "Or in the garden. Someone who is *careful* might have noticed that they were there."

The Scar muttered something I didn't understand.

"And now they've flown away," Danby said. "And they no longer trust me, and it's impossible to get answers when your prisoner has taken those bloody muting pills."

Benjamin and I looked at each other. The mute prisoner must be his father. He'd taken a pill like Shiskin's, to make him unable to speak. Danby's cigarette appeared through the open window, and he knocked the ash to the ground. I wondered how I had ever found his long, pale hands appealing. They seemed so sinister now.

"*I* could get answers," the Scar said.

Danby sighed. "The drug makes speech impossible. It's very clever."

The passenger door opened with sudden decisiveness, and I flew, panicked, into a nearby tree. Benjamin and Pip scattered, too. Danby didn't seem to see us. He got out of the car and ground out his cigarette with his heel, then straightened his tie and walked around the corner.

The three of us left our trees and flew after him, keeping our distance, and Danby walked to the end of the block. He stopped outside a boxy-looking building, turned a key in the door, and vanished inside.

There was a large tree that looked like a sycamore outside the building, and I landed on a leafy, low branch beside

Benjamin and Pip. I didn't know what the building might be, but I was sure it was where they were keeping Benjamin's father.

We couldn't communicate in speech, but I knew that Benjamin wanted to fly in as a skylark as soon as someone opened the door, and I knew Pip thought it was a bad idea. I can't explain now exactly how I knew all of that, but it was clear in their eyes and in the movement of their heads and their wings.

At some point during this avian battle of wills, a stealthy orange tabby cat must have been climbing our tree. We were oblivious, thinking only about the locked door and the question of whether to go in.

Then a man pushed open the bunker's door and came outside. Benjamin spread his wings to fly in the open door, but Pip chirped and fluttered to stop him. And then the giant tabby reached our branch and pounced on Benjamin's back. Benjamin screeched, in his thin bird's voice, and tried to fly away, but she had him in her claws.

I was paralyzed with fear, but Pip wasn't. He flew straight at the cat's huge yellow eyes with his sharp beak. She yowled in pain, dropping Benjamin to the ground. Then she swiped at Pip with her paw, pinning him to the branch.

The man leaving the bunker stopped to watch the commotion for a moment, but it was only a cat after a couple of birds in a tree, and he walked away, lighting a cigarette inside a cupped hand.

I grabbed the cat's soft ear with my talons just as she took Pip's neck in her sharp white teeth. I squeezed her ear, and her yowl of pain turned to one of surprise as Pip started to grow, right under her claws. He lost his feathers and grew clothes, and suddenly the cat had a full-sized boy in her clutches, crouching precariously on the branch.

The cat scrambled back in a panic and fell out of the tree. I watched her twist in midair and land heavily on her feet. She didn't stop to contemplate what had gone wrong, but raced off down the street, an orange streak.

Benjamin, too, had become a boy again, and was sitting on the ground. Pip lowered himself by his arms off the branch, then dropped the remaining distance. They both seemed a little dazed, and Pip was rubbing the back of his neck, where he had four small puncture wounds from the cat's teeth. I thought the stress of the attack must have caused the boys' bodies to change back. I hadn't changed yet, but I had become a bird last and I hadn't been seized by a cat. I flew down to the grass, where Benjamin felt his legs. "No broken bones," he said. "I don't think."

"That cat put holes in me!" Pip said.

I flew to his shoulder to look. Benjamin peered at them, too. "They're tiny."

"Says you!"

"We still have to get inside that building," Benjamin said. "Janie could fly in, when that man comes back."

"She can't!" Pip said. "I've been tryin' to tell you, it's a secret bunker. She'll get caught if she turns human, and she can't carry your da out with her little wings."

Benjamin stared at him. "It's a secret bunker?"

"Sure. It's a military bomb shelter, underground. For Churchill and that lot, if there's another war."

"How do you *know* that?" Benjamin asked.

Pip shrugged his narrow shoulders, nearly dislodging me. "*Everybody* knows. To put a bloody enormous bunker right under Bethnal Green, you need builders, right? And the builders all say the job's *top secret*, mind your business, till they get a few pints in 'em. Then they spill it. They swear all the barmaids to secrecy, like."

"How big is it?"

"The whole block, underground."

I had an idea, but I couldn't speak. Then the idea was interrupted by a strange sensation coming over me. It came in a wave, and I couldn't control it. I hopped off Pip's shoulder as my heartbeat started to slow, and my arms prickled in a thousand places where the feathers were disappearing, retracting back into my skin. I grew fingers and toes, and my skull thickened and expanded, and hair grew from my head.

And then I was sitting on the grass in my school uniform.

"Right," Pip said. "Good. She can't fly in."

Through the fogginess in my new human head, I remembered my idea. "What if we could be invisible?" I asked.

"That would solve a lot o' things," Pip said, as if I was joking.

"We'd need the Pharmacopoeia," I said.

"The farm-a what?"

"It's a book," I said, "and Sergei has it."

"We *hope* he still has it," Benjamin said.

CHAPTER 18

The Opera Game

School was just getting out when we got back to St. Beden's to recover the Pharmacopoeia, and students were streaming out into the gray afternoon, released for the day. They were all going about their lives, heading off to field hockey practice or choir rehearsal, and I felt that an enormous, unbridgeable gulf had opened up between us. Wearing the wrong clothes and not knowing Latin seemed like enviable problems to have.

Pip stopped at the bottom of the stairs, looked up at the tall, imposing Victorian building, and shuddered. "I'll just wait out 'ere," he said.

It struck me as funny that Pip had no problem running across a peaked roof three stories off the ground, or attacking a monstrous cat as a tiny bird, but when confronted with a school, even after hours, he looked scared. It was as if someone might come after him with a butterfly net and pin him inside a case.

"But school's out," Benjamin said. "It's safe."

Pip looked doubtful.

"They're not going to kidnap you and make you go," I said. "No one will notice one more kid."

Benjamin and I started up the stone steps, but Pip hung back.

Then Sarah Pennington came out the front door, and the February clouds momentarily parted—they really did. I'm not making this up. A shaft of sunlight caught her golden hair as she stopped at the top of the steps.

Pip stared, openmouthed, at this paragon of schoolgirl beauty. A few strands had escaped from Sarah's long braid, and they sparkled around her face. She blinked her long eyelashes in the unexpected light.

Then her eyes met Pip's bright hazel ones. I doubt she could have avoided it, given the intensity of his unconcealed longing. She seemed startled by what she saw, and she glanced at me, then at Benjamin, then back at Pip. We were all standing on the steps below her, like acolytes before the queen. I thought it might be good for Pip that she couldn't see how short he was.

"Hello," she said.

"Hello," Pip said, as if in a dream.

"How do you do?" she asked.

He nodded, paralyzed with love.

"This is our friend Pip," I said.

"Pip?" she asked, tilting her head fetchingly. "As in *Great Expectations*?"

"Why not?" Pip said.

She smiled. "Do you have great expectations?"

"I do now."

"Do you go to this school?"

"Not yet," he said. "But if you go here, I will."

I noticed that he had pronounced the *h* in "here," and wondered how much he changed his accent to suit his situation each day.

Sarah blushed, flustered. Having started the flirtation, she didn't seem to know how to keep it up. "My car is waiting," she said, and she skipped lightly past us, down the steps, ignoring Benjamin and me but glancing one more time at Pip.

Pip gazed after her. Then he scampered down to the black car that waited at the curb, slid in front of the chauffeur, and opened the back door for her, saying something I couldn't hear.

"Is that a limousine?" I asked Benjamin.

"A Daimler," he said. "It picks her up every day."

As the Daimler pulled away, with Sarah safely inside, Pip clutched his heart and staggered backward, with the mock-clumsiness of a vaudeville performer. Then he ran back up the stairs.

"I think I should go to this school," he announced.

"What did she say?" I asked.

"She told me 'er name. Sarah Eleanor Pennington!" He sighed.

"She told you her *middle* name?" Benjamin asked.

"Benjamin fancies her, too," I explained.

"I do not!"

"Yes you do. You know how she leaves school every day."

"I *don't* fancy her," Benjamin said. "I *did*."

Pip sized up his new rival, then shrugged. "May the best man win," he said.

Benjamin stalked into the building, letting the door swing closed behind him, and I wondered if he was pretending not to like Sarah because he envied Pip's success, or if he really meant it.

"What was that she said about great spectations?" Pip asked.

"It's a novel," I said. "*Great Expectations*. About a poor boy named Pip who falls in love with a beautiful rich girl."

"And the girl falls in love with 'im, too?"

"I can't give away the ending."

"Huh," Pip said. "Then I'll 'afta read it."

We found Sergei at chess club in one of the history class-rooms. Six unassuming boys sat at chessboards set up on three desks. Sergei was across from the pimply kid from our Latin class, about to make the first move, but he jumped up from the desk when he saw us.

"Benjamin! Janie!" he said. "I have your—"

He caught Benjamin's look of displeasure.

"Oh!" he said. "Sorry! But it's only chess club. They're my friends!"

Benjamin drew Sergei to the back of the room, out of ear-shot, and Pip slid into the vacated chair.

"Is this game like checkers?" he asked the pimply boy.

The boy rolled his eyes. "No. Well, only superficially."

"What's superficially?"

The boy thought about it. "On the surface."

"Aright," Pip said. "What do you play for?"

"Nothing," the boy said. "For pleasure."

"*Pleasure*," Pip said. "That's daft. Let's say half a crown. Can I move this little round-headed one?"

I left them to their game and followed Benjamin and Sergei to the back of the room.

"I have the book right here!" Sergei whispered. "I've kept it with me! I was worried. Where did the police take you?" His face was flushed with excitement.

"Has anyone asked you about the book?" Benjamin asked.

Sergei thought about that. "No! What should we do next?"

"Nothing," Benjamin said. "I just need it back."

Sergei reluctantly handed over Benjamin's satchel. "I didn't even get to look at it," he complained.

"I also need to borrow your Latin book."

Sergei dug in his bag and produced *Kennedy's Latin Primer.* "Can't I help you? Please? I'm good at Latin."

"We promised your father we'd leave you out of it," Benjamin said.

"He doesn't have to know!"

"Is he okay?" I asked Sergei. "I mean, did he get in trouble for what we said in your house?"

"I don't think so," Sergei said. "And he can talk again."

"You should tell him to be careful," I said. "He's in a lot of danger."

"Really?" Sergei asked.

Across the room, Pip said, "Checkmate!"

His pimply opponent was staring down at the board. He looked up at me in protest. "He asked if the game was like *checkers*!"

"That's half a crack, please," Pip said smugly.

"I don't *have* half a crown."

"S'all right," Pip said. "I'll take your marker. I think you're good for it."

We stood over their chessboard and Sergei studied it for a moment, then looked at Pip with respect. "Is it the Opera game?"

"The *what*?"

"It's outright thievery!" the pimply boy said.

"The Opera game was played in sixteen moves," Sergei said, "by an American master against two amateurs, in an opera box. Where do you study chess?"

"I don't *study* it," Pip said. "My uncle taught me down the pub."

"Will you join our chess club?"

"Don't let him!" the boy said. "He tricked me!"

"He can't join chess club," Benjamin said. "He doesn't even go to this school."

"I will soon!"

"Let's go," Benjamin said, and he nudged Pip toward the classroom door.

Sergei caught my arm. "Please take me with you."

"I'm so sorry, Sergei," I said, and gently pulled my arm free. "We can't."

So we weren't, as you see, very good at being sneaky. We'd interrogated our own ally in a bugged house, and turned into birds in front of the entire population of Turnbull Hall, and now we'd hustled the St. Beden's chess club in the space of five minutes. We left Sergei looking brokenhearted, the pimply boy looking fiercely indignant, and the rest of the club looking like they weren't sure what had hit them. If we were going to do anything unseen and unnoticed, we needed help.

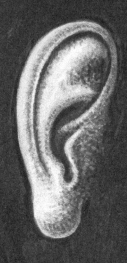

CHAPTER 19

Invisible

Mr. Gilliam's chemistry classroom was locked, but it only took Pip a few seconds to open the door with a bent paper clip. The room was empty, and Benjamin relocked the door and lodged a chair under the knob.

I remembered that the invisibility spell the gardener had shown us in the Pharmacopoeia was on the page just after the Smell of Truth, and had the Greek letters Αιδος at the top. I remembered because invisibility appealed to me—much more, even, than flying. We found the page, and the instructions were in Latin, so Benjamin started translating with Sergei's primer.

"*Balineum* means 'bath,'" he said. "I think we have to prepare a bath."

"A *bath*?" Pip said. "Don't you just drink a lickser?"

"Maybe you have to soak in this one, to be invisible," I said.

We considered the classroom sink, which wasn't deep enough.

"What about that?" Pip asked, pointing to a big garbage can in the corner.

We emptied the crumpled paper out and carried the can over near the book. It was large enough to get inside, and it wasn't even too disgusting.

"Now what?" Pip asked.

"*Liquefac aurum.*" Benjamin flipped the primer's pages. "*Liquefac* means 'melt.' We have to melt something. We'll need a Bunsen burner. Here, take the dictionary, Janie, and I'll set one up. What's *aurum*?"

I looked it up. "Gold!" I said, my heart sinking. "We don't have that."

"If we were decent alchemists, we could make it," Benjamin said.

"We need two drachms."

Benjamin looked at the ceiling, calculating—he'd retained at least some knowledge of compounding medicines, from working for his father. "That's about a quarter of an ounce, I think. Not much."

"Janie's got gold earrings," Pip said.

I reached for my ears and felt the small, round studs. "They were my grandmother's," I said. "She's dead."

There was a silence in the room. My nana Helen was my mother's mother, and she'd tried to act elegant and sophisticated when she came to visit us, because that's how she thought Hollywood was, but she couldn't help being warm and silly, because that was her nature. The earrings were the only things of hers I had.

Benjamin looked uncomfortable. "You don't have to give them up," he said.

"Yes I do," I said, and I took off an earring. "Here. Melt them."

"Are you sure?"

"Yes." And I almost *was* sure, now that I'd made the offer. "She'd want us to find your father."

"Thank you," Benjamin said, holding them for a second in indecision before he dropped them in a clay crucible over a Bunsen burner. I looked away.

There were other ingredients, and I helped translate the rest of the instructions, but I can't tell you what they were, because I was thinking about how my nana Helen had made me promise to wait to pierce my ears until I was twenty. I had promised, but only because I thought she'd live to see me grown up, well past twenty. She died when I was twelve, and it seemed unfair. At a slumber party that same year, I let Penny Meadows numb my earlobe with ice and then pierce it with a needle and dental floss, using half a potato as a backstop. I almost fainted—not from the piercing, which didn't hurt as much as the ice did, but from the feeling of the floss being pulled, dragging slightly, through my ear. I let Penny do the other one, too, because I was going to be elegant like my nana Helen had always wanted to be. My mother was upset, but she came around. "A sewing needle?" she'd said, inspecting the neat holes. "And you didn't faint? You take after your father."

Benjamin ground the melted gold with something else until it became a powder, which he mixed into a solution that he poured into the garbage can and diluted with water from Mr. Gilliam's chemistry lab sink.

"Now what?" I asked.

"*Lava vestibus depositis,*" Benjamin read. "That's the last thing on the page."

I flipped through the primer. "Oh no," I said.

"What does it mean?" Pip asked.

"It's a command to wash . . . um, the clothes having been dropped," I said. "I think it means 'get in the bath naked.'"

We all looked at one another.

"The bird thing worked on clothes," Benjamin said in a tone of protest, as if being naked was my idea.

"The gardener said there are different ways of changing something," I said. "I think he called the avian elixir a

transformative process, and said that this one is only a masking process. Maybe it only works on your body."

"So if it wears off, we'll be starkers inside a military bunker," Pip said.

"We might feel it wearing off," Benjamin said. "And have
some time."

"What, three seconds?" Pip asked. "Time to put your
hands over your willy?"

Benjamin shook his head, dismissing the objections. "I
have to find my father," he said. "You don't have to do this,
but I do." He shrugged off his school blazer and started unty-
ing his tie.

"We'll go with you," I said.

"Maybe you should turn around, Janie."

"Wait!" Pip said. Mr. Gilliam had a freestanding blackboard in the room, the two-sided kind that moves on wheels,
and Pip rolled it between the garbage can and us. "We've got
a screen like this at home," he said. "'Cause the bath's in the
kitchen."

Benjamin stepped behind the rolling blackboard, and we
could only see him from the knees down. His white shirt
dropped to the floor, and he kicked off his shoes and pulled
off his socks. His feet were pale, and looked vulnerable. His
blue wool pants dropped, and he climbed into the garbage
can with a slosh.

"Benjamin!" I said, remembering. "The note in the mar-
gin said to leave one part of your body out!"

"What part?"

"I've got a funny idea," Pip said.

"That's *not* funny," Benjamin said. "And it's too late anyway."

I blushed in spite of myself. Pip giggled.

"Maybe part of a hand," I said. "Something you can see, so you'll know when other people are seeing it."

"My hands are already wet."

"A shoulder?" Pip suggested.

"I'll try," Benjamin said. "It's awkward in here."

There was more sloshing, and we heard the thud of a knee or an elbow against the inside of the metal trash can. Then a wet footprint appeared on the concrete floor beside Benjamin's clothes, and another. There were no feet making the footprints.

"Benjamin!" I said. "It works! We can't see your feet!"

There was silence from behind the blackboard, except for the dripping.

"Benjamin?" I said.

"It's so strange," he said. "I can't see myself."

"Come out an' show us," Pip said.

"But I'm naked."

"But we can't see you!"

The wet footprints came slowly around the side of the blackboard. A pale smudge of pink skin floated five feet above the ground. I knew it must be part of Benjamin's shoulder, but I wouldn't have noticed it if I hadn't been looking for it. The pink spot moved, and a wet handprint appeared in the white chalk dust on the blackboard. There was no other sign of him. "It's as if I'm not here," he said, wondering.

"Brilliant!" Pip said. "I'm goin' in!" He disappeared behind the board.

"I can't tell you how strange this feels," Benjamin's voice said, from just above the pink floating spot of skin.

The two of us stood there awkwardly. I was as awed by the fact that he was naked as that he was invisible. There was a slosh as Pip climbed into the can.

"Remember to leave some part of your body out," I said.

"Right," Pip said.

"I don't know if I can do this," I said. "It might be too embarrassing."

"You think it isn't embarrassing for me?" Benjamin asked.

There was another sloshing behind the chalkboard, and Pip's wet footprints came scampering around the side. He was laughing delightedly.

"I *love* this!" he said. "I always *wanted* this!"

At first I couldn't see what was visible on him, but then I saw one floating ear. It was more identifiable as a body part than Benjamin's shoulder was, but it was also smaller and harder to see, especially when he was facing us and we weren't seeing the ear from the side.

"I want to go everywhere!" Pip said. "We can sneak into the cinema! An' the casino! An' the races!"

"First we can go to the bunker and find my father," Benjamin reminded him. "Your turn, Janie."

I went around the blackboard and looked at the two piles of clothes on the floor. Experimentally, I dunked a corner of my sleeve into the bath. It came out soaking wet, but unchanged. If I kept my clothes on, I'd be invisible, but in wet, visible clothes.

"Come on, Janie," Benjamin's voice said. "Before Mr. Gilliam comes back. We can't see you."

I looked once more into the garbage can full of solution, and thought that if my grandmother's earrings had been melted down for this, I might as well make use of it. I took off my clothes and climbed in. I decided to keep the pinky finger on my right hand out, as it seemed small and easy to hide. The water was cold, and I held my breath and tucked my knees so I could dunk my head under and get my hair wet. I waited a few seconds and then stood up, dripping, and looked down at myself. There was nothing there. It was disorienting. When I touched my arm, it felt slippery and wet, but I couldn't see it: I only saw water dripping in the shape of an arm. The clash between what I knew and what I saw made me dizzy. I climbed out, watching the water fill in the space in the can where my body had been, and saw the telltale footprints appear on the classroom floor.

"Did it work?" Pip asked, and his ear came around the screen.

"Hey!" I said. "You're not supposed to come back here!"

"But you're *invisible*!"

Benjamin's clothes seemed to be picking themselves up off the floor, and I could see his pink shoulder, leaning over.

"I didn't barge in on you guys!"

"We don't know how long it will last," Benjamin's voice said. "We have to go." A low cupboard below the sink opened, and his clothes seemed to throw themselves into it. "We should dump the bath."

"I wish we could keep it for later," Pip said wistfully.

"We can't leave a trail," Benjamin said.

I put my clothes in the cupboard, wanting to take them with me, although they would have looked like a bundle of clothes floating bizarrely down the street. The heavy garbage can seemed to levitate as Pip and Benjamin lifted it together and poured it out in the laboratory's sink.

Then we heard a thump from across the room: the thwarted noise of wood jamming as someone shoved the classroom door against the propped chair.

"Who's in there?" Mr. Gilliam's voice called.

Benjamin and Pip threw the paper trash back into the wet garbage can. I put away the Bunsen burner and the crucible and the beakers we'd used. Then I saw the Pharmacopoeia on the lab table.

"The book!" I said. We couldn't carry it out without it being seen.

The teacher rattled the doorknob again. "Open this door!"

The book seemed to float in Benjamin's hands to a high shelf with some other heavy chemistry books. I saw the logic: It looked like it belonged there, and blended in.

Mr. Gilliam was pounding on the door by now. We moved cautiously toward it.

"I'll move the chair," I whispered. "You go out after he comes in."

We got in position and I reached for the chair. It was like reaching for something in the dark, knowing approximately where it is. But it was the opposite: I knew exactly where the chair was. It was my own hands I couldn't see. The pinky finger, at least, was reassuring. When I had a good grip, I pulled the chair free.

Mr. Gilliam, who was so perfectly round that his belt looked like it bisected a beach ball, burst into the room and stood looking around. I saw Pip's ear, then Benjamin's shoulder, glide out of the room. I stayed very still.

"I know you're in here!" Mr. Gilliam said.

I dodged him as he came near. He stormed past me, looking for the rascally students who were surely crouching behind the lab tables, and I slipped out.

The school was empty—even the chess club was gone—and we ran down the hall in bare feet. It was disorienting, running without being able to see my legs. It almost made me forget about being naked, but not quite. The secretary with the sheep's curls came out of her office, and we slowed down so we'd make no noise. I slid my visible pinky along the wall, but she didn't seem to notice anything. I could see that Pip had kept his paper clip for picking locks. But no one expects to see a finger or a paper clip floating down the hall, so no one does.

We pushed open the front doors of the school and stepped out into the February day, and it was *freezing*, being damp

and naked. I hugged my arms. I'd anticipated the embarrassment of nakedness, but I'd completely forgotten about the
cold. Pip let loose a shocking string of words, most of which
I'd never heard before. "Is there some trick that makes you
warm?" he asked.

"I only know one," Benjamin said.

"Well?"

"Running to Bethnal Green," Benjamin said.

The patch of pink shoulder set off down the steps at a fast
clip, and Pip and I followed. I tried to think about how we
were rescuing Benjamin's father from evil forces, and *that* was
what mattered—not that the cold concrete stung my feet, and
not that we were running naked and freezing into the wind.

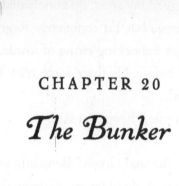

CHAPTER 20

The Bunker

We ran, invisible, through the streets of London, dodging people in warm hats, scarves, and woolen greatcoats, who couldn't see us and would have walked right into us. Benjamin was right about the running warming us up: By the time we got to the bunker, I was out of breath, but I wasn't cold anymore.

Pip's ear went straight to the lock on the bunker's door, and his paper clip looked like a tiny worm wiggling in the air as he worked. Benjamin and I kept an eye out for passersby. "Oh, come on, now," Pip said to the lock. "Right—*there* it is." The door swung open, and his ear went inside.

I bumped into Benjamin's bare shoulder as we tried to go through at the same time.

"Sorry!" we both said.

"Shh!" Pip said.

Inside the door there was a small room with an elevator, but instead of a button to call the car, there was a place to insert a key.

"Can you pick that?" Benjamin asked.

"I dunno," Pip said. "It's a switch for the lift."

As he said it, we heard the elevator cables running, and we stepped back. I held my visible pinky behind my back, not sure if that would do any good. Then I pressed it against the wall, so at least it wasn't floating. The doors opened, and Mr. Danby came out with a young man who looked puzzled.

"Stand outside and watch for *birds*?" the young man asked.

"Three small ones, all together," Danby said. "One is a red-chested American robin. Captain Harrison thinks he saw a cat attacking them. I don't understand why he didn't report it right away."

"I'm sorry, sir, but—I don't think I would have reported a thing like that either."

"*That*'s why you're only a lieutenant," Danby snapped.

I felt Pip's hand grab mine, and he pulled me around the two men, toward the open elevator door. The three of us tiptoed silently into the car.

"So, if I see three birds, I call you?" the young man said.

"Try to capture them first," Danby said.

The lieutenant, who wasn't in uniform—I guessed because of the bunker's "secrecy"—went unhappily outside. It was clear that he thought Danby had lost his mind.

Danby turned a key in the switch and got back into the elevator with us, glancing up at the upper corners of the car. He was looking for birds, I supposed. The doors closed and we started to sink down under the ground.

Below ground, the elevator opened onto a small room, in which a row of orange hard hats hung over brown canvas jumpsuits on hooks. Heavy boots were tucked neatly under a bench along the wall. Danby went out of the room into a hallway and turned right. We followed him, padding barefoot past framed pictures of Queen Elizabeth, Princess Margaret, and Winston Churchill.

Then, abruptly, Danby stopped and turned around, as if he'd sensed someone behind him. I tucked my visible pinky behind a picture frame and held my breath. He scanned the hallway.

Another man leaned out of a doorway and called, "Danby! If you please."

"Yes, General," Danby said, giving the hallway one last searching look.

We followed him into the general's office, where he sat down. The general had gray hair and an air of authority, but like the others, he wore no military uniform. There was a map of the world on the wall, with thumbtacks stuck in it. There were a few blue tacks in what seemed to be New Mexico, and a few red ones in Russia. There was a blue one stuck in an island in the Pacific, and a white one off the coast of Australia.

"Any luck with the prisoner?" the general asked.

"Not yet, sir," Danby said. "The muteness should wear off soon."

"Did you try getting written answers?"

"With no success, sir."

"I heard you questioning Captain Harrison about birds."

Danby flushed crimson. "Yes, sir."

"Something to do with your investigation of the apothecary and his doings?"

"Yes, sir."

"I'm sure you have your reasons, Danby, but the men are starting to talk."

"But they—" Danby began, and then he seemed to think better of it. "Of course, sir."

"Just so you know. You're one of our best men, and I don't want you compromised."

"Thank you, sir."

"And your East German contact? What does he report?"

"That the apothecary isn't working for the Soviets, sir. Also that Leonid Shiskin, an accountant at the Soviet embassy, has been serving as a messenger, but seems to be working on his own, out of personal conviction. He isn't running the network."

"I see."

"We know that the Soviets are looking for the apothecary. They expect the conspirators to gather soon, and they believe Leonid Shiskin might lead them to the group. But as it stands, I don't think the group can proceed without the apothecary."

"No?"

"No, sir. He's their—their Oppenheimer, if you will."

I was pretty sure Oppenheimer was the physicist who'd made the atomic bomb. I tried to look at Benjamin to see what he made of the comparison, and realized that the strangest thing about being invisible wasn't being naked in a military bunker. It was that we couldn't make eye contact. There was no way of sharing all the information I had grown used to sharing with him in a glance. I didn't know where Benjamin's eyes were, and he couldn't see mine.

The general raised an eyebrow. "I see." He looked at his watch. "D'you suppose the silent treatment might be ending yet?"

"I'll go check, sir," Danby said, rising. He seemed anxious to be out of the office.

"Danby," the general said.

"Yes, sir?"

"You're sure your Kraut is entirely on our side?"

"Yes, sir," Danby said. "And he's quite ruthless."

The general smiled to himself. "Good," he said. "Wish we could bring him in here to do some interrogating. We could use some of that ruthlessness."

Danby smiled uncomfortably.

"And do we know who killed the poor old gardener?" the general asked.

"Not yet, sir," Danby said. "But we'll find out." I knew that he knew the Scar had done it, and thought what a very good liar he was. He sounded completely convincing.

"Strange business, that," the general said. "Well, carry on."

"Yes, sir."

We followed Danby out and tiptoed behind him down the hallway. When I think now about how much eavesdropping we did, I realize that being fourteen had prepared us for it. To be a kid is to be invisible and to listen, and to interpret things that aren't necessarily meant for you to hear—because how else do you find out about the world?

We passed an enormous telephone switchboard, with empty chairs waiting for operators to sit and make connections, and I wondered if the switchboard was meant to run all the calls of London in the case of an atomic bomb—and if there would be anyone left to make calls.

Farther down the hall, Danby knocked at a door. A young woman in a neat green dress came out and closed the door behind her. She had wavy light-brown hair cut short around her ears.

"So?" Danby asked her.

"I'm so bored!" the girl complained. "I thought that stuff was meant to wear off. But we're just sitting there *staring* at each other."

"I'd think you'd like that," Danby said. "You could talk all day, with no one to interrupt you."

The girl pouted. "It's no joke," she said. "I need a coffee."

"Go on then," Danby said.

The girl flashed him a grateful smile and darted off down the hall.

Mr. Danby went into the room, and we silently followed him in, ready to rescue Benjamin's father—somehow. I was so busy finding a place to stand where I wouldn't bump into Danby or anyone else that when I finally looked up at the prisoner, I was shocked.

It wasn't the apothecary.

The prisoner was a woman, and she looked Chinese. She was young, maybe in her twenties, with her hair in a shiny black braid, and she wore a black shirt and black trousers. I could have sworn that she looked at my visible finger, but only for an instant, and then she fixed her eyes on Mr. Danby. She was beautiful, in an austere way, and angry. She sat straight-backed in a chair at a metal table that was bolted to the floor.

Danby took a seat on the table, with one foot on the floor, affecting a casual stance. "Would you like a coffee?" he asked her. "Or tea?"

The prisoner shook her head.

He asked her something in a language I guessed was Chinese, and the woman gave him a look of contempt.

"My Mandarin's rotten, I know," Danby said. "But I'm curious—the muteness didn't last this long on Shiskin. Perhaps it's because you're so much smaller?"

The woman shrugged.

"The things you wrote for me, in such elegant Chinese

calligraphy, I had them translated," he said, tapping his knuckles on the table. "Some of the curses were rather primitive—the ones about dogs and pigs, for example—but some were rather good. I liked the one insulting my ancestors to the eighteenth generation."

The woman glared at him.

He reached forward and put a hand on her pale throat, as if he were a doctor, examining it. "It's been suggested that I hurt you, to make you talk," he said. "It isn't my way, but I'm under a great deal of pressure." He pressed his finger and thumb into the soft recesses of her neck in a way that seemed both very expert and very painful.

The woman's eyes watered and she blinked, but she said nothing. I couldn't believe I had ever found Danby *dreamy*. Now his handsomeness only made him more horrible.

He dropped his hand. "Amazing how long the pill has lasted," he said. "But it's only a matter of time before it wears off. I'll be back."

He left the room, and we heard the door lock behind him. The prisoner's manner immediately changed, and she coughed and put a hand on her throat, then turned to where I was standing.

"Why you here?" she demanded hoarsely.

Pip already had his unfolded paper clip out, and was working on the lock.

"You can talk!" Benjamin said.

"Of course I talk."

"Do you know my father, Marcus Burrows?"

The woman paused, as if unsure whether to trust us, then nodded. "Where is he?"

"We don't know," Benjamin said. "We thought he was in here."

"You're the chemist!" I said, remembering Shiskin's note, and the gardener. I wondered if they had known she was a woman. "You're Jin Lo!"

"How long have you been able to talk?" Benjamin asked her.

"Whole time. They think I have pill. So I pretend."

"Can you make yourself invisible?" I asked. It was a long shot, but she *was* a chemist. It seemed worth asking.

She shook her head, her braid snaking on her shoulder.

"The door's unlocked," Pip announced.

Jin Lo frowned. "This is not trap?"

"You think it's the kind of trap the British military's likely to lay on?" Benjamin said. "Three invisible kids?"

"We just need some way of hiding you," I said.

Jin Lo seemed to consider the problem, then untucked her shirt and removed several tiny glass vials from the sewn-up fold of the shirt's hem, pressing them out of the slot in the fabric one at a time. She chose two, and stuffed the others in her pocket. One of the vials contained something orange, and one was a clear liquid.

"Smoke flare," she said. "To signal plane. Will fill all of bunker."

She poured the clear liquid into the orange vial, sealed it with her thumb, and shook it up. When she took her thumb away, a thick orange smoke started to pour out of the vial. In a few seconds it had filled the room. I held my breath so I wouldn't cough.

"Open door," she said, and Pip did.

There was no guard in the hall when we looked out—just Queen Elizabeth and Princess Margaret and Winston Churchill gazing at us from the wall. Jin Lo held up the vial, and the orange smoke filled the hall, obscuring the pictures. I'd never seen so much smoke pour out of such a small container. It surrounded us as we started silently down the corridor.

We were almost to the telephone switchboard, with the smoke billowing out behind us, when Pip whispered, "Look!"

He held out his arm, and I saw him do it, because there was a dusting of orange on his invisible skin. I could see his head, too, as if cast in orange mist. The smoke was clinging to us, and we were becoming visible, as orange ghosts. I looked down at myself and saw my hands and forearms, nearly transparent but outlined in smoke dust. I crossed my orange arms over my naked chest. The dusting had started at the top, where the smoke was thickest. I could see Benjamin's head and shoulders, too.

"We have to get clothes!" I whispered.

We were outside the general's office, where we'd heard Danby talking, and I peeked in. No one was inside. A long black wool overcoat was hanging by the door, and I grabbed it and put it on. It was enormous, but I didn't care.

There were voices back down the hall, beyond the smoke screen.

"Look at this *smoke*!" the girl who'd gone for a coffee said.

"Is it a fire?" a man's voice asked.

We ran silently toward the elevators, the smoke billowing behind us. Benjamin grabbed a jacket off one of the switchboard chairs and pulled it on just as his legs became orangely visible.

An alarm rang out, making me jump. There was coughing and shouting in the obscured hall behind us.

We reached the elevator lobby and Pip pressed the call button. It didn't require a key to go up. I grabbed two khaki jumpsuits and two hard hats off the hooks on the wall. Jin Lo was still waving the vial into the hall, spreading smoke.

"Take this," I said, handing her one of the jumpsuits. "And put your braid up under the hard hat. Pip, you take the other."

She started pulling the jumpsuit on over her clothes.

"You look like the invisible man," Benjamin said to me, looking at my long coat.

"Well, you look like the invisible girl," I said. The jacket he had stolen was actually a woman's light blue raincoat, cinched at the waist, with a full skirt.

Pip, still naked and half visible, was busy brushing the orange dust off his skin. "It comes off!" he said. His arm had vanished again. "Brush it off and take those stupid coats off! Quick!"

We scrubbed ourselves clean as quickly as we could—the orange dust came off easily—and handed our clothes to Jin Lo as the elevator opened. She still wielded the smoke-spewing vial in one hand.

I heard a shriek from the female guard down the hall. "The prisoner's gone!" she cried.

But the elevator doors closed, and we were on our way out.

CHAPTER 21

The Oil of Mnemosyne

The elevator took us up to daylight, and Jin Lo left the vial of orange smoke by the front door of the bunker so that it poured out into the street. She looked boyish in the khaki jumpsuit, with her long braid up under a hard hat, and she walked purposefully away, carrying her bundle of clothes, as if she were a workman going for help in controlling this strange chemical fire.

A few people came out of houses, staring at the orange smoke rising into the air, but no one stopped Jin Lo, and we were around the corner before we heard shouts coming from the building, and a man's loud voice asking if anyone had seen a Chinese girl in black. No one had, and Pip and Benjamin and I were still invisible.

A bus came by and stopped, and we climbed aboard. Jin Lo nodded to the driver and walked past him with her armful of clothes.

"You've got to pay!" the driver said, but Jin Lo ignored him. The rest of us filed invisibly after her.

There were seven or eight other people on the bus, including a white-haired woman with a curly white dog in her lap. The dog started to bark hysterically as we passed, and she murmured and hugged him close.

"It's just a Chinaman, my angel, selling clothes," I heard her say.

The dog kept barking—smelling, I was sure, all four of us.

We found a place near the back of the bus where no one was going to bump into us, and the driver gave up and drove on, flummoxed by the inscrutable Chinaman and late for his route. The old lady got the curly dog to be quiet, but it gazed back over her shoulder, panting.

Jin Lo dumped the pile of clothes beside her and sat down.

"So who are you, exactly?" Benjamin whispered, under the rumbling noise of the bus's engine. "How do you know my father?"

"Only letters," Jin Lo said. "I come from China to meet him."

"Are there lots of girl chemists in China?" I asked. This was 1952, after all.

Jin Lo frowned as if the question had never occurred to her. "I am apprentice, very young, to chemist in Shanghai. I have no other school. When he die, I finish his work, write to colleagues."

"What was his work?" I asked. "He wasn't a normal chemist, right? Was he an alchemist?"

Jin Lo shrugged, as if the idea of normality was unimportant. "Everyone work different. Where you last see apothecary?"

"In his shop," Benjamin said. "He was given a message saying you had been taken, and he would be next, so he hid us in the cellar. Some Germans burst in, and when we came upstairs, my father was gone."

"Germans—they say what?"

"We don't know," Benjamin said. "It was in German."

Jin Lo frowned. "Why you not speak German?"

"I don't know," Benjamin whispered. "I guess because of the war. No one wants to. Do you speak Japanese?"

Something I couldn't identify passed over her face, and I remembered that parts of China had been occupied by Japan. "Yes," she said. "When soldiers come, better to know what they say."

"Oh," Benjamin said, abashed. "Well, I don't speak German."

"You take me to shop," she said.

The dog up front gave a petulant bark, and the old lady sneaked a look back at the Chinese rag seller. Then her gaze seemed to shift to me, and I looked down at my two visible fingers, which were holding on to a pole. It wasn't just my fingers anymore, but a whole stretch of my hand and forearm that was visible—*actually* visible, not just dusted with orange. My other arm was visible in patches, too, and so was part of my left knee.

"Jin Lo!" I whispered. "Stare at that lady with the dog, quick."

Jin Lo did, glaring so fiercely that the old lady whirled to the front, embarrassed and confused, pulling her dog down into her lap. I grabbed the blue raincoat from the top of the pile and wrapped myself in it, tying it at the waist. It covered me to the knees, and I crouched down on the seat, trying to blend into the pile of clothes.

"You'll draw attention without a head," Benjamin whispered.

"Not as much as you'll draw in a second."

He looked down at himself and saw that his shoulder patch was growing, down his biceps to the elbow. Half of his smooth, pale chest had appeared: the shadow of a collarbone, a pink nipple, and his belly button, which was a neatly sewn inny. He grabbed the general's coat and pulled it on.

I looked at Pip, and half of his face was visible, too, spreading across his cheek from his ear. "Aw, all the *pockets* I could've picked," he whispered. "Another hour and I'd be rich!" He pulled on the spare jumpsuit and rolled up the cuffs on the arms and legs.

By the time we filed off the bus near Regent's Park and the apothecary's shop, we were fully visible and fully clothed. The Chinese rag seller seemed to have spawned three non-Chinese teenage children, in strange costumes, all riding for free. The little dog barked wildly at us, vindicated, and the old lady and the bus driver watched us go in disbelief.

We surveyed the door to the apothecary's shop from across the street. Jin Lo looked around to all the neighborhood windows that might have a view of the front door. No one seemed to be watching the building, but still I was afraid to go inside. The Germans could come back, or Danby and the British officers.

The door to the shop was unlocked, the latch forced by the Germans, and my heart pounded as Jin Lo pushed it open. We all slipped inside and stood in the dark chaos, listening. Things were overturned and broken, as the intruders had left them. Jin Lo's soft braid spilled over her shoulder like a snake when she took off her hard hat, and she brushed it away. I imagined she would brush away a real snake with the same disinterested calm.

The shop seemed to be empty, so Benjamin ran upstairs to his flat to get some clothes to replace the general's overcoat. He brought me a pair of his trousers, a shirt, and a sweater, and I went behind a ransacked shelf to change out of the pale blue raincoat. I liked having trousers on again, even if they were loose and I had to belt them tightly. I had never felt quite right in the pleated skirt.

Jin Lo finished her inspection of the shop. "So—you hear voices," she said.

"Right," Benjamin said.

"And you see German with scar."

"Yes."

"But you don't see them take apothecary away."

"No, we were in the cellar."

"We go down now to see," she said.

We went back to the office, and Benjamin opened the iron grate that led to the cellar. We all climbed down. We showed Jin Lo and Pip where we'd been hiding against the wall. Jin Lo looked up at the grate.

"So," she said. "You hear them say, 'Ha! I got you now, apothecary!'"

Benjamin and I looked at each other.

"No," I said. "We heard an explosion."

"What kind? Small? Big?"

"Medium."

"You see explosion?"

Benjamin thought about it. "No. Also there was a police car's bell! That's what made them leave. But the police never came."

"Sit here," she said. "Wait."

She ran up the ladder, and we heard her light footsteps in the shop, and the clinking of jars. Then she climbed back down, with one arm on the ladder, carrying an armful of things in the other, including a mortar and pestle.

She sat cross-legged in front of us and tapped some herbs from three different jars into a stone mortar. With the wooden pestle, she ground the herbs together, then poured clear oil over them and ground up the mixture some more. She dipped her finger in the oil and applied it to my left temple. When I started to draw back, she said, "No! Stay." Then she dipped her finger again and put a smear of oil on my right temple and on each of my wrists.

"It smells strong," I said.

She turned to Benjamin and applied the oil the same way: to the sides of his forehead and the insides of his wrists.

"Now," she said. "You remember more."

"Can I have some?" Pip asked. "I need to remember things, too!"

"What things?"

"Racing tips! Poker tells!"

She shook her head. "Very dangerous, remember too much," she said.

She took one of my hands and one of Benjamin's so that the insides of our wrists pressed against hers. Her arms were wiry and strong.

"You hold, too," she commanded, nodding at our loose hands.

Benjamin took my wrist, and I took his. It was soft and warm, and I could feel his pulse beating through his skin. The three of us were now sitting in a triangle on the cellar floor, cross-legged and linked at the wrists. Pip sat on the outside, pouting and bored.

"Close eyes now," Jin Lo said. "Think."

I closed my eyes and felt the oil on my wrists and my temples. It tingled slightly. I wondered if Benjamin could feel my pulse, too.

"Apothecary says hide," Jin Lo said. "You go in cellar."

I felt a little dizzy and disoriented, as if something was happening to the part of my brain that was just behind my eyes, and also to the backs of my eyelids. The present started falling away, and I was vividly in the past. It wasn't like normal memory, superimposed on the present, able to co-exist with other thoughts and experiences. It was more like an intensely realistic waking dream, of a time and place I'd been before. I remembered the terror of that night in the cellar, and the nervousness about being with Benjamin, this strange boy. I felt his shoulder brushing mine as he tried the locked doorknob. And then I heard voices, too distant to make out, in the front of the shop, and I heard the explosion. Then the German voices were closer.

"*Wo ist er?*" one of them asked.

"*Ich weiss nicht,*" another said. "*Er ist verschwunden.*"

"So?" Jin Lo said, beside me, startling me out of the past.

I opened my eyes and blinked, and tried to imitate the words the Germans had said. Jin Lo listened.

"They don't see apothecary," she said. "They say, 'Where is he?' Go back. Before."

I closed my eyes and felt the odd, swooning feeling, and again I was climbing down the cellar stairs with Benjamin in the dark, before the Germans arrived. Just as he brushed my shoulder, I heard a hoarse whisper from above, in English. I hadn't heard it before, in all the confusion.

"*The shelter, Benjamin,*" his father whispered. "*I'll be in the shelter.*"

Then there were the distant voices, and the explosion, and the sounds of things being knocked over. The German voice asked, "*Wo ist er?*" again.

I opened my eyes. "Did you hear it?" I asked Benjamin.

"The shelter!" he said.

"Isn't this it—the cellar?"

"No," he said. "There's an old Morrison shelter up there, from the war. My father uses it as a table."

We scrambled up the ladder, and Benjamin went to a corner of the office. There was a wide, low table there, with an oilcloth covering, and books and papers scattered across it. Benjamin pulled the oilcloth back. The table underneath was actually a giant metal cage, with wire mesh sides and a flat steel top.

Pip whistled. "You had this in your *house*?" he said. "My mum and da had to fight their way into the Underground."

"The shelter wouldn't withstand a direct hit," Benjamin said. "But it was supposed to keep the walls from crushing you if, you know, one of the V-1s hit your block. My father and I used to get inside and sleep in it at night. He made it like a game." He paused, and I guessed he was thinking of his mother. "But he isn't in it now," he said finally.

"He said he'd be in the shelter," I said.

"Maybe he was there and he's gone. Maybe we heard it wrong. Anyway, the Germans would have found him in here."

I looked around for Jin Lo, and realized she hadn't come up with us. I went back to the iron grate and looked down, and saw her crouched in the cellar, staring into the darkness with a terrible look in her eyes.

"Jin Lo?" I said.

She recoiled from my voice, looking haunted.

"Are you all right?"

She shook her head and said something I couldn't understand. I climbed down the ladder and saw that she was trembling. I sat beside her.

"What happened?"

She opened her hands in front of her face and gazed at her wrists. They were shiny with the oil from Benjamin's arm and mine. The austere strength in her face was gone and replaced by something wild and vulnerable. "Things I do not wish to remember," she said.

Pip and Benjamin were at the top of the ladder, looking down.

"Is she all right?" Benjamin asked.

"She's shaking," I said.

"Soldiers come," Jin Lo said, in a little girl's voice. "Japanese army. I am eight years old. They kill everyone. Father, mother, baby brother. They think I am dead. So many guns. At night, everything quiet. I climb out from under body, our neighbor, and I look. Whole city . . ." She stopped, and her narrow shoulders danced and trembled. She pressed her hands into her eyes, as if to block out what she had seen, smearing the oil down her cheeks.

I didn't know what to say that could help. I put my hand on her shoulder and I could feel how overcome she was. I didn't know if she'd be able to move.

"Janie," Benjamin said, after what seemed like a long time. "We can't stay here. They might come."

I reached in the pocket of my trousers—Benjamin's

trousers—and found another of the folded handkerchiefs his father must have neatly ironed. I gently pried one of Jin Lo's hands from her face and wiped the oil off the delicate skin inside her wrist.

"We have to go," I said. "It's dangerous for us to stay here."

I took the other wrist and wiped away the oil, and then I cleaned the tears and oil from her face. She let me do it, as if she were a small child. Her eyes were still spilling tears.

"I'm so sorry about your family," I said. "And your city."

She blinked vacantly.

"We need your help," I said. "The apothecary said he'd be in the Morrison shelter, and we found it, but he isn't there."

I thought I could see her eyes slowly returning to the present, from the distant past. I could feel that I was coming into focus.

"Come and look," I said, and I helped her stand up. She was unsteady on her feet, as if all strength had been drained from her. "Can you get up the ladder?"

"I try," she said.

I stood behind her, making sure her feet were on the rungs, and Benjamin and Pip helped pull her up when she reached the top. Upstairs, we all stood in front of the Morrison shelter, and Jin Lo crouched to peer through the wire mesh.

"We open," she said, and together we lifted one of the long side walls of the shelter off its hooks. Jin Lo peered inside again. There was a flat board making a floor in the bottom of the shelter, and I imagined a tiny Benjamin and his father sleeping on it.

"See this," she said, and she pointed to a cone-shaped pile of white dust on the shelter's floor. "Japanese call 'Morijio.' Like Shinto offering. But English say 'Lot's wife'—you know this meaning?"

"Is Lot the one who had all the bad luck?" Benjamin asked.

"No, that's Job," I said.

"Lot's wife turned to a pile o' salt," Pip said.

I looked at him, surprised. "How do you know that?"

Pip shrugged. "I 'ad to go to church lessons once, for stealing, like. The stories were all right, though."

"This salt your father," Jin Lo said.

"What?" Benjamin said.

"You find one glass beaker now," she said. *"Clean."*

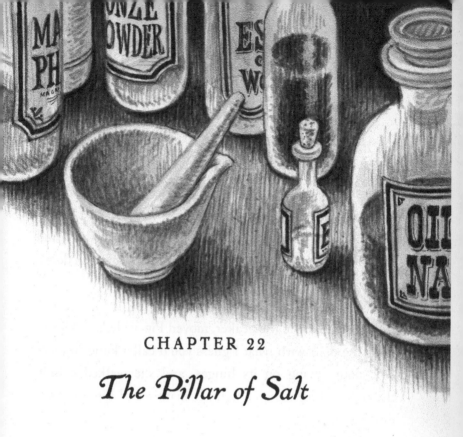

CHAPTER 22

The Pillar of Salt

Jin Lo climbed into the Morrison shelter and gathered all of the salt onto a piece of paper, carefully brushing up every loose grain with her finger, even after I was sure she had them all. I still didn't believe that the salt was the apothecary, but I could see how she wouldn't want to leave a whole leg behind. She bent the paper and poured it into the clean beaker. Then she brought the beaker out of the shelter. She still had the marks of tears on her face, but she was steady again.

"Where he work?" she asked.

Benjamin looked around the paper-strewn office and raised his hands to offer it up. "Here," he said.

"No," she said. "*Real* work. Laboratory."

Benjamin shook his head. "I don't know."

"Must be in house."

"It's not upstairs. That's where we live."

I looked around the room, which had no doors except the one to the shop. "What about the locked door in the cellar?" I asked.

We all climbed back down the ladder into the dark, and Pip got out his wire to start working on the heavy iron door's lock.

"No time," Jin Lo said. "Hold please."

She handed me the beaker, moved Pip aside, and kicked open the door with what I guess you'd call a kung fu kick. The door swung on its hinges, and she walked calmly through and turned on a light. Benjamin and Pip watched, impressed.

We all followed her into what was, as she had promised, a laboratory. Where the cellar looked dusty and unused, the lab was spotless and orderly, with rows of shining bottles and jars. It had an oven against one wall, a sink, and a row of gas burners. There were beakers and vials and crucibles, and mortars and pestles in different sizes: Some were made of wood and some of white marble, but one bowl looked like black onyx, and one like green jade.

Jin Lo started to move around the lab like a chef moving around her own kitchen, pulling out an enormous copper pot. She emptied the white liquid from a large bottle into it, and a clear liquid from another, and lit a burner underneath.

"You're not going to put my father in there," Benjamin said.

"We wait too long," she said, pouring black seeds into the green jade mortar, "harder to change. You want him like this?" She handed me the mortar and pestle. "Crush," she said.

"But what if we do something wrong?" Benjamin persisted.

Jin Lo surveyed the shelves again, and slapped Pip's hand away from a jar that said LICORICE ROOT.

"Just one little bit?" he pleaded.

She ignored him. I started grinding the black seeds with the heavy pestle.

"I need a minute with the beaker," Benjamin said.

Jin Lo looked at him. "Is *salt*," she said.

Benjamin's jaw was set firmly. "I still do," he said. "It's my father."

Jin Lo sighed at this sentimentality and let him have the beaker. Benjamin held it in both hands and turned away from us. He was telling his father something, but even in the small room, I couldn't hear the words.

The liquid in the pot had started to boil, and Jin Lo added a dark red powder, and then a yellow paste that she measured in spoonfuls from a jar. She took the mortar and inspected my work, then gave it a few more emphatic grinds with the pestle and poured the powdered seeds in. She stirred the pot, and lifted the wooden spoon experimentally: As it boiled, the solution had started to thicken into a greenish-brown ooze. It glopped off the spoon back into the pot. She leaned over and sniffed it. "Now," she said to Benjamin.

He looked at the pot. "I can't," he said, clutching the beaker.

"Now," she said. "Will be too late, too thick."

"Have you done this before?" he asked.

"No," she said. "I read how."

"What if you remember wrong?"

Jin Lo shrugged. "Then he stay salt."

I could feel Benjamin's fear of letting his father go, and of never being able to get him back. Finally he handed the beaker to Jin Lo and turned away, unable to watch as she dumped his father into the goo.

Pip pulled over a footstool so he could see inside the pot, and I stood on tiptoe. As Jin Lo stirred, the mixture took on a stickier consistency. At first, nothing happened. I realized I wasn't breathing. I didn't think Pip was either. I thought of the witches in *Macbeth*, hunched over the cauldron, waiting for their evil magic to happen. Was it "eye of newt and tongue of frog"? Something like that.

Jin Lo pulled the glop up out of the pot with the spoon, working and stretching it like taffy. Each time she pulled, some of it stayed stretched for a moment. Benjamin couldn't stand it and turned to look. I thought I saw something like a knee forming as Jin Lo pulled. It held its shape for a second before sinking back into the pot. I blinked, thinking I'd imagined it. Then I was sure I saw part of an arm, before it sank back in.

Then the whole mixture started to boil up over the lip, and the shape of the apothecary's head emerged and sank down again. Then his head returned with both shoulders.

Two sticky hands gripped the sides of the pot and pushed his torso and then his legs up out of the ooze. He stepped onto the counter, towering over us, and Jin Lo handed him a linen towel to cover the nakedness that would be revealed when all the goo dripped off. He wrapped it around his waist automatically, like a man at the beach, and she handed him a second towel to wipe his face and arms. Pip stared with his mouth open. I'm sure I did, too. Jin Lo had reconstituted the apothecary out of a tiny pile of salt, and he was standing there in front of us, whole and alive.

He looked around, dazed, and held out his hands in front of him, staring at them. Then he saw his son looking up at him from below. "Benjamin!" he said.

Pip stepped off his footstool and offered it to the apothecary, who climbed down from the counter. He wiped ooze off his pale chest, and it plopped to the floor. Benjamin threw his arms around his father, and the apothecary looked surprised, then wrapped his arms around Benjamin, too. I remembered their argument in the shop, and how little Benjamin had wanted to be an apothecary, and I wondered if it had been a long time since they hugged like this. Benjamin was as tall as his father, but rested his head on his shoulder with his eyes closed, like a kid. I had a pang, thinking of my own parents, who were out in the country knowing nothing about where I was.

When Benjamin and his father released each other, Jin Lo stepped forward and extended her hand. "I am Jin Lo."

The apothecary blinked at her. "You are?"

"Not safe here," she said. "We go now. You have clothes?"

"I'm so sorry," he said. "In our correspondence, I had thought you were—well, a man."

Jin Lo shrugged, as if she got that all the time. She was extraordinarily pretty, especially when she stopped looking annoyed and looked relieved, as she did now that the apothecary was back.

Mr. Burrows took in all of us now. "You're the American girl," he said to me.

"Yes," I said. "Janie. This is Pip."

"Pip," he said, still dazed, and he turned to Jin Lo. "How long has it been? Have I missed the test?"

"No," she said. "We meet at boat tomorrow."

"What test?" Benjamin asked.

The apothecary rubbed his sticky forehead. "I haven't finished preparing."

"You have things you need?" Jin Lo asked.

"Yes, of course," he said, wiping his face. Most of the ooze had dripped off him now, onto the floor. Benjamin found him a spare pair of spectacles. He took a folded change of clothes from a cupboard and quickly pulled them on, then looked around at his shelves. From another cupboard, he took a black leather medical bag and started filling it with bottles. Jin Lo helped, suggesting items.

"I have to go to the Physic Garden," the apothecary said, and I realized he couldn't know.

"The gardener's dead," I said.

The apothecary stared at me.

Just then Pip looked up, with a twig of licorice root in his mouth. "Shh!" he said. He pointed to the ceiling.

We listened. There were footsteps upstairs.

"Is there a way out, down here?" I whispered.

The apothecary shook his head. He took a jar of gray powder off the shelf and handed it to Jin Lo, who opened it and nodded, as if she understood. She took a long glass tube from a rack of tools and stuck it into the powder like a drinking straw.

The apothecary picked up his medical bag in silence.

Jin Lo climbed the ladder first, carrying the jar of powder, and I followed close behind her. I saw the backs of two men crouched in the shop, inspecting the disturbed Morrison shelter. I couldn't see their faces, but I knew from their shapes that it was Danby and the Scar.

Jin Lo crept silently toward the door. I climbed out of the cellar, but I wasn't as soundless as Jin Lo. A floorboard squeaked, and the men heard me and turned.

The Scar lunged for me, but Jin Lo pulled the straw from the jar and blew a cloud of gray powder in their faces. Both men clutched their eyes. Danby shouted, and the Scar said something in German. He stumbled toward Jin Lo, trying blindly to grab her, but she slipped past him.

We ran through the ruined storefront and out the front door, followed by Benjamin and his father and Pip. Danby and the Scar tried to chase after us, but crashed blindly into the standing shelves, unable to see.

"Is that stuff permanent?" Benjamin asked as we walked

quickly down Regent's Park Road, but not so quickly that we would draw attention.

"Oh, no," his father said. "It would be a terrible thing to blind someone."

"Not so terrible to blind *those* two," Benjamin said.

"Oh, yes," his father said. "Even them."

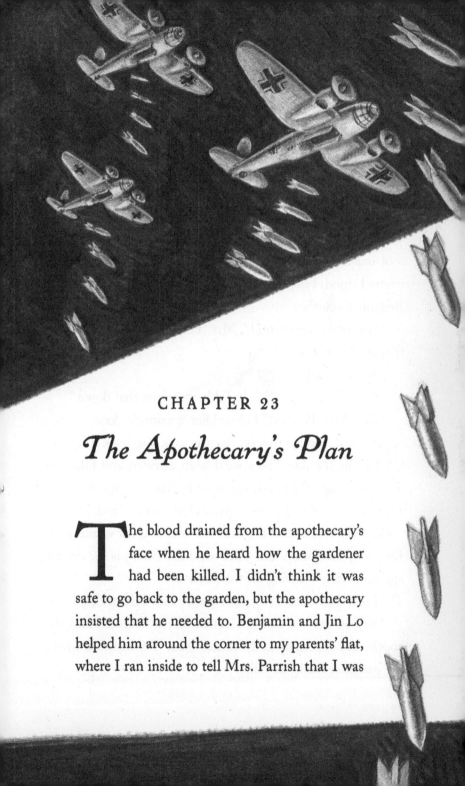

CHAPTER 23

The Apothecary's Plan

The blood drained from the apothecary's face when he heard how the gardener had been killed. I didn't think it was safe to go back to the garden, but the apothecary insisted that he needed to. Benjamin and Jin Lo helped him around the corner to my parents' flat, where I ran inside to tell Mrs. Parrish that I was spending the night with my friend Sarah so we could do our Latin homework together.

"Your parents won't mind?" Mrs. Parrish asked.

"No, not at all," I said.

"In my day, a girl with any looks on her never bothered with Latin," Mrs. Parrish said. "Boys didn't like a girl was *too* smart."

"Things have sure changed!" I said, smiling brightly, one foot out the door. I could smell the gin on her breath from where I stood. I hoped she wouldn't notice that I was wearing Benjamin's clothes.

"Oh, brave new world," Mrs. Parrish said. "Susan, your friend's name was?"

"Sarah," I said.

"Right," she said. "Sarah. I'd better write that down."

"Bye, Mrs. Parrish!" I closed her apartment door.

We told the apothecary, as we took the back alleys to Chelsea in the dark, how we'd been arrested and taken to Turnbull, and then nearly captured by Mr. Danby, our Latin teacher who seemed to be a spy, and his Stasi friend.

"Danby told us that the Scar is a double agent working for England," Benjamin said. "But we think *Danby* is the double agent, secretly working for the Soviets."

"I see," his father said, but I wasn't sure that he did.

We had arrived at the Chelsea Physic Garden, and the apothecary looked up at the locked gate. "I need to see where the gardener died," he said.

I shuddered at the idea of going to the cottage, but we helped him over the fence. Pip and Jin Lo scaled it easily by themselves, and dropped down to the other side.

The garden was quiet, and we walked on the grass that bordered the paths, to avoid the crunching of the gravel. We showed him the broken sundial, and he peered through the window at the floor where we had found the gardener. There was still a dark stain I knew must be blood. It didn't seem like a good idea to go trooping through a crime scene.

"There wasn't any need for them to kill him," the apothecary said. "He was the gentlest man I ever knew."

"They killed him because he was helping us," I said. "It's our fault."

"No," he said. "It's mine."

We showed him where the avian elixir had been hidden among the green rows of the *Artemisia veritas*.

"Have you—?" he asked.

"I was a skylark," Benjamin said. "That's how we escaped Turnbull."

His father smiled sadly. "My father showed me the avian elixir to win me over to his practice. I was planning to do the same with you."

"It would've worked," Benjamin said.

"Yes, I see that now. I was going to tell you when I thought you were ready. But you—well, you seemed to be headed in a different direction."

"If you'd told me the truth, I might not have been."

Being near the cottage was making me nervous. "I don't think we should stay here," I said. "Someone will find us. How long will the blindness last on Danby and Scar?"

"It depends on the dosage and the accuracy of the delivery," the apothecary said.

"Very accurate," Jin Lo said. "Full dosage."

"Then perhaps overnight," he said. "But I must be in the garden at first light."

"We can hide in the white mulberry tree," Benjamin said. "I used to play inside it." He led us away from the cottage and out of the inner garden to a tree with long branches draping down to the ground. He held one of the branches aside, and we walked into a hollow that was like a green cave, with room for all five of us to sit around the trunk.

"What a hideout!" Pip said, and he flopped onto his back to look up at the canopy of leaves overhead.

"So tell us why the British military and Soviet security are both after you," Benjamin said to his father.

The apothecary sat on the ground and seemed to gather his thoughts. "My father," he said, "and his father before him, and generations of our family going back to the Middle Ages were engaged in a study of matter, as it grew out of the attempt to heal the human body. The work has always been secretive, and has often been considered a threat by the various authorities— with the exception of Henry the Eighth. He was very interested in medicine, and open to creative solutions to his various woes. The trouble was that he changed his mind so often about what the solutions should be. As he did about his wives."

"Our ancestors knew the *king?*" Benjamin asked.

"Royal favor has come and gone," the apothecary said. "The secrets, meanwhile, were kept in the Pharmacopoeia." He looked suddenly anxious. "You do have the book?"

I could tell from Benjamin's face that he had forgotten about the Pharmacopoeia. "It's safe," he said.

"Safe where?"

"At school."

The apothecary looked aghast. "Where your Mr. Danby works?"

"Mr. Danby is blind and doesn't know it's there," I said.

"I hope you're right," the apothecary said, and went on. "Over time, as travel and correspondence became easier, we began to seek out people in other countries who were engaged in a similar study. The work has always been accelerated by wartime, when the offenses to the human body are increased. When new and innovative ways are found to hurt, we find new and innovative ways to combat injury and pain. And there have, of course, been offshoots of the practice, and discoveries that have nothing to do with medicine. Temporary alterations."

"Like becoming birds," Pip said.

"Precisely," the apothecary said. "Tell me who this boy is again?"

"We were locked up in Turnbull together," Benjamin said. "He helped us escape. He's a friend."

"Then I owe you my thanks."

Pip nodded. "Go on with the story."

"When you were very small, Benjamin, the war began," he said. "Children were sent to the countryside by the thousands, with labels tied around their necks. You were too young to go alone. Some mothers went, of course, but your mother helped me in my work. She didn't want to leave, and I—well, I didn't know what I would do without you both. And for a long time, nothing happened. We were given an infant's gas mask for you, and your mother carried the horrible thing everywhere, but we never had to use it.

"Then the Blitz began, and the bombs came every night. Hundreds of German planes carrying hundreds of tons of explosives and incendiary bombs. We finally decided that you couldn't stay in London, that your mother had to take you out of the city. We were making the arrangements for both of you to leave when a bomb fell one night, unexploded, in the middle of Regent's Park Road."

The apothecary paused and looked at his hands.

"Your mother had nursing skills and worked for the Women's Voluntary Service. She was out after the air raid was over, helping to see who was hurt, when the bomb suddenly went off and threw her against a wall. Her neck was broken, and she was killed instantly."

There was a silence under the mulberry tree that seemed to fill my ears and take away all sounds.

"People were putting out fires," he said. "And I was sitting there in the street, in the chaos, with my dead wife in my arms. I've never known so much pain. I was struck by the senselessness of the bombing. And the fear. And all those young men dying in France and Italy and Greece and Africa and Germany, for victory—I was in a kind of nightmare, in those years. A kind of shock.

"Then the bombs were dropped on Hiroshima and Nagasaki, to end the war in the Pacific. And there was great celebration and relief. It seemed—monumental. Such enormous power the Americans had. I had known, from my correspondence with other scientists, that the nuclear experiments were happening, but I was not prepared for the bomb. The first thing I remember thinking is that the unbearable pain I had felt when your mother died was spread over those two Japanese cities, hundreds of thousands of times over, in two horrific clouds. All over the whole country, really."

Jin Lo had started to weep silently, and the apothecary turned to look at her. I thought she was remembering the Japanese soldiers in China, and I tried to think how to explain that to the apothecary. She seemed to read my mind.

"I am fine," she said, and she wiped her eyes. "Tell story."

"There was so much anger and grief and outrage and loss," the apothecary said. "And now there was this terrible bomb with which angry people could simply wipe each other out. I had this small boy, you see, being raised in the grief and the rubble, and I couldn't imagine letting him grow up with such fear. It wasn't a world that deserved to have such an awful bomb."

He paused. "So I began to work," he said. "I knew in a

general way what the atomic scientists were doing, and I knew how to rearrange atoms, and manipulate them, to make one thing into another. It was my father's work, and his father's. And as I worked, there were rumors spreading. The Soviets were making their own bomb, and the Americans were building bigger ones. Both countries were arming themselves with weapons that could destroy the world. People said that as long as they both had such terrible weapons, no one would ever use them. But I thought I knew something about people and their weapons. They *want* to use them."

"Course they do," Pip said, listening with his legs crossed under him, his chin in his hand, like a child listening to a storybook.

"I wanted to develop a way to make a whole city safe," the apothecary said. "But this is difficult to do. I thought first of creating a kind of shield—an area in which it would be impossible for an atom to split. A small shield was possible, but a large one, big enough for a city, was very difficult.

"Then I thought of a kind of containment, something that could be done *after* the bomb was dropped, as long as it was done very quickly. I knew from being an Air Raid Warden that there would be some warning when an airplane was spotted. So perhaps, if I couldn't maintain a shield to protect a city, I could at least contain the damage and the radiation from the bomb.

"I started writing to the people in other countries who were doing this kind of work. And I began to correspond with Jin Lo." He looked to the young woman, with her long dark braid. "Whom I imagined rather differently, as an eminent, gray-haired man."

Jin Lo shrugged. "This is not important."

"You have developed the most elegant net," he said. "Would you like to describe it?"

"You tell them *everything*?" she asked.

"Just the broad strokes."

She shrugged. "It makes a polymer."

The apothecary waited for her to go on, but she wasn't going to.

"The idea is brilliant in its simplicity," he explained. "She puts particles into the air that react with radiation to create, as she says, an extremely strong polymer, which then contracts as it solidifies. The contraction pulls the explosion tightly back in on itself. If it works, it will be a thing of great beauty."

"And if not, we die," Jin Lo said.

The apothecary ignored that. "My role was to absorb the radiation that would be released, even if the net contained the explosion," he said. "I was convinced that the solution was botanical. Just as plants mop up our carbon dioxide for us, I was sure I could find one to absorb radiation. I tried various methods and finally settled on the flower of the jaival tree, which is a white lotus brought by traders from India in the last century. The air around the jaival's blossom is particularly rich with the Quintessence." He waited, as if we were supposed to understand what he meant and respond with awe.

"And—what's the Quintessence?" I asked.

"The fifth element!" he said, amazed at my ignorance. "The source of all life. A life force to combat a killing force, you see. But the jaival in this garden, here, is the only one in England, and it has a very long, slow life cycle. It blooms only once every seven years. It isn't due to bloom again until 1955, which is three years from now. I thought that shouldn't matter, as I believed we had time. But then Russia began to test its own bombs, and England started developing atomic capabilities. I had no choice but to try to force the bloom— which turned out to be very difficult."

The apothecary sank into silence, apparently preoccupied with all the complications of the jaival tree's life cycle.

"And then?" Benjamin prompted.

"Yes, then," he said. "Leonid Shiskin, our contact within the Soviet embassy, brought news that the Soviet Union would be testing a new bomb in the north, on an archipelago called Nova Zembla. So we had to accelerate our plan. Jin Lo and our Hungarian physicist, Count Vilmos, who had been living in Luxembourg, would come to London."

Benjamin and I looked at each other—a Hungarian count! The man in the hotel!

"But then Jin Lo was captured on arrival," the apothecary went on. "And I was nearly so. The British authorities must have intercepted our letters and broken our code. We underestimated them. If Count Vili is safe, then the boat may still be a secret. It was never mentioned in the letters. But we have no way of knowing if he is safe."

"Is he a bit fat, and dandyish?" Benjamin asked.

The apothecary brightened. "That's him! Have you seen him?"

"We saw Shiskin pass a message to him in a newspaper," I said. "The day before he passed one to you. We followed him to a hotel but couldn't find out his name."

The apothecary frowned. "Why were you spying on me?"

"We weren't, we were spying on *Shiskin*," Benjamin said crossly. "I thought he was spying on *England*."

"But you must have known that these were my colleagues."

"I knew nothing, because you *told* me nothing!"

"Tell us more about Count Vili," I said, to keep the two of them from going around again in the same argument. "He's not a normal physicist, right? He's a physicist like you're an apothecary."

"His name is Count Vilmos Hadik de Galántha," the apothecary said. "He was orphaned during the first war, and was sent to Luxembourg with a German tutor and a great deal of money. His tutor was, as you say, not a normal physicist, and he took the boy on as an apprentice. Vili had a talent for the work."

"Like you," I said, turning to Jin Lo. She had taken out her braid and was combing her fingers through the silky strands that hung to her waist. Whenever I unbraided my hair, it held the unruly kinks of each braid until I washed it, but Jin Lo's was like a sheet of smooth black water.

"I met Vili when he came to England to go to Cambridge," the apothecary went on. "He was immature and unfocused then. He liked to spend all his time drinking and floating in punts down the river. My father thought him a disgrace to our craft. But like many men, he eventually found his purpose and his way. And he has accomplished what none of us thought possible. He has discovered a way to stop time."

"That's impossible," Benjamin said.

"Well, yes," his father said. "It's more precisely that he *freezes* time, as when we supercool some chemical reactions so that they happen very slowly. He creates a temporal lag in his immediate vicinity, from which he is exempt, so that he can move quickly. It's remarkable. The Hungarians are so adept at physics, and also at mathematics and music. I've always thought it must be because so few people speak their language. They've found extralinguistic means to interact with the rest of the world." He smiled at this thought.

"So he freezes time," Benjamin said, pulling him back to his story.

"Well, it would obviously be very useful," the apothecary said. "You could get your ducks in a row, as it were. He also has a great deal of money, which is more immediately useful. He has engaged an icebreaking research vessel to take us to the north. He knows and trusts the Norwegian crew, and has chartered the boat on northern cruises to the fjords. It's our only hope of getting close to Nova Zembla."

"But first we need jaival tree," Jin Lo reminded him. She had braided her hair again, with swift deft fingers, into a silken rope.

"Yes, of course," the apothecary said. "We'll begin at dawn, in the sunlight. For now, I think we should stay here and sleep."

"But we haven't had any *tea*," Pip said.

The apothecary looked perplexed. He could turn himself into salt, and he believed he could stop an atomic bomb, but he couldn't produce a dinner for three children out of thin air, under a mulberry tree. "We'll get breakfast in the morning," he said. "We can't risk anyone's leaving the garden. You all know too much."

Pip narrowed his lemur's eyes at the apothecary and said, "Look, mister, you do what you want, but I'm not sleeping on the ground, without my tea." Then there was a rustle of branches and he was gone, as if he'd never been there.

No one went after him—no one could have caught him—but the apothecary turned to us accusingly. "What do you know about that child?" he asked. "How do you know he wasn't planted in that cell with you?"

"We thought he was at first," I said. "But he really wasn't."

"You vouch for him?"

"I do."

"I do, too," Benjamin said.

"Is he likely to get caught out there?"

"No one less likely," Benjamin said.

"Still," his father said, "it was careless to bring him in."

"Not careless," Jin Lo said. "I vouch, too."

Then she wrapped her coveralls tightly around her slender

body, tossed her braid over her shoulder, and rolled over as if she slept under trees all the time. The apothecary, outvoted, lay on his back with his head on his doctor's bag. That left an area about three feet square for Benjamin and me.

I spread the stolen blue raincoat on the ground and curled up with my arm for a pillow. There was no way I was ever going to get to sleep. An owl hooted outside in the night, and I was glad at least that I wasn't a tiny bird anymore, and prey. The ground was cold, and I started to shiver inside Benjamin's shirt and sweater.

"You'll freeze," he whispered, and he put his arm under my head, and moved his jacket over so I could share it. It was warm under the jacket, and I could smell his boyish smell. It didn't sound like he was any closer to sleep than I was.

"Benjamin," I whispered.

"Yes?"

"Will everything be all right?"

"I hope so," he said, and I could feel the pulse in his arm against my cheek. "I really do."

CHAPTER 24

The Dark Force

I must have slept, finally, because I dreamed of being on a boat in the vast sea, among seals and walruses that rose up out of the water and spoke Norwegian. For much of the dream I was panicked that I didn't have the Pharmacopoeia, and when I did have it, its pages were terrifyingly blank.

I woke at dawn to a racket of birds and didn't know where I was until I saw Benjamin's face, blinking and frowning close to mine. The early light filtered through the mulberry leaves. I sat up and saw the apothecary and Jin Lo waking up, too. Jin Lo was brushing dirt off her coveralls. Neither of them seemed to notice that I had slept under Benjamin's jacket with him. The apothecary was too distracted, and Jin Lo, I was pretty sure, would never notice such a thing.

"That boy isn't back," the apothecary said. "Your friend."

"He will be," I promised, though I wasn't sure.

We emerged cautiously from our little cave of leaves, and there were no police officers waiting to arrest us, no Danby with his sight returned, no Scar. The apothecary led us across the dew-soaked garden to a leafless tree I hadn't noticed before. His eyes were locked on it as if he were facing a formidable adversary. There wasn't a single bud on the tree, or even a bit of warm brown color in the bark. It could have been a sculpture made of stone or concrete: an expanse of smooth, gray, bare branches, reaching up to the sky.

"You can make that bloom?" I asked.

He didn't answer, but started to methodically unpack his bag.

Jin Lo went to the gardener's shed and brought back a long metal rod with a T-shaped handle. She walked around the tree, making deep holes in the earth among its gnarled gray roots. The apothecary followed her with a bottle of green powder, tapping the powder down into the holes.

Then he circled the tree a second time, with a bottle of clear liquid, pouring it into the same holes where he had sprinkled the powder. Green foam bubbled up out of the ground, until there was a ring of popping, fizzing bubbles around the roots and the thick trunk.

The apothecary walked around a third time, with a trowel, and covered all of the holes with dirt so that the fizzing and foaming was trapped underground. And then he stood back with us and waited. I remembered a poem we'd read in school: "Weave a circle round him thrice, and close your eyes with holy dread."

But nothing happened. We watched and waited.

"That's the jive-o tree?" a voice said behind me, and I turned and saw Pip, holding a paper bag. He'd approached without any of us noticing, and he'd changed out of the rolled-up coveralls into his own clothes and shoes.

"You're back!" I said.

"You think I'd miss the show? Have a popover."

He held out the bag, and I brushed off my dirty hands and took one. It was hot and soft and smelled delicious, and I realized I was starving. "Where'd you get these?"

"Portuguese lady makes 'em on the King's Road," he said, and he took a bite of golden dough.

Benjamin said, "Look!"

I did, and tiny green leaves had started to pop out and unfold on the tree. As they unfurled, they grew, until there were thick, green, waxy leaves on every branch. Then, while the leaves were still unfolding, tiny white flower buds appeared.

"Take this," Benjamin's father said, handing him a glass bell. "I don't know how long the bloom will last."

The buds grew into tight fist-sized bundles of petals,

which then burst open, all over the tree. It was as if the great tree had spontaneously burst into flame, but the fire was made of white flowers as big as my head. The air smelled heady and sweet, like spring.

The apothecary pulled down a branch with one of the white blossoms on it, and showed Benjamin how to hold the glass bell over the flower. Then he snipped it free. They cut two more like that, and the apothecary fastened a piece of cloth tightly over the open base of the bell and dampened the cloth with something from a bottle.

As soon as he'd sealed up the three blossoms, there came a rumbling noise from deep in the earth, among the roots of the tree, and the thick trunk seemed to shudder.

The apothecary looked concerned. "Stand back," he ordered, and we all moved a step away, transfixed.

One of the white blossoms on the tree trembled and started to wither, then another. As each blossom shrank, turning gray and shriveled, a thick black smoke rose up into the air. The apothecary rushed forward and snipped one more flower while it was still white and fresh. He quickly dissected it with a pocketknife, squeezing oil from the bulb at its center into a vial.

Then he looked up, and we all watched the smoke from the tree gather itself into a dark cloud. Again there was a rumbling noise, and this time it came from inside the cloud, like thunder. But it wasn't thunder: It was more like an expression of disapproval. I can't describe the cloud accurately except to say that it seemed to have *intelligence*. It seemed like a great being, made of cloud vapor, embodied with the power of intention, of will. That idea seemed foolish to me at the time, but I couldn't ignore the feeling, and now it doesn't seem so foolish. The cloud moved away deliberately, as if it knew where it was going, into the sky.

The apothecary pushed his spectacles up on his nose, watching the cloud glide over London. "I was afraid that might happen," he said.

"What is it?" Benjamin asked.

"A consequence of forcing the bloom. It's something like the radiation released when they split the atom, I suppose. The Pharmacopoeia calls it the Dark Force."

"Is it dangerous?"

"I'm not sure," the apothecary said. "I've never seen it happen like that before." He plucked one of the withered gray blossoms from the tree to inspect it, but it crumbled to dust in his hands.

I looked at the three blooms in the glass bell, which were still perfect and fresh, with thick, waxy petals. "It didn't affect your flowers."

"I took precautions," the apothecary said. "Now we have to collect our provisions and get to the boat."

"We'll need warmer coats for Nova Zembla," Benjamin said. "And boots."

The apothecary blinked at him. "We? *You're* not going to Nova Zembla."

"Yes, I am," Benjamin said. "You need me."

"If Benjamin goes, I go," I said.

"Me too!" Pip said.

The apothecary, who had been so un-parentlike until now, gathered up all his fatherly indignation and seemed to grow several inches taller. "You think I would take *children* to the testing of a nuclear bomb?"

"We can help you," I said. "Jin Lo, tell him we're helpful!"

Jin Lo shrugged. I was getting tired of her eloquent shrug. "They help some," she admitted.

"We helped a lot!"

"It's out of the question!" the apothecary said. "Enough! I need to go over my notes." He patted his pockets but found nothing. We waited.

"They are lost?" Jin Lo finally asked.

"Oh, dear," the apothecary said. "They're in the Pharmacopoeia."

CHAPTER 25

Science Team

Benjamin and Pip and I went to St. Beden's for the book while the apothecary and Jin Lo set off to collect provisions for the trip. In two hours, they were to meet Count Vili at the icebreaker *Kong Olaf,* docked in the Thames—assuming Vili was safe and uncaptured. We were to go there to hand over the Pharmacopoeia, assuming the book was safe and uncaptured, too.

It was still early and school hadn't started, but

students were arriving and talking in little groups in the yard. I kept an eye out for Mr. Danby as we walked up the school steps. I tried to look nonchalant, as if this were just another day at school, but I was uncomfortably aware that none of us had a uniform. I was wearing Benjamin's clothes, and they looked dirty and slept-in. A mother dropping her daughter at school gave me a pinched look of censure.

We made our way to the chemistry classroom, where the door was open. Benjamin peered inside, then waved us in. The room was empty, and I looked anxiously to the shelf in the back, terrified that we'd let the apothecary down.

But the book was there, right where we'd left it. The Pharmacopoeia's old brown leather spine blended in among the heavy textbooks and binders. Benjamin pulled the book down and put it in his satchel, where it stuck out as usual.

"Good morning," a Russian voice said behind us, and we whirled, expecting the worst.

But it was only Sergei Shiskin, standing in the door of the chemistry classroom. The shock of hair over his eyes was greasy, and he looked unwell.

"Sergei," I said. "What's wrong?"

"Nothing!" he said, but his face twitched and he grimaced as if he was trying not to cry. "I don't know anything!"

"Did something happen to your father?"

"No!" he said, too quickly.

"You can tell us," I said. "We're your friends."

Pip tiptoed around behind him, unnoticed, and closed the classroom door.

Sergei jumped at the sound. "I can't tell you anything!"

"Yes, you can," I said. "We have no secrets in science team." I sounded sinister even to myself, but we had to know what he knew.

Benjamin reached for a beaker full of clear liquid on a lab table and held it up. "We just made up some Smell of Truth," he said. "A fresh batch."

"No, please!" Sergei begged.

"You know how it works," I said. "You might as well tell us."

"I can't!"

"Then you leave me no choice," Benjamin said, and he threw the liquid to the floor at Sergei's feet, where it splashed on his heavy black shoes. I hoped it was just water and not some kind of acid. "Smell that?" Benjamin said. "You'll have to tell us now."

Poor Sergei looked stricken. We had surrounded him, so he couldn't get away from the spill without knocking one of us over. The clear liquid didn't smell like anything, but it did spread slowly and ominously over the floor.

"You saw your father break," Benjamin said. "And he's strong. You won't be able to resist telling us."

Sergei put his hands over his face and moaned.

"That strange feeling must be coming over you now," I said.

"Please," Sergei begged. "Don't make me. My mother—" He stopped.

"What about your mother?" Benjamin asked.

When Sergei finally succumbed, I thought it was to the need to talk to someone as much as to the idea of the Smell of Truth. "They have her!" he wailed. "The MGB does. Soviet security. In Moscow. They know about your father's plan, they know everything. They told my father to play along and help the Soviets take the boat, or they will kill my mother and my sister."

We stared at him.

"Is that true?" Benjamin asked.

Sergei gestured to the water on the floor. "How can I lie?"

"We have to tell my father," Benjamin said.

"No!" Sergei cried. "He will send my father away, and my father *must* be on the boat! They will have watchers to see him go."

"Then we have to go along and stop him, once the boat has left," Benjamin said.

"But my mother!" Sergei said.

"We'll think of some way to protect her," Benjamin said. "Don't worry."

There was a pause as we all tried to think of what way that might possibly be.

"First we have to get aboard," Pip said.

"We could use . . . the garbage can," I said. It didn't seem right to talk about being invisible in front of Sergei.

"We'd freeze to death, naked," Benjamin said.

"What garbage can?" Sergei asked, sniffing away tears. "Why naked?"

"We'd need to find really warm clothes," I said. "Fur coats or something, and get them on board somehow."

We all looked at each other, stumped—except for Sergei, who was too traumatized to be stumped. The bell rang for class, but no one came in.

"There's that girl, Sarah," Pip said finally.

"Yes?" I said.

"That's a girl who'd have fur coats."

"But not a girl who'd give them to us."

Pip grinned. "I've got half a crown says she does. Or I *will* have half a crown, from that spotty chess bloke. I'll give you odds."

Benjamin's and my school uniforms were still in the cupboard, and we changed into those behind the rolling chalkboard to look less conspicuous. We agreed that Sergei should go to class and try to act normal, and not cry. Pip would go look for Sarah Pennington—watching out for Mr. Danby—and Benjamin and I would stay in the chemistry classroom to make more of the invisibility solution. We couldn't use it right away because we still had to take the Pharmacopoeia to the apothecary, but we could take a concentrated version with us, and find something later to use as a soaking tub.

Before Pip left, I remembered that we'd already melted down my earrings. "We need gold!" I said.

"I'll get that, too," Pip said. "But the bet's now at five bob."

Benjamin opened the Pharmacopoeia to the page with the invisibility solution, and the process went more quickly this time. We remembered the words, and didn't need to go step-by-step with the Latin primer, or wrestle with my feelings about my grandmother's earrings. We ground and dissolved and titrated until Pip came back with Sarah Pennington.

As they walked into the room, Pip was talking to Sarah, and even though he was shorter than she was, he had a confidence that matched hers. It didn't come from having money, it came from having no money, and from knowing how to survive. She couldn't take her eyes off him.

"I didn't know there was a science competition," she said.

"Course there is," Pip said. "We won last year, at my old school."

Sarah looked up and realized there were other people in the room. "Hi, Janie," she said. "Did you win, too? Back in California?"

I was getting tired of her mocking tone. "Why do you keep saying 'California' that way?"

Pip shot me a warning look—for challenging his girl? For messing with his bet?

"What way?" Sarah asked.

"Like it's a joke. It's a real place."

Sarah rolled her eyes. "Sorry," she said. "So what's your project?"

"We melt down a piece of jewelry," Pip said. "And then we bring it back, just as it was."

Sarah fingered the gold necklace around her neck, with its heart-shaped charm. "*Exactly* as it was?"

"It's a project on the conservation of matter," Benjamin said.

"Do you have a jeweler remake it?"

"No."

"Then it's impossible."

"No, it's not."

"Yes, it is!"

"So give me your necklace, and I'll show you," Pip said.

Sarah pressed her lips together. Then she ducked her head to unfasten the gold chain. I glanced at Benjamin to see if he was looking at the mesmerizing back of her neck, but he was peering into the crucible. Sarah dropped the necklace into Pip's hand, and his fingers closed over the little heart.

"It's still warm," he said.

Sarah laughed. "Go on. You can really bring it back?"

"We can do *way* more than that," Pip said, which I realized wasn't technically a lie. We could do more than recover a melted necklace—we just couldn't do *that*.

Pip handed the necklace to me, and I held it over the hot ceramic crucible.

I hesitated for a second, but Benjamin caught my eye and nodded. What did a rich girl's necklace matter, against the possibility of his father being captured in the North Sea, or of a Soviet atomic bomb going off because Leonid Shiskin had decided that his wife's life was more important than the apothecary's? I dropped the necklace in. Sarah could always get another one. It didn't look like it had been her grandmother's.

"So when do you bring it back?" she asked.

"At the competition," Benjamin said. "It'll be very dramatic."

"Did you come from Mr. Danby's class?" I asked her. I wondered if he was still blinded.

"Yes, but we have a substitute, Miss Walsh," she said. "You know, I don't believe you can bring that necklace back."

"We have another favor to ask you, Sarah," Pip said.

"Oh?"

"This lot said you wouldn't help us," Pip said, "but I said you would. I said you're the kind of girl who would naturally help."

"I gave you my necklace, didn't I?"

"This is more important."

"All right."

"It's *really* important."

"So what is it?"

"They didn't even think you'd have what we need."

Sarah stamped her pretty foot with impatience. "Why don't you just *tell* me!" she said.

CHAPTER 26

At Lady Sarah's

We left school without being stopped, and Sarah Pennington led us to her house to look for warm clothes. It was as if Pip had his own spell, a love potion that made her agreeable to whatever he wanted. He caught my eye when Sarah wasn't looking and mimed money crossing his hand—five bob. I mimed putting on a warm coat to indicate that he'd get his money when we had everything we needed. Pip laughed and walked ahead with Sarah.

"I don't even know what five bob is," I said to Benjamin. "How much am I in for?"

"About a hundred dollars," he said.

I stopped walking. *"What?"*

It was Benjamin's turn to laugh. "No," he said. "Maybe a dollar. Come on."

I caught up to him. "I believed you!"

Benjamin looked pleased.

"Keep an eye out for truant officers," Pip called back to us.

"Oh, they won't bother *us*," Sarah said.

The Pennington house, when we got there, was the biggest house I'd ever seen. It was in Knightsbridge, and it took up much of a city block. A butler let us in, looking Benjamin and Pip over suspiciously.

"These are my friends," Sarah said. "They need some warm clothes to go out on a boat. We'll just go look in the old wardrobes."

The butler nodded. "Don't you have school?"

"We were excused," Sarah said.

"Ah," the butler said. "Shall I take your things?"

I felt Benjamin, beside me, tighten his grip on the strap of his satchel.

"No, thank you," Sarah said. "We won't be long."

We started up a grand staircase, past old portraits of pink-cheeked young men in tailcoats and willowy maidens in long dresses: generations of Penningtons who had been the richest and most attractive students at their schools. At the top of the stairs was a small painting of a little girl in a blue dress who crossed her ankles and gazed at the artist with a bearing that was already regal.

Pip stopped in front of it. "That's you."

"Oh," Sarah said. "I was so bored, sitting for that."

"You looked lonely," he said.

"Lonely? I had a nurse or a governess with me every second!"

Pip said nothing, and raised his eyebrows at her.

"It was a perfectly ordinary childhood," she snapped.

I bit my tongue to keep from reminding her that she had a butler and a nurse and a governess, which wasn't very *ordinary*. I reminded myself we needed the clothes.

She led us down the hall to a bedroom done all in flowered upholstery, with a canopied bed and an enormous window seat. The room seemed unused and in perfect order. I went to the window and pushed the curtain aside to look outside. There were two men in suits standing on the other side of Knightsbridge, and I wondered if they were watching the house. But after a moment, they shook hands and walked in different directions without looking up at the windows. I let the curtain fall.

"This was my aunt Margaret's room," Sarah said, opening a wardrobe that ran along one wall. "She went off to America in the twenties, to Vassar or someplace, and brought back all kinds of shocking clothes."

"Is she dead?" I asked.

"Oh, no," Sarah said. "She's just married. She lives in Scotland and she's old and dull. But she used to be *so* glamorous." She pulled out what looked like a diaphanous white silk handkerchief with spaghetti straps, embroidered with silver thread. "That's one of her dresses. I don't think she could get one arm in it now."

"But we need *warm* things," I said.

Sarah dropped the silver dress to the floor. "Where are you going again?"

"My uncle's a fisherman," Pip said. "He's taking us on his boat."

"Ugh," Sarah said. "I get seasick in the bath. It's tragic for my father, who's terribly yachty." She pulled out a long, dark fur. "That's a raccoon coat. Everyone wore them in the twenties. I think it's for a man."

She handed the coat to Benjamin, who put it on and stood in front of a long oval mirror beside the wardrobe. He looked like a bear escaped from the zoo, and raised his arms as if to lumber forward in attack. Pip convulsed with laughter.

"Now *this* might be suitable for a boat," Sarah said, pulling out a lined wool peacoat. "Here, Janie, try it."

I shrugged the peacoat onto my shoulders, and it fit me. I put my hands in the pockets and came out with a navy blue watch cap, which I pulled over my hair. It was a good feeling, to be enshrouded in thick military wool like that—I felt oddly safer.

Sarah tilted her head to consider me. "That's not terrible, actually," she said. "It's rather chic."

Against my will, my eyes went to Benjamin in the mirror, to gauge his reaction. He stood with his arms hanging at his sides in the raccoon coat.

"What do you think?" I asked.

"Looks warm."

"But your legs will be cold," Sarah said. She pulled out some silk long underwear and a few pairs of heavy wool pants, and she added them to the growing pile on the floor.

"Try those on," she said. "I'll take the boys to my brother's room."

They left, and I tried the warmest-looking pants on under my skirt. They fit fine, and I folded the warm clothes and sat on the end of the bed. The mattress was soft and inviting, and the room was quiet, and I had an overwhelming urge to lie down. It felt so luxurious just to be alone. I lay back and let my body relax into the bed's silk coverlet, and looked up at the flowered patterns in the canopy overhead.

I thought it would be very restful to be Sarah Pennington for a little while. There would be no worries, no running naked through the cold, no fear of what would happen if the apothecary caught us and wouldn't let us on the boat. I could feel myself sinking into the soft bed, as if I were falling very slowly, floating into oblivion.

Then I heard a slight cough, and I shot upright to see the long-faced butler standing in the door. I felt that my hair was askew and tried to smooth it with my hand.

"Did you find what you need, miss?" the butler asked.

"I think so."

"May I ask, will Miss Pennington accompany you on this boat trip?"

"Oh, no. She gets seasick."

"That's a relief," he said. "I answer to her father, you see."

Sarah came back down the hall with the boys, who looked like Eskimos in heavy trousers and ski coats with fur-lined hoods. They were carrying warm boots. "We'll need a trunk," Sarah said.

"Of course," the butler said. "I can have it delivered to the boat."

I looked at Benjamin and Pip. It might actually work. The others would have luggage, too, and the crew wouldn't know which trunks were coming from where.

"The boat's called the *Kong Olaf*," I said. "It's at the Port of London."

"It's Norwegian?" the butler said, frowning thoughtfully. "Then I daresay they'll have dried codfish aboard, but have you arranged for proper things to eat?"

CHAPTER 27

The Port of London

The trunk was sent ahead, and the chauffeured Daimler waited for us in Sarah Pennington's drive. We crowded into the backseat, with Benjamin on my left, the side of his leg pressed against mine. Pip was on my right, with Sarah squeezed between him and the door.

"One of you can sit in front," the driver said. He had clearly met a few charming pickpockets in his time, and he wasn't amused by Sarah's slumming.

"We have plenty of room," Sarah said imperiously.

The driver sighed and pulled out into the street.

At St. Beden's, Pip stole a kiss while the driver wasn't looking, and Sarah blushed crimson as she climbed out of the car. "Have fun!" she said, and she waved good-bye and skipped up the steps.

Pip looked at me. "What?" he said.

"Nothing," I said, trying not to laugh. "I owe you a dollar."

Benjamin did laugh, and I felt it in his body, through the leg that rested against mine. We didn't need to sit quite so close together anymore, but it didn't seem urgent to move away.

"To the port?" the driver asked.

"To the port," Benjamin said, and the car swung away toward the river.

There was a guard at the gate, but he took one look at the shiny chauffeured Daimler and waved us through. We drove slowly past the docks, past the hulking boats and barges and cranes. There were little sailboats in one section and big industrial-looking cargo steamers in another.

Then we saw a steel boat about a hundred feet long, tucked in against the dock. It was painted bright blue, with a long white deckhouse on top. In crisp white letters on the blue hull, it said KONG OLAF. The bow was rounded and sledlike,

I guessed for breaking the ice, but the boat itself was long and narrow, and looked like it might go fast.

Two crewmen were carrying Sarah Pennington's trunk, with its mahogany leather sides, up the gangway. I guessed they were used to nice luggage, with Count Vili aboard, and no one stopped them. So that was progress at least: Our warm clothes were on the boat. We thanked the driver and walked down the dock as the Daimler purred away.

A longshoreman carrying a coil of rope over his shoulder bumped into Pip, knocking him forward a few steps.

"No bloody nippers on the docks," he growled. "'Less you fancy a swim."

Pip called the man something shocking.

The longshoreman grinned and called, "Same t'you, mate!"

I looked down into the murky water of the Thames and remembered my father telling me that the river had always been the city's sewer system and that London's toilets still flowed, ultimately, into it. I definitely didn't fancy a swim.

There was a man standing beside the short gangway for climbing aboard the *Kong Olaf*, and we walked over to him. His hair was sun-bleached white, and his skin weathered, and his lips so thin he seemed not to have any.

"We're meeting my father on board," Benjamin said. "Marcus Burrows. I'm supposed to bring him something."

The man called up to the deck, "Ask the count if he wants a delivery!"

The plump, elegant man we had seen in Hyde Park appeared at the rail. He was as well-dressed as before: His three-piece suit was dark green, and over it he wore a long trench coat, unbuttoned, lined with dark silky fur. His eyes were friendly, and he didn't have the manner of someone who was sought by both the British and the Soviet authorities.

"Ah, the children!" he said. "Thank you, Ludvik, send them up. Tell me, have you ever seen such a marvelous boat?" His voice reminded me of expensive furniture, something that belonged in Sarah Pennington's house: rich and soft-textured.

Ludvik the guard stepped aside, and we climbed aboard the blue icebreaker, our footsteps ringing hollowly on the metal gangway. I made a mental note that we would have to step quietly when we were invisible.

The apothecary met us on deck, his face looking anxious beside the happy, complacent count. "Were you followed?" he asked.

"I don't think so," Benjamin said.

"You have the book?"

Benjamin nodded.

"Jin Lo is still collecting provisions," his father said. "I hope she's all right."

"I'm sure she's fine," I said, just because he seemed so nervous and agitated.

The *Kong Olaf* wasn't fancy, but it was orderly and clean, the steel deck painted and scrubbed, and the chrome metalwork polished. The skipper's name was Captain Norberg, and he had a cragged face that looked as if it had spent years squinting into the wind. Aside from him, I counted five crewmen, including the guard at the bottom of the gangway, who all seemed to speak English. The bridge was at the foreward end of the deckhouse, with a tiny galley behind it. Next was a little sitting area Vili called the "saloon," with built-in couches and a square table.

Beyond the saloon was a corridor with doors to the cabins on either side, and the apothecary led us back toward his cabin. Everything was small and crowded, and smelled of things that had been damp once. But Count Vili clearly loved the boat, and rhapsodized about its usefulness and efficiency, pointing with his knobby walking stick. As he gushed, Pip touched my arm and pointed to an open cabin door.

The cabin was piled with duffel bags and suitcases, including Sarah Pennington's mahogany leather trunk. They were using the room for storage. I nodded. That was where we would hide and recover our warm clothes when we got on board.

"We can talk freely here," Count Vili said. "The crew knows of our plan. They come from northern Norway, which will suffer from the effects of radiation if the test proceeds. The reindeer will be affected, and the fish, not to mention the children."

We crowded into the apothecary's cabin, which had twin bunks and a small washstand. There was barely room for all

of us to stand. Benjamin pulled the worn leather Pharmacopoeia from his knapsack.

Count Vili reached for it with awe. "May I?" he asked.
"I haven't seen it since I was an undergraduate. I was far too
stupid to appreciate it then."

"You were very young," the apothecary said.

"So were you," Count Vili said, sitting on the bunk and
crossing one plump leg over the other to prop up the book.
"But you weren't a fool."

"You'd lost your parents," the apothecary said.

"What did Oscar Wilde say? 'To lose one parent may be
regarded as a misfortune; to lose both looks like carelessness.'"

"How did they die?" I asked. I couldn't imagine not having any parents to care deeply what happened to me. I thought
I would feel unmoored, like a boat allowed to drift free.

Count Vili opened the book and scanned a page. "My
mother was carried off by the Spanish flu," he said, as if he
had told the story many times, "in the epidemic of nineteen
eighteen. She was a bit inbred, in the way of the aristocracy,
I'm afraid, and had never been terribly strong. My father was
executed without a trial by the Communists who came to
power in Hungary after the first war."

"The Communists *executed* people?" I said.

"Of course," Vili said. "But then they themselves were
executed, by the counterrevolutionaries who called themselves the Whites. It was a dreadful time in Hungary. We
have not yet recovered. I love telling the story to Americans.
You are so sweetly innocent, always aghast." He turned a page

of the book. "Ah, the avian elixir! I always wondered, in my dissolute youth, if it were really possible to become a bird."

"It is!" Pip said. "It's *great*!"

"You've done it?" the count said. "How wildly unfair that I haven't."

"Can you really stop time?" I asked.

"It's more like slowing it down briefly," he said. "It does nothing about wrinkles." He put a hand to his round, smooth face, which was too cheerily plump to be wrinkled.

"How do you do it?" Benjamin asked.

"My boy, it's taken a lifetime of study."

"But you'll do it to stop the bomb?"

"That's the plan!"

"Oh, *please* take us with you!" I said. It was partly what I thought I should be saying, as someone who wasn't allowed to go and didn't have a secret plan. And it was mostly what I really meant—because if they would just let us stay, then we wouldn't need to find a place to become invisible and run freezing and naked through the streets.

"Absolutely not," Benjamin's father said.

"What if you don't make it back?" Benjamin asked his father. "What am I supposed to do then? I don't want to be an orphan!"

"Oh, it isn't the end of the world, to be an orphan," Count Vili said, still flipping through the Pharmacopoeia.

"Easy for you to say," Pip said. "With your magical tutor an' your great bleedin' pile of money."

Count Vili looked up from the book and broke into a

delighted smile. "True!" he said. "Well, then, we'll just have to make it back safely."

"Can Benjamin stay with one of you?" the apothecary asked. "With your parents?"

Pip and I looked at each other and said, "Sure" at the same time.

Then they herded us out of the cabin, through the saloon, just as Jin Lo came aboard with her arms full of bags and parcels, which she set down in the little galley.

"Good luck, Jin Lo," I said. "Good luck, Mr. Burrows."

"Look out for my son, will you, Janie?" the apothecary said. "You too, Pip."

Then he sent us off down the steel gangway. We passed the guard at the bottom, with his thatch of white hair, and walked away up the dock before turning back to look at the boat, with its round blue icebreaking hull.

"Now," Pip said, rubbing his hands together. "How 'bout a nice hot bath?"

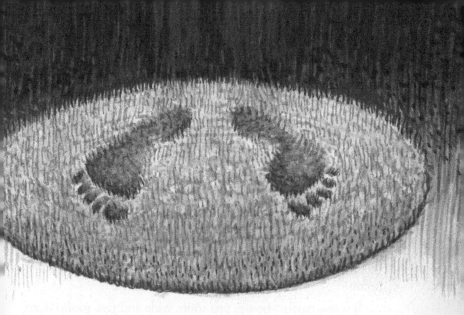

CHAPTER 28

Breaking and Entering

Across the Lower Thames Road from the Port of London's gate, there was a narrow street, and down that narrow street was a row of terraced houses, all attached to each other. Pip eyed them, looking for one in which no one was home, and no one would be. Finally he stopped in front of a house with lace curtains and dark windows. "That's the one," he said.

"How do you know?" I asked.

"How d'you ever know? It's just a feeling you get."

"Should we go around the back? It's broad daylight."

"*Burglars* go in the back," Pip said. "Act like you're doing nothing wrong. It's our auntie's house, and we've got our key. Sticks a bit, it does."

So I tried to look as innocent as possible, chatting with Benjamin on the stoop, while Pip made picking the lock look convincingly like struggling with a sticky key. Then he pushed the door open, and we went inside.

"Auntie?" he called, but he was right that no one was home.

It was a narrow house, one room wide and two rooms deep on each floor. Pip locked the door behind us. A steep staircase led straight up from the front hallway, and we found a bathroom just off the second-floor landing. The bathtub was old but clean—much cleaner than a high school garbage can.

The pipes screeched as we turned on the water, then thundered as the water poured out, and I hoped the neighbors were away. Benjamin set the lever that stopped the drain, then poured the bottle of invisibility solution under the tap, like bath oil. I thought about the fact that Sarah Pennington's necklace had been melted and ground into powder, and was now suspended in the water. Once, I would have teased Benjamin about taking a bath in it, but now it didn't seem right. Sarah wasn't Benjamin's crush anymore; she was Pip's—*girlfriend*? The thought was bizarre.

When the bath was full, we turned off the water, and the doorbell rang downstairs. "Mrs. Jenkins?" a woman's voice called, muffled by the glass in the front door. "Are you in there?"

We all froze.

"Mrs. Jenkins?" the voice called again.

"Let's find another house," I whispered, in a panic.

"We can't!" Benjamin said. "The bath is drawn!"

"I'll go talk to 'er," Pip said. "Get in the tub." And he was gone.

Benjamin pulled his jacket off. "I know this is awkward," he said. "You can turn around if you want. But you should undress, too. I won't look. We need to move quickly."

I turned to face the towel rack, which had a blue towel hanging from it, under a framed needlepoint of a basket of flowers. Each blossom was made of tiny cross-stitches. I felt frozen with shyness and indecision, and wished we still had the rolling chalkboard as a screen.

"Hullo!" I heard Pip say downstairs. "Can I help you?"

I couldn't hear the woman's exact words, but she sounded surprised to have the door opened by a smallish boy. I heard Benjamin step into the water behind me, and imagined his lean body sliding into the tub. I took off my school blazer and dropped it to the floor. Then I slipped off my shoes.

"My auntie Jenkins isn't home," Pip said downstairs. I could tell he was making his voice a little sweeter and more childish than usual, and his accent more like Benjamin's. "She'll be here soon. I'm meant to have a bath. Is there a message?"

The woman stammered an uncertain apology.

I managed to roll my tights down under my skirt, and hopped on one foot to pull them off my toes. I pretended I was just slipping a swimsuit off under a towel, after junior lifesaving, with a bunch of other kids on the sand in Santa Monica. It was the same as that, I told myself—but of course it wasn't.

The tub water sloshed, and I turned and saw wet, foot-shaped depressions form on the tufted blue bath mat. I stood there in my skirt with the cool air on my bare legs, knowing I had to unbutton my shirt next, and that Benjamin was standing naked—invisible, but still naked—in front of me. I could see one of his knees.

"I promise I won't look," Benjamin said. "But you should hurry."

I fumbled with my shirt buttons, wondering if he really wouldn't look, then slid the shirt off my arms and dropped the pleated skirt. As I moved toward the tub, my bare shoulder brushed Benjamin's invisible one.

"Sorry!" we both said at once.

I stepped into the bath and sank down into its enveloping warmth, with my eyes closed and the world silent and sealed away. I left the tip of my nose out, and when I sat up and opened my eyes, the rest of me seemed to be gone.

A towel floated in the air as Benjamin held it up for me. I pushed myself up out of the bath and accidentally kicked the lever that controlled the drain plug, stubbing my toe.

"Ow!" I said.

"Janie!" Benjamin said.

The mechanism behind the wall of the tub had opened the drain, and the water was rushing out at an alarming rate.

"Oh, no!" I tried to push the lever down again to stop the drain, but it was stuck. I tried to close the drain itself, but it wasn't one you could push into place.

I felt Benjamin's arm slide wetly against mine as he tried to force the lever down, but he couldn't do it either. I held my hands over the drain, but it wasn't a small one, and the water went through my fingers. I put my foot over it, and that finally stopped the water, but by then there was only an inch or two left in the bath—not enough for Pip to get fully invisible in.

"What do we *do*?" I asked.

Downstairs, Pip's voice said, "I'll tell her you called round, then. It's time for my bath. Ta!" We heard his footsteps on the stairs, and he came into the bathroom.

"You two in here?" he said, pulling off one boot. "I don't think she believed me. She might come back." Then he saw the bath, and heard the last of the bathwater draining away. "You didn't save none for me?"

"I kicked the drain lever and it stuck," I said. "I'm so sorry!"

He looked around the empty bathroom. "There's no more potion?"

"We used it all," Benjamin's voice said.

Pip sighed. "All right, then. I'll jus' find another way onto the boat."

I took the towel from Benjamin, thinking that if anyone

could get on that boat visible, it was Pip. But I also thought that if Pip had gotten in the tub before me, *he* would never have kicked the lever. "I'm so sorry," I said again.

"S'all right," he said. "Dry your hair off. It's cold out."

There was another knock at the front door, downstairs. A stern male voice called, "Who's in there?"

"Let's go!" Pip said.

"What about our clothes?" They were scattered all over the floor, and they were traceable to St. Beden's.

"I'll take 'em," Pip said, and he bundled them under his arm. Then he turned the noisy water in the bathtub on again, and let it run.

We crept quietly downstairs, watching the doorknob rattle as the man outside tried to get in. Pip whispered to us to stay out of the way, and then stood close to the hinge side of the door. He unlocked it, and the man pushed, and the door swung open, hiding Pip with the bundle of clothes.

"Hello?" the man said, stepping into the house.

Upstairs, the bathtub water was rumbling. The man tiptoed up to catch the bathing boy-housebreaker, and as he did, the three of us slipped out onto the stoop. Pip stashed our clothes behind the first likely low wall, and we ran back toward Lower Thames Street. The cold pavement stung my bare feet, and I thought that if we were going to keep doing this invisibility thing, I had to find some invisible shoes.

"What time do you think it is?" I asked. The boat was leaving at three.

"Half past two," Pip said.

I saw a new watch buckled on his wrist. "Where'd you get that?"

"From my auntie Jenkins," he said. "Can't be late."

I was very cold, and all I could think about was getting onto the boat and burrowing into the enormous raccoon coat, but then I noticed a familiar car parked on our side of the street, just across from the Port of London's gate.

"Look!" I said.

It was the green sedan with three men sitting in it: two in front and one in back.

"Go listen," Pip said. "I'll see that the boat don't leave."

He sauntered off across the street, and Benjamin and I moved invisibly closer to the green sedan. The passenger side window was open a few inches to let the smoke from Mr. Danby's cigarette out. The Scar was in the driver's seat, so I assumed he had his vision back. And the man in the back was Leonid Shiskin, in a warm wool coat.

Mr. Shiskin looked nervous, and twisted a fur hat in his lap. "The apothecary is very clever," he was saying.

"I agree," Danby said. "He's a formidable opponent. I thought he'd blinded us for life."

"He is also my friend."

"*That's* what makes you so valuable," Danby said. "You can take him directly to the Soviet authorities, in his own chartered vessel, without unnecessary loss of life. You're perfectly positioned. It's a stroke of genius on Moscow's part."

"If I fail, please try to save my wife and daughter," Mr. Shiskin said.

"You won't fail."

"And please look after Sergei. He's only a boy, and not a very bright one."

"I will, of course."

Mr. Shiskin looked miserably at the hat in his lap. "You know that the ninth circle of hell is reserved for those who betray their friends."

"Think of it another way, Leonid," Danby said. "Russia is your country, and your family is your family. This isn't a betrayal of the apothecary, but an act of loyalty. There comes a time when we must choose."

"But Russia isn't *your* country," Mr. Shiskin said.

"It's the country of my heart."

I tried to look to Benjamin in silent amazement at Danby's claim and ran into the impossibility of eye contact again. You don't know how much you rely on it until you're invisible.

"But why *is* that?" Mr. Shiskin asked. "What is Russia to you?"

Danby took a long, thoughtful drag on his cigarette. "What is Russia to me?" he said, exhaling. "A good question. There's a literary answer, since we're discussing Dante's hell. I read *Anna Karenina* one summer in the country when I was fifteen, and it had such an effect on me, that book. I thought I had to marry a woman like Anna, with those round, soft arms, and dark eyes, and that passion."

"But," Mr. Shiskin said, "no one sells out his country for *Anna Karenina*. And that Russia is gone, you know."

"Yes, of course," Danby said, tapping ash out the window. "There was also a very lovely ballerina named Natasha, when I was studying in Leningrad. Also with beautiful arms, though less round. That had some effect, too. But it was really the Russian soldiers I met as a prisoner of war, when I was shot down. They were kept on the other side of a great fence from us. We got packages of food and cigarettes from the Red Cross, but the Russians got nothing, and we used to throw them food, when we got it. But even starving and imprisoned, those Russian chaps were *certain*, in such a pure, strong way, that their country would be a great power after the war. Again, that passion. I admired them terribly. They were like the ardent young men in Tolstoy. I wanted to be like them, to believe like them, not always to be halfhearted, ambivalent, reticent, *English*. I didn't want to be that."

Mr. Shiskin looked at him sadly. "You've been taken in," he said. "Fooled by this Russian passion."

"Perhaps," Danby said. "But Moscow wants the apothecary, so that's where he must go. If England discovers his secret, they'll hand it over at once to the Americans, who will then have everything—both the power to destroy the world, which they have already, and the power to stop all other countries from protecting themselves. They will become even more monstrous than they already are. We mustn't let that happen."

"We," Shiskin repeated bitterly. "There is no *we* here."

"Of course there is," Mr. Danby said. "We're all on the same side. Now you must be going. Don't disable the boat until you're *positive* you're in Russian waters. We don't want to start an international incident. And think of your family."

Shiskin sighed, pulled his fur hat down over his great head, and got out of the car. He stood waiting for a break in the traffic, then crossed the street toward the port, carrying a small, heavy brown suitcase that bounced against his good leg.

The Scar said something in German.

"He'll manage all right," Danby said, flicking the rest of his burning cigarette out the window. I made a small, inadvertent noise as I jumped away from the hot ember, which made Danby look up, but he saw nothing.

Benjamin and I crossed the street, following Shiskin at a distance through the port's gate and along the docks toward the *Kong Olaf.* It was a long walk in bare feet.

"What do you think's in his suitcase?" I whispered. "A gun?"

"Maybe a radio transmitter," Benjamin said. "To signal the Soviets about the boat's position."

I thought about Benjamin's fascination with espionage, and his old disdain for his father's work. "Do you still want to be a spy?" I asked. "Or do you want to be an apothecary now?"

Benjamin thought about it for a second. "I'm not sure," he said. "Right now there doesn't seem like much difference."

We had almost reached the *Kong Olaf*, picking our way over rusted nails and bits of glass, when we heard the clang of a police car's bell. We jumped out of the path of the car, and watched it screech to a halt in front of the boat. Mr. Shiskin froze.

"Oh, no," Benjamin said.

The wispy-haired detective who'd arrested us at school jumped out of the police car, ignoring Shiskin, and approached the guard on the dock. "I'm Detective Montclair, Scotland Yard," he said. "This is Officer O'Nan. We've had a truancy report from port officials. Three children were spotted near this vessel, two boys and a girl."

"They were here," Ludvik said. "But they left."

"I'll search the boat then."

"I'm sorry, sir, we're just casting off."

"I'm afraid I must insist," Montclair said.

Count Vili came to the rail and leaned over. "Is there a problem, officer?" he asked, his voice full of courtesy and money.

Mr. Shiskin seemed paralyzed by indecision about whether to board the boat, which might be searched at any moment, or to stay where he was and risk not getting aboard at all.

"We're looking for three children," Detective Montclair said to the count. "They escaped from Turnbull Juvenile Hall yesterday."

"Oh?" Count Vili said mildly, in his interesting accent. "Then they couldn't have been the children who were here."

"Why not?"

"Because I had them out on the boat fishing all day yesterday."

"In the *Thames*?" Detective Montclair asked, disgusted.

"Just for perch and pike," the count said. "The fish are there if you know where to look."

"Didn't the children have school?"

"A holiday. They've gone back to their studies now."

Montclair frowned. "May I ask where you're *from*, sir?"

"Certainly," said the count. "I am from Luxembourg."

The detective didn't seem to know what to do with that information. He had no opinions about Luxembourg. "I really must search the boat," he said, striding toward the gangway.

Count Vili's face lost some of its composure. The descriptions of the apothecary and Jin Lo would have been circulated to the police by now. If Detective Montclair came aboard, he would take them all in, and the voyage would be over.

But then Pip appeared beside me with a bright look in his eyes. I don't know how he spotted me, when I'd left only the tip of my nose out of the invisibility solution, but I was no longer surprised by anything Pip did. "Get ready," he whispered.

Before I could ask, "Ready for what?" Pip strolled down the dock with his hands in his pockets, passing the policemen as if he hadn't noticed them. He stood at the bottom of the *Kong Olaf*'s guarded gangway.

"Hey, mister!" he called up to the count at the rail. "I left my cap on the boat! Throw it down, will you?"

Vili glanced at the detective on the dock. Pip followed his glance and jumped in surprise, as if noticing Montclair for the first time.

"Crikey!" he said stagily. "Coppers!"

He ran back up the dock, zigzagging between the two policemen. Detective Montclair tried to grab his sleeve, but missed and chased after him. Officer O'Nan hesitated, looking at the boat, then took off after Pip, too.

Grateful to Pip for the distraction, we followed Mr. Shiskin invisibly up the gangway to the boat, our light footsteps masked by the clang of his wooden leg. I looked back to see if Pip was coming. He had a good lead on Detective Montclair and was running toward the Port of London's gate, just out of the detective's reach. He had given all of us the chance to get away.

On board, Benjamin and I avoided the crew and went straight through the saloon to the cabin full of empty suitcases where we'd seen our trunk. We closed the door while no one was looking, climbed into the pile of luggage, and dug into the trunk. I pulled on silk long underwear, wool trousers, a sweater, and the peacoat over my freezing invisible nakedness. The *Kong Olaf's* engines rumbled to life.

"Soon we'll be at sea," I said, feeling better and warmer already.

"*Soon?*" Benjamin said, his invisible head shrouded in the hood of Sarah's brother's ski coat, and his hands missing at the ends of the sleeves. "We're in London, Janie. We've got forty miles to go before we get out of the Thames."

"Forty *miles*?"

"Have you ever looked at a map of England?"

I had, of course, but not closely. I hadn't realized there would be such a long stretch when the police could stop us or the apothecary could put us ashore with train fare home. We heard the calls of the crew casting off, and I pushed the blue curtain away from the cabin's porthole, to look out at the busy port. The whole world, the boats and docks and cranes, seemed to be gliding past us as the boat began to move out into the Thames, with the sound of the churning engines reverberating through the hull. The effect made me a little queasy, and I let the curtain drop.

I pulled a blanket from the trunk and drew it over my legs. We just had to stay hidden for forty miles, that was all. And then we had to stop Shiskin from disabling the boat and turning us over to the Soviets. And then, presumably, we had to help the apothecary with his plan. And meanwhile my parents would be getting home from their location shoot to a tipsy Mrs. Parrish, who would tell them that I'd spent the night with my friend Sarah (or Susan) No-last-name, at no given address, to do my Latin homework, and had never come back.

CHAPTER 29

The Kong Olaf

Sarah Pennington's butler had included a bundle of things to eat in the trunk. We found tinned salmon and crackers from Fortnum & Mason, bottles of apple cider, and a pack of playing cards. I thought I would enjoy having a butler to think of everything I might need, but then realized that my parents mostly did that.

We sat among the empty luggage and played silent games of gin rummy as we waited for the *Kong Olaf* to get out of the endless Thames. As parts of Benjamin returned, one at a time, I noticed the way his sandy eyebrows brushed up toward his forehead. It was part of what made him look so curious and intent, as if he was looking hard and slightly skeptically at the world. There were two freckles joined into one on the left side of his nose. His fingernails were round and still clean from the bath, in spite of our running around the dockyards. He caught me looking at him, over his cards.

"What?" he whispered.

"Nothing!"

"Do I have something on my face?" He brushed the back of his hand across his cheek.

"No."

"Am I all here?"

"Yes," I said. "You're all—"

"Shh," he said, and he looked to the door. People were talking outside, and Mr. Shiskin was one of them.

We couldn't hear the exact words, but from the voices and the thumping of the wooden leg, it was clear that Shiskin had taken the cabin next door. I wondered that the others couldn't hear the anxiety in his voice. I could hear it through the door, without even knowing what he was saying.

The voices faded, and we went back to the cards. Eventually, the corridor grew quiet as people went to bed. Through the porthole we could see the open sea; we were out of the Thames and motoring north.

I had just been dealt a beautiful hand, with three eights and a run of four, and was waiting to go out. Benjamin frowned and moved his cards around in his hand, as if shifting them was going to change what they were. I felt a sudden giddy pleasure at doing something as ordinary with him as playing cards.

Benjamin must have felt something of the same happiness, because he said, "I've got a hand like a foot," with his vowels flattened out like an American poker player, so it came out, "Ah've got a *hayand* like a *fuht*."

I started to giggle at the fact that he was doing American impressions, and at how funny he sounded doing it.

"Shh!" he said.

"You started it!" I whispered.

Then he held up his hand for silence. There was a faint movement out in the silent corridor. We both listened, alert and tense, but the sound was gone. A minute passed, and I dared to breathe again.

But just as I did, the luggage cabin's door flew open and we were staring at Jin Lo over the cartoonishly wide barrel of a gun. When she saw who we were, she dropped the gun and glared at us. "Why you here?"

I was too stunned to say anything.

Benjamin managed to say, "To help you."

"Apothecary say no!"

"But he needs us!" Benjamin said. Even in the panic of the moment, I thought he was wise not to suggest that *she* needed us.

"Is that a real gun?" I asked.

"Flare," she said. "For signal." She shook her head as if disappointed with herself. "I *know* there is trouble. I go tell apothecary." She turned.

"Wait!" I said. "The trouble isn't us, it's Shiskin."

She turned and eyed us, then stayed and closed the door. Benjamin told her in a whisper what we knew about Mr. Shiskin: that he was acting as a saboteur, and that the Soviets had kidnapped his family and were forcing him to disable the boat in Russian waters so that they could quietly capture the apothecary without attracting attention. And that we had promised Sergei we would try not to get his family killed.

Jin Lo listened carefully, then said, "We throw him into sea." And she vanished out the cabin door.

"No, wait!" Benjamin said.

We scrambled out of the luggage bunk, over trunks and bags, but Jin Lo was already in Mr. Shiskin's cabin and had dragged him out of bed by the time we got there. He had taken off his wooden leg for the night, which gave her an advantage, but still I was amazed at how strong she was. She twisted his arm behind his back in a way that looked painful, and he struggled to stay upright on one leg. She still had the flare gun, and she held it to his head.

"You *bú yàolian*," she said. "I not know how say this in English. You have no shame."

"*Shame?*" he said, incredulous. "I risked my life for you and you were *careless*. You were discovered." He couldn't see Jin Lo, who was twisting his arm behind his back, so he glared fiercely at Benjamin and me. "And my family will not be punished for it. *I* will not be punished."

"And *I* will not go to Russian prison," Jin Lo said.

"Then you shouldn't be interfering with their nuclear program," Shiskin said. "If I don't send a radio signal every six hours, they will know I am captured."

"You think I am fool?" Jin Lo said, tightening the twist of his arm. "I know you signal them to come."

Shiskin winced. "They'll come, whatever you do."

The two of them stood welded together, caught in a stalemate of contempt and fury. "Find rope," she finally said to us. "We tie him."

Shiskin tried to struggle away, and Jin Lo looked ready to pull his arm out of the socket. Benjamin and I found a long cord in the luggage cabin, and Jin Lo trussed Shiskin up with the speed of a calf-roping champion, leaving him immobilized and attached to his bunk. On her way out of the cabin, she picked up his wooden leg. Then she closed the door on him and marched us down the hall to the apothecary's cabin.

The apothecary opened the door sleepily, wrapped in a dressing gown. His eyes looked naked without his spectacles, but then they grew wide. "Benjamin!" he said.

We sat on the spare bunk and told him about Shiskin.

Benjamin's father listened and shook his head. "You should have told me before."

"Then you wouldn't have let Shiskin aboard," Benjamin said. "And they would have killed his family."

"We could have abandoned the mission."

"It's what you've been working for all these years," Benjamin said. "I want to help you."

We all sat in silence, listening to the rumble of the engines. The apothecary's spirits seemed very low. "We have to tell Captain Norberg," he said.

CHAPTER 30

The Anniken

We woke Captain Norberg, who was sleeping in his clothes and came instantly awake on seeing two stowaways on his boat. The apothecary apologized for our presence, and told him that Shiskin had been assigned by the Soviets to disable the *Kong Olaf.*

The captain rubbed a hand over his yellow hair and considered the news. "I suppose you could take it as a compliment," he told the apothecary. "They must be afraid of you. They could have arrested us in Russian waters without sending a saboteur."

The apothecary shook his head. "They've overestimated my powers. I'm no match for the Soviet Navy."

Captain Norberg studied Benjamin and me. "In all my years at sea, I've never had a stowaway bigger than a cat."

"We're sorry, sir," Benjamin said.

The captain sighed. "I can't lead my men into an ambush without telling them what to expect," he said. "I'll wake the ones who aren't on watch and assemble them on the bridge, and you can tell them where we stand." He put on his coat and hat and went forward to the crew quarters.

The apothecary stood in the middle of the corridor and stared morosely at the floor. "We should abandon the plan," he said.

"No," Jin Lo said. "We have come so far."

He shook his head.

Benjamin and I left them there and went to wake Count Vili. We explained the situation while he pulled a burgundy silk dressing gown over striped pajamas and knuckled sleep out of his eyes.

"Shiskin? I trusted that man!"

"They kidnapped his family," I said.

The count yawned. "That's why it's best to be free of attachments. Much safer that way. How did you get aboard?"

"Invisibility," Benjamin said.

"Ah," the count said. "You're hardier than I thought, running around naked in this weather. You'll do well on that freezing rock of Nova Zembla—if we ever get to Nova Zembla."

"Does anyone live there?" I asked.

"Samoyeds," the count said. "They were reindeer breeders on the mainland, the best in the world, until the Soviets moved them to Nova Zembla and forced them to work on collective farms. The people rose up, so the Russians shot them down from airplanes. Charming, no?"

"How can the Soviets test a bomb where people live?"

The count shrugged. "You Americans have done it, too. And if the Soviets were willing to shoot unarmed citizens from airplanes, perhaps they don't care if the rest are poisoned by radiation. Do you suppose it's cold on the bridge? What an ungodly hour for a meeting."

"*You* should talk to the crew," I said. "You could be convincing and inspiring. The apothecary seems . . . discouraged."

"Oh, he'll be fine," the count said, pulling his fur-lined trench coat over the dressing gown and taking up his black walking stick.

But I wasn't sure. The crew crowded into the wheelhouse in varying degrees of sleepiness and disarray. A piratical sailor with silver hoop earrings in both ears had the wheel. There was also a skinny boy who looked about seventeen, the sun-bleached Ludvik, a man with a nose like a lump of dough, and the old cook, who looked ready to retire. They all looked as if they had better things to do than spend the rest of their lives in a Siberian prison.

The apothecary, standing in front of them, polished his spectacles anxiously with his sleeve. The count found a spot inside the wheelhouse, but Benjamin and I had to stand in the galley with Jin Lo, the men's backs partly blocking our view of the apothecary. I wished we had coached him, wished we could have given him some of the fervor Benjamin had against the lunch lady.

He put on his spectacles again. "As you know," he began, but the engines and the wind drowned him out.

"Speak loud," Jin Lo said.

The apothecary coughed. "As you know," he said more loudly, "our plan is to contain an atomic bomb being tested on Nova Zembla, and to counteract its destructive effects. That is the task we have been working toward for many years, and I am confident that we have the correct approach."

The men waited. They knew this part, and he sounded like a boring teacher. I wished he would use fewer long words. He was going to lose them. "But now it seems that our friend Leonid Shiskin has been sent by the Soviet authorities to stop us. He is restrained in his cabin at the moment, but we are exposed. The Soviets know we are coming."

The men looked at one another in silence.

"I know that many of you have children in Norway," the apothecary went on. "I realize that the danger of the trip is now heightened to the point of impossibility, and I can't ask any man to risk his life for me. My best advice to you is to take us back to England, and go home to your families."

I winced. It was one thing to lose the men's faith, but another to *try* to send them home. He was supposed to talk about the radiation, the fish, the reindeer, the Samoyeds, the children!

"Actually, that's my request to you," he said. "That we go home. It's the only rational thing to do."

A clear, loud voice came from beside me. "This *not* our request," Jin Lo said. She was standing very straight. "Not mine."

"It isn't mine either," Count Vili said, his fur collar up, leaning on his walking stick just inside the door.

The apothecary looked surprised by the objections. I wondered if he had worked alone for so long, getting only letters from disembodied scientists, that he'd forgotten he had colleagues and friends. "Well," he stammered. "I suppose—I suppose we could go on. That is what I intended to ask you to do, in the first place. But the immensity of what we are facing . . ." He trailed off and I realized he had caught sight of Benjamin, standing behind the men. He hesitated, and his eyes softened, and something seemed to shift in him.

When the apothecary began speaking again, his voice had become oddly strong and thrilling. "You have children," he said. "And you want to be able to protect them. I want you to be able to go home and protect them. But I believe what my colleagues are saying is this—that we should not stop at our desire to protect our own children in their immediate world. We want the streets they walk to be safe, and the walls around them to be sound, and we want to be able to put food in their bellies. These are natural desires." He paused.

"But if we truly want them to be safe and well, we must make the greater world a different place. As it stands, we are all threatened, at every moment, and nothing we do to lock our own doors and earn our pay and tuck our children in bed will make the slightest difference. I believe we can achieve a safer world, on this voyage, if we succeed. But I can't guarantee success. The Soviet Navy, as I have said, is waiting for the *Kong Olaf.* They have our description and will be very difficult to elude. So I leave you all to make your choice."

No one spoke, and we kept moving north toward the waiting Soviet ships. Suddenly, I heard my own small voice in that crowded wheelhouse of grown men. "Could we make the boat invisible?" I asked. The men turned to see where the voice had come from, and I felt myself blush.

The apothecary shook his head. "It's too big, I'm afraid."

The sailor at the wheel with the earrings said, "We could disguise her."

"I'm sorry?" the apothecary said, blinking behind his spectacles.

"The boat," the skinny young crewman said, understanding. "We could disguise the boat, like pirates and warships used to."

"That would be difficult," the apothecary said.

"Not so difficult," Jin Lo said.

"It can't hurt to try," said the captain.

"We need paint," Jin Lo said. "Not blue, not white."

The crew sprang into action, opening the storage bins

on deck. They produced two cans of red paint from beneath piles of rope, plus several paintbrushes.

"Not those," Jin Lo said, dismissing the paintbrushes. "Too slow." She took the paint cans to the little galley, where she chose the largest cooking pot and dumped the paint into it.

"But I make the oatmeal in that pot!" the cook complained.

"Your oatmeal already tastes like glue," Ludvik said. "So what if it tastes like paint?"

There was a strange air on board of anticipation and growing willingness. The apothecary brought his black leather bag from the cabin and joined Jin Lo, who took a bottle of gray powder from him and tapped some into the pot.

"What's that?" I asked.

"Is like magnet," she said. "But not magnet."

She stirred the pot, smelled it, and added something else from the apothecary's bag. The paint seemed to move almost restlessly in the pot. She let it run in ribbons off a wooden spoon to test the consistency. The red liquid was a little less bright now, and a little runnier. "It's good," she said.

The apothecary helped her decant the heavy pot back into the paint cans. The boat was still moving north into the wind through the dark night, and Jin Lo asked the captain to bring it nearly to a stop. He nodded to the man with the earrings and the boat slowed. Then she carried her can of paint forward to the bow and leaned over the starboard rail. She waited for the men to gather around her—she had a sense of occasion, and knew her audience—and then she carefully tilted the paint over the lip of the steel hull. The red color didn't drip or run down, but spread so rapidly and evenly over the vertical side of the boat that it looked like water spreading over a flat floor. It continued, as far as I could tell, beneath the surface of the waves, unaffected by the water.

The men watched, mesmerized. They'd spent *years* of their lives scraping and painting boats, but this paint moved on its own, as if drawn to any surface. "Can you teach us to do that?" Ludvik asked.

"After Nova Zembla," Jin Lo said. "*Then* I teach you."

She took the second can to the port side to run the paint down over the hull, watching it spread and wrap itself around the hull, then studied her work. She found that she had missed a spot, and poured a little more until she was satisfied. At the stern, she poured the last of the paint, and the boat was entirely red. The words KONG OLAF were gone.

The men stared at Jin Lo and the apothecary with shining eyes, in silence. It was a job that would have taken them a week in dry dock. If they'd had doubts about the apothecary's abilities before, those doubts were gone.

Then the skinny young crewman piped up. "She needs a new name," he said.

"Who does?" the apothecary asked.

"The boat. It's a dead giveaway if she doesn't have a name."

"Of course," the apothecary said. "What should it be?"

Again there was a silence.

"The *Anniken*," Ludvik ventured.

"Is that a suitable boat name?"

"It's my little girl's name. She's a fierce little thing." He looked around at his friends. "I always told her I'd name a boat for her. I didn't think it'd be so soon. But if we do this, I'd be doing it for her."

"Does that mean you'll go with us then?" the apothecary asked. "On the *Anniken*?"

The men looked at each other, and at the same moment they all threw their arms in the air and a great cheer rang out on deck. "The *Anniken*!" they cried. Their voices were hoarse with emotion. I looked at Benjamin, beside me, and I could tell he was proud of his father.

Count Vili elbowed me. "See?" he said. "I had a feeling the soft sell would work."

"I don't know," I whispered. "I think it was Jin Lo's paint that did it."

The apothecary stood blinking at the men, overwhelmed. "The *Anniken* it is, then," he said.

Ludvik's tanned face broke into a blinding smile. He went to put his daughter's name on the side of the boat, looking enormously proud. The captain took over at the wheel, and the others started to drift back to bed. It had gotten so late that it was early: A glow of light appeared in the east. Ludvik called, astounded, "The red paint is already dry!"

"We still have to do something about Shiskin's family," I said.

"I've been working out an idea," Benjamin said. "Who's the nicest of all of us? I mean the softest touch?"

"Jin Lo," Count Vili said, and we stared at him in disbelief until he burst out laughing at his own joke. It was my father's kind of joke, and I couldn't help smiling.

"I think it's Janie," Benjamin said.

"Of course it's Janie!" the count said. "It isn't you, and it certainly isn't *me*."

I frowned, secretly pleased. "I'm not *that* nice," I said.

"Here's what we'll do," Benjamin said.

CHAPTER 31

The Execution

In the morning, after breakfast, I knocked softly on the door to Shiskin's cabin. The men were taking turns guarding it with a revolver, and the skinny young crewman, whose name was Niels, was on guard duty. I nodded to him and went inside. Shiskin lay listlessly on his bunk, his hands and leg tied, his head on the pillow. I closed the door behind me.

"Ah, the little girl," Shiskin said. "Who thinks she is saving the world and instead has ruined my life."

I tried to ignore that, and tried not to feel hideously guilty. "I wanted to ask you to change your mind and help us," I said.

"Ha," Shiskin said bitterly.

"You used to believe in the apothecary," I said.

"That was before my family was held hostage."

"The crew is willing to help us."

Shiskin rolled on the bunk to look at me. "I could lie and say I would," he said. "But your friends would not believe me. Jin Lo especially knows that every person acts for himself, and his family."

"The apothecary isn't acting for himself."

"Of course he is. For himself and for his dead wife. Every minute of every day is for his dead wife."

"He's trying to save humanity."

Shiskin scoffed. "Humanity is not worth saving."

There was a pause. Finally I said, softly, "They're going to kill you. I tried to argue, but they won't listen. They're worried about our survival."

Shiskin sat up as well as he could, bound as he was. "Janie," he said, alarmed. "Untie my hands. You *must* let me signal."

"I can't!"

"The radio is in my suitcase. Janie, listen. If the Soviet kidnappers think I have helped the apothecary, there is no hope for my wife and daughter. But if they know I have been murdered in their cause, perhaps they will have some pity and free my family."

I hesitated, so as not to seem too eager. "You swear on Sergei's life you won't do anything but signal?"

"I swear on Sergei's life."

It was all going perfectly. I untied his hands, and he rubbed his wrists, bringing blood back to them.

Then I turned to pull the little suitcase close to him, as Benjamin had told me to do, but Shiskin had loosened the rope tying his leg to the bunk, and he launched himself at me. I felt one powerful arm tighten around my neck and tried to scream, but Shiskin clamped his free hand over my mouth.

"Tell them to open the door," he said.

"Mmph!"

"Any tricks and I will kill you, I swear." He released my mouth.

I didn't know what to do. "I'm ready to come out," I called weakly.

Niels opened the door carefully, with the revolver raised, but Shiskin grabbed the barrel and wrested it free. I screamed, and Shiskin crooked his arm around my face, smothering my mouth. He leveled the gun at Niels. "Put your hands on your head," he said. "And find my leg."

Niels lifted his skinny arms. "But I don't know where it is!"

"*Find* it," Shiskin said. "Or I kill her."

"Benjamin!" I shouted, my mouth full of the wool of Shiskin's jacket. "Jin Lo!"

Shiskin knocked me in the side of the head with the butt of the gun, making my eyes fill with tears, and he tightened his elbow around my face. I had no doubt that he could break my neck if he wanted to. Niels had disappeared into a cabin, looking for the leg, and we were alone in the corridor.

Count Vili came into the saloon and said something calm and placating in Russian, which Shiskin ignored. Vili held up both hands, one empty and one dangling his walking stick, in a gesture of peace or surrender. He looked inconsequential—soft and whimsical, with his expensive clothes and his unnecessary walking stick, facing the hardness and desperation of a man with nothing to lose.

"Comrade," the count said. "Friend. Please."

In the meantime, Niels had returned with the prosthetic leg.

"Put it on," Shiskin said, nodding down toward his left thigh. "And try nothing, or I will kill you."

The boy's hands were trembling as he fumbled with the unfamiliar straps, trying to attach the leg.

Benjamin appeared from the wheelhouse and said, "Janie!"

Shiskin still had the revolver pointed at my head, and my mind was strangely detached. I thought what a peculiar way this would be to die, and how it was the last thing I would have expected: to be killed at sea by a one-legged man, while a teenaged boy tried to get the other leg on him. Who would explain it to my parents?

Then something even stranger happened. The sound of the struggle with the straps stopped, and a deep calm came over the corridor. I couldn't hear Shiskin's breathing anymore, and everything was still. The ship had stopped rolling, and the birds had stopped crying. It wasn't that I couldn't move, exactly—but I *wasn't* moving. And my heart wasn't beating.

Nothing moved except Count Vili, who came at us so quickly he looked like a flash through the air. He had knocked Shiskin's gun out of his hand with the walking stick before I knew what was happening, and had pulled me free. The gun hung in the air, motionless.

Just as I formed the thought that the count had frozen time, there was a rush of noise in my ears. Everything came unstuck, and Count Vili caught the flying gun, and the momentum of his pulling me away from Shiskin threw me against the wall of the corridor. I put my hands up to stop myself before my face hit.

Shiskin lost his balance without me to hold him up, and fell to the floor. Vili stood over him with the gun—no longer a racing, superhuman blur, but a round Hungarian count in a rumpled three-piece suit.

Benjamin, who had been frozen across the saloon, rushed forward. He threw himself at Shiskin on the ground, gripping his throat with both hands.

"Stop!" Shiskin's strangled voice said.

"Benjamin!" Vili said.

"I'm all right!" I cried, thinking Benjamin might kill Shiskin with his bare hands. I knew he didn't want to do that, and would regret it later. "Really, Benjamin, I'm fine!"

"Get—him—off—me!" Shiskin gasped, with what sounded like his last breath.

Vili pulled Benjamin away, and up to his feet, and the young crewman tied Shiskin's hands with expert sailors' knots. Benjamin didn't look at me. I could see a muscle working in his jaw, in anger and maybe in embarrassment.

As they moved Shiskin back into his cabin, I slipped my hand into Benjamin's. "Thank you," I whispered.

Shiskin was allowed to signal the Soviets to tell them he had been discovered and was going to be executed. He seemed subdued and resigned to his fate, and I pitied him, even if he had held a gun to my head ten minutes earlier. Vili, who knew Russian Morse code, monitored the transmission.

When Shiskin signed off, Count Vili took off his earphones and switched off the radio. "That was very good," he said. "Very moving and patriotic. Now you have died a hero, and your family is of no use to the Soviets. With luck, they will set your wife and daughter free. And with more luck, they won't find us and discover that you're alive."

Shiskin blinked. "You're not going to shoot me?"

"You think we are barbarians?" Vili said. "The children promised your son that they would try to help your family. We are trying to help them keep their word."

Shiskin looked to Benjamin and me, amazed. Jin Lo took his radio out on deck and we heard a splash as she dumped it overboard.

"We do have to keep you locked up, you understand," Vili said. "I apologize for that. We can't have you taking hostages all the time."

But Shiskin had his face in his hands and didn't seem to hear the count, so overwhelming and torrential was his relief. He might not think humanity was worth saving, but that didn't mean he wasn't happy, himself, to be alive.

CHAPTER 32

Genii

awn broke clear and cold over the North Sea, and the red *Anniken* plowed steadily north-northeast through the waves. Seagulls flew overhead, calling, and two fought over a fish in midair, wheeling and turning on each other. The light shimmering on the water was so bright, it made me blink.

A man took sun sightings with a sextant at noon to determine our position, and studied charts, trying to keep us from straying prematurely into Russian waters. An albatross soared in our wake. I had come to look at birds in a new, suspicious light in the past few days, but this one seemed genuinely like a bird. It wheeled in our slipstream as if for the pleasure of it, making endless, effortless figure eights with its vast wings.

Jin Lo showed me a vial she had brought, to be used if we were stranded at sea. She dipped a cotton thread into the clear liquid and lowered it, wet, into a beaker of seawater. Salt crystals began to form on the treated thread, and grew until they looked like a piece of rock candy hanging in the water. Jin Lo pulled out the hardened salt and handed me the beaker of water.

"Drink," she said.

"It's safe?"

"No, I poison you."

I smiled, used to Jin Lo's sense of humor by now, and drank the water. It was cold and tasted clean and silvery, but not salty.

"People could use that," I said, excited. "All over the world!"

Jin Lo frowned. "Is new. Difficult to make more than small amount."

In the afternoon we watched her send her particles up into the air so she could practice with her net. Count Vili explained that large amounts of radiation were required to make the net contract sharply, so the low levels of radiation from the sun just made it hang like gossamer in the light. It was barely visible, but cast a golden shimmer against the sky.

The crew of the former *Kong Olaf*, who knew a good fishing net when they saw one, asked Jin Lo to try to snare some fresh fish.

"This is not purpose of net," she said.

"Just try!" begged Ludvik.

Jin Lo sighed. "Okay," she said. "You find fish."

So the men scanned the surface of the water intently, until they saw herring gulls feeding in the distance. "There'll be a school right there," Ludvik said. "The birds always find them."

They steered the *Anniken* toward the gulls and stopped the boat. Below the birds, we saw small baitfish leaping from the water in silver showers, trying to escape the larger fish below. The big ones flipped at the surface and sometimes cleared it, and meanwhile the gulls went crazy trying to snatch the flying baitfish.

Jin Lo, unmoved by the spectacle, showed two of the men how to hold the net's nearly invisible golden edges. Together they swung it out over the sea, where it fell like a light rain on the surface of the water. After a few tries they gathered it in, full of fat, shining fish, which flipped and wriggled on the deck.

The cook prepared the fish on an open grill on the deck, grumbling about how Benjamin's father had taken over his galley as a laboratory. The apothecary had extracted the Quintessence from the preserved flowers in the glass bell, but he was still experimenting with it. Thinking about how intently he concentrated on his work made me think about my own parents, and how soon they'd be back in London to discover I was missing, and what they might do.

When the fish came off the grill, hot and salty and delicious, Count Vili and Benjamin and I took our plates to sit on the storage bin. The brief noonday sun was out, and the count held up a fish by the tail, then stripped off the flesh with his teeth like a great happy cat, basking in the light. I'd grown fond of the count on the voyage. He was sardonic and jaded sometimes, but he was also endlessly willing to be pleased.

"*Kings* do not have finer lunches than this one," he said, licking grease off his fingers. "I can promise you that."

"What do you know about the bomb the Soviets are testing?" I asked.

"Only that it was designed by a physicist named Andrei Sakharov," he said. "Their young genius. I have longed to meet him under other circumstances. I think he has a very flexible mind. We thought for some time that we might win him over to our work. But I fear he's rather entrenched in the Soviet system."

"Maybe he'll be interested when he sees what you can do," I said.

The count gave a wry smile. "When we have sabotaged his work? I don't know how *you* make friends, but I don't think that's the best way."

I thought of something else that had been bothering me.

"When the apothecary made the jaival tree bloom," I said, "to harvest the Quintessence, it released something he called the Dark Force. It was like a cloud."

The count looked startled. "You *saw* it?"

"We watched it float away," I said. "Except it didn't really float. It seemed to know where it was going."

A momentary frown crossed the count's face. "Have you noticed ill effects from your experiments with the Pharmacopoeia?"

Benjamin and I glanced at each other. "You were missing the feathers around your neck," Benjamin said. "When you were a bird."

"But that was because Mr. Danby grabbed my scarf," I said. I thought about the other things we'd done. "I kicked the drain before Pip could become invisible, but that was my fault, and it ended up helping us, because he was still visible and could distract the police."

"The memory oil paralyzed Jin Lo," Benjamin said.

"Whenever we tamper with natural laws, there are consequences," the count said. "The larger the disruption, the larger the consequence. The name of your Pharmacopoeia, for example, comes from the ancient Greek *Pharmakon*, which meant both 'drug' and 'poison': the power to heal and harm. I have never seen the Dark Force as a cloud before. But I have seen its effects, in small ways. My tutor, Konstantin, compared it to the Roman idea of the 'genius,' or guardian spirit. He felt that something like those genii resided in matter, and were released and disturbed when matter was transformed. It explained, for him, the effect of the cloud seeming to know where it is going. There is a kind of intelligence to what is released, and sometimes it has a mischievous or irritable character. But these genii have a strange kind of loyalty. The fact that they bother to tease us with ill effects means they are inextricably linked to those who disturb them, if you see what I mean. I'm not sure of any of this, of course. We work in the dark—we do what we can, as Henry James said."

"Mr. Danby told me to read Henry James," I said.

"Ah, you see?" Count Vili said. "The dreadful Mr. Danby reads good books. Even the darkest forces are never all bad."

That night, Benjamin and I stood on the rail in the dark, bundled up against the cold, watching the water break and foam beneath the *Anniken*'s bow. It poured away along the sides of the hull, bright white against the black sea, as if the boat had wings. Overhead, the stars were impossibly clear, brighter than any stars in smoky England or smoggy Los Angeles, and they gave me an odd feeling, as if something was expanding inside my chest and spilling over. It would seem very unfair to be killed at fourteen when the world had so much loveliness in it.

Benjamin broke the silence, saying, "I'm sorry I lost control yesterday, Janie. I couldn't stand it, watching Shiskin hold that gun to your head and not being able to move or do anything. It was my plan that had put you in danger, and—I sort of snapped."

"It was a good plan," I said. "I just wasn't careful enough."

"You were brave to do it."

"I wasn't brave. I was scared to death."

"He believed you the whole time. Did you ever want to be an actress?"

I thought about the vain and silly Maid Marian, with her false eyelashes and her obvious flirting, and the other versions of her who'd been in my parents' shows back home. "No," I said. "I mean, I used to practice walking like Katharine Hepburn. But that was more about wanting to be the characters she plays than about wanting to be *her*."

"Show me the walk!" he said.

I shook my head. I couldn't believe I'd told him about the Hepburn walk.

"Please?" he said.

"No!"

Benjamin smiled. "Someday."

I couldn't help smiling back. "Maybe."

We watched the bow wave a while longer, and then Benjamin said, "Listen, Janie. Remember that thing I said about Sarah Pennington? Under the Smell of Truth?"

I nodded. My heart was pounding inside my coat.

"I just wanted to say," Benjamin said, staring hard down at the water, "that—well, that you're the one I'd want to be here with."

It was exactly the thing I might have wanted him to say,

but wouldn't have dared to wish for, back when I'd had time to worry about whether he liked me or not. Hearing it out loud, I didn't know how to answer. He turned to look at me, and his dark, serious eyes had the same effect on me as they had in the lunchroom that first day. The wind blew my hair against my cheek and he pushed it away and smiled.

"*This* is what I mean by 'American hair,'" he said, tugging the strand lightly. His fingers touched my face and then slid around to the back of my neck, and he pulled me close and kissed me.

His lips were warm and soft against mine, and the night air was cold. Shivers went down my spine from the place where his fingers were tangled in my hair and pressing against my skin. It felt infinitely sweet. We were on our way to a nuclear test site with an untested antidote. The Soviet Navy was looking for us in submarines and spy planes, and my parents would be frantic with worry, but there was nowhere else I wanted to be. There is still, to this day, nowhere I would rather have had the first kiss of my life.

Benjamin pulled back and his face was turbulent with emotion. He seemed to be frowning and smiling all at once. I knew he was thinking the same things I was. And then he was kissing me again, and the world fell away.

When we were too tired and cold to stay on deck, Benjamin went to his father's cabin and I went to the one I shared with Jin Lo. She opened one eye, then the other, when I came in, and I wondered if she ever truly slept. She gave me a once-over.

"Something good happen?" she asked.

"Um," I said. "Yes."

"That's good," she said.

I undressed down to my silk long johns and climbed into my little bunk, where I lay awake, staring at the rivets in the cabin's ceiling.

"Jin Lo?" I said after a while.

"Mm-hm?"

"Do you still miss your parents?"

There was a silence in the dark cabin. "Sometime," she said.

"Do you remember them well?"

There was another pause. "I remember smell of father's shirt," she said. "Combing mother's hair. Sometime faces not so clear. I am eight. I remember baby brother's feet. Very small toes and very funny."

"What was his name?"

"Shun Liu," she said. "It mean 'willow tree.' But he is so fat, not like willow."

"Maybe he would've grown up to be tall and skinny," I said. There was no answer, and I thought maybe I'd said the wrong thing.

"Your mother know where you are?" Jin Lo asked finally. "Your father?"

"No."

"They worry."

"I know."

"You don't know," she said. "You are child."

I resented that for a little while, but I knew she was right, and I couldn't really imagine what they'd be going through. I tried to summon some comforting idea, but could only picture them angry and frantic, and I didn't want to think about that. I rolled back and forth on my bunk's thin pillow. My mind drifted back to the look in Benjamin's eyes on deck, and his soft lips on mine, and his warm hand touching my face in the bitter cold. And finally I fell asleep.

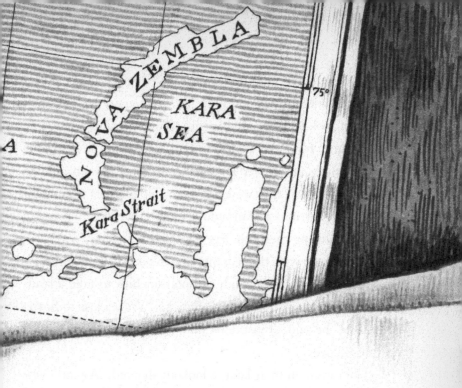

CHAPTER 33

Nova Zembla

The next morning we crossed an invisible line, after which the air didn't just have the nip of the Arctic in it. The Arctic had seized us in its icy teeth and wouldn't let go. Even in our furs and woolen clothes, it was impossible to be on the deck of the boat without ducking our faces and hunching our shoulders against the freezing wind. If I breathed too deeply, I felt as if icicles were stabbing me in the lungs. Actual icicles formed on my eyelashes when my eyes watered, and if I took off my gloves, within seconds my fingers became too cold to function. The cook kept hot coffee and hot cocoa on the stove, and passed it around in mugs. The men coddled the engines as if they were unpredictable toddlers who might erupt in tantrums any minute or simply shut down, refusing to do anything their minders wanted.

The mate with the sextant tried to take his sun sightings, but the sky was too cloudy at noon for him to take a reading. He frowned over his calculations. "We're close to Soviet waters," he said. "I just don't know how close. We may have crossed over."

Not even an hour later, a lookout shouted, "A patrol vessel, sir!"

Captain Norberg took a pair of binoculars from the lookout and peered at the horizon. The apothecary stood beside him. I could see the vessel, too. It was on the horizon, but it was making a direct line for us.

"It's Soviet," the captain said, without putting down the binoculars. "However you're going, I need you off the boat, *now*. The children also. There's no place a boarding party won't find them."

So we hurried to the apothecary's cabin, where Jin Lo was already a swift-looking bird with fierce eyes and a cap of dark feathers. She must have gone below to take the avian elixir the moment the patrol was spotted.

"A falcon!" Count Vili said. "How terribly exciting."

"It's appalling that you've never done this before," the apothecary said. "I do hope you won't be a flightless penguin."

"Oh, dear, is that possible?" Count Vili said. "I'd hate to be stuck here. I do want to see Andrei Sakharov."

"And you want to help us stop Sakharov's bomb," the apothecary reminded him. "This is not a fan club."

"Of course I want to stop it!" the count said, hurt. Then he took up the bottle of elixir and drank, making a noise of surprise. His shining face and plump body began to shrink and shift. Thirty seconds later, he was a large gray bird with a rounded bill and an enormous wingspan, like the albatross we had seen soaring in the wind off the stern. It was exactly the bird he would have wanted to be, and when he stretched his wings with delight, he smacked the falcon in the face with his wing tips. Jin Lo gave him a savage look. The albatross instantly drew in his wings and ducked his gray head in apology.

The apothecary handed me another vial. "Janie," he said, "please give this to Shiskin."

"Is he coming with us?"

"We can't very well leave him here."

"I bet he becomes a stool pigeon," Benjamin said.

I ran to Shiskin's cabin. He was still tied up, but the bonds would be too big for whatever kind of bird he became, so I didn't bother to untie him. "A Soviet patrol is coming," I said. "We can't let them catch you. You have to take this."

Shiskin frowned at the vial. "What is it?"

"There's no time to explain. But I've taken it, and it's fine. I promise."

I helped him drink and waited for the slow, fascinating transformation, but instead there was a small explosion in the cabin. I flinched and covered my eyes. When I looked back, Shiskin wasn't on his bunk. The knots that had held him were empty.

I looked around the cabin for a bird, wondering if Shiskin had become something Russian, and what a Russian bird might be, but I couldn't find him. Then I saw it on the bedcover: a tiny pile of salt. I scooped every grain carefully back into the vial, pressed the rubber cap on tight, and ran back to the apothecary's cabin.

"It's Lot's wife!" I said. "I thought it was the avian elixir!"

"Shiskin would never have agreed to become salt," the apothecary said. He was packing things in the cabin away. "And we can't have the Soviets find him. Put him in that small backpack, please."

I picked up the little backpack, which was a miniature harness attached to a hard, cylindrical case wrapped in leather, and I slid the portable Mr. Shiskin inside. The backpack would fit a large bird, and had tiny buckles. "Where'd you get this?" I asked.

"I adapted it from a design by a German apothecary." He shoved his medical bag into the bottom of a sea chest and covered it with blankets. "He used to send medical prescriptions by carrier pigeon. Will you put the rest of those vials in?"

Each of the vials on the bunk fit in the palm of my hand, and I slid them one by one into the little backpack, alongside Mr. Shiskin's vial. One contained something golden, the color of Jin Lo's shimmering net. One was full of clear liquid, which I knew was the Quintessence. I could smell its sweetness even through the seal. One was so cold it burned my fingers, and I had to pick it up with my sleeve. I wondered if it helped Count Vili freeze time. The fifth was an amber color and I didn't recognize it.

"That's an emergency supply of the avian elixir," the apothecary said, "in case it wears off inconveniently early."

I was going to ask him how we were going to get the elixir out of the backpack and drink it before plunging to an icy death, but Benjamin said, "The Pharmacopoeia! Where do we put it?"

I didn't have to think. "With Captain Norberg's logbooks," I said. "Like in the chemistry lab." Benjamin ran out of the cabin with the book.

The apothecary looked around the cabin to be sure everything looked ordinary and unsuspicious, then turned to me. "You'll be the smallest bird, Janie," he said. "The bomb will be in a wooden shed on the southern tip of Nova Zembla. The shed has been there for years, and therefore looks harmless to spy planes. We will need to discover how the bomb is triggered, and how much time we will have until it goes off. If you can find a way to get into the shed, I may ask you to do so. I hate to keep making use of you, and I know Benjamin will object to putting you in danger again, but you may be the only one small enough to get inside."

"I'll do it," I said. "I want to help."

"Thank you." He handed me the little backpack. "You'll fit me with this," he said. Then he drank from the bottle of elixir. After a moment, he shrank and shifted until he was a snowy white barn owl with a heart-shaped face and piercing black eyes.

In my nervousness about fitting the harness, I pinched one of his wings, and he pecked at my hand. "Ow!" I said. "I didn't mean it!"

His owl face looked sorry, and I realized pecking had been a reflex.

When Benjamin came back, he looked startled for a moment by the snowy owl, but then recognized it as his father. "Captain Norberg says he'll stay near Nova Zembla until sundown, in case he can pick us up. Then he'll wait in Kirkenes, in Norway, just this side of the Russian border."

The owl nodded and pushed the bottle of elixir toward him with his beak.

Benjamin and I drank the rest of the elixir and became, once again, a skylark and a robin. Benjamin had thought to prop open the doors to the cabin and to the deck, and the five of us flew out and off the bow just as the Soviet boarding party came alongside.

A few of the *Anniken*'s crewmen stared up at us, with mouths dropped open, until their friends elbowed them.

Then they fixed their eyes stonily on the patrol, as if nothing extraordinary had happened. They were just some innocent Norwegians who had wandered mistakenly into Russian waters on a cloudy day.

The air was bracing in my feathers, although it didn't feel as cold as when I was human, and the sky was overcast. I was smaller than the other birds, and it was difficult to keep up. Gusts of wind knocked us off course, until Benjamin, flying a little higher, zipped ahead. We rose to his altitude and found a wind moving steadily north, and rode it until we came upon a great gray ship idling in the water, with gun turrets and a monstrous gray helicopter crouched on the stern. Count Vili had said that the Soviets would station a destroyer off Nova Zembla as an observation post for the test, and I guessed this was the destroyer, which meant we were close to the island.

We could see farther as birds than as people, and soon came upon Nova Zembla. It was more desolate than any place I had ever seen before: frozen, treeless, and windblown. I couldn't believe anyone lived there. The archipelago had open water along its long northern side, but it was almost completely connected to mainland Russia by ice on the south and east. There was a landing strip at the southernmost tip of land. Farther north, there seemed to be tiny houses, spread out in little clumps. I guessed they belonged to the Samoyeds.

Near the landing strip was the nondescript wooden shed the apothecary had described as the secret housing for the bomb. The Soviets had chosen well: It looked like nothing important would ever happen there.

As we flew lower, we saw a sentry standing under the eaves of the little shed. He was wearing a white coat and a white cap as snow camouflage and seemed to be the only guard. Beside the shed was a mound in the snow, which revealed itself to be a sort of bunker as we grew closer, probably for the sentry to sleep in, with a door dug out into the ground.

When the guard was looking the other way, we landed behind the bunker, but I hadn't mastered stopping yet, and I bowled into Jin Lo. She stepped disdainfully away on her sharp talons as I rolled through the snow. I could tell she considered all of us hopeless amateurs.

We heard the sound of helicopter rotors chopping through the air, and the sinister gray machine appeared. It hovered near the bomb shed like a giant angry insect. The sentry clutched his white cap tightly to his head against the rotors' churning wind. Then the helicopter settled down, blowing snow into the cold air.

Two Soviet officers climbed out, one wearing a pilot's helmet and goggles, followed by two men in civilian clothes. One of the civilians was tall and elegant, even in heavy winter clothes, and I recognized him with a start.

It was Danby, and with him was the German with the scar.

The fifth and last man was young and thin, in a long nubbly fur coat and a gray wool hat. He had a restless, distracted manner, and longish hair sticking out from the hat. From the albatross's excitement beside me, I guessed this was Andrei Sakharov, the Russian genius Count Vili had wanted to see. In his gloved hands, the young physicist held a small metal box.

The helicopter pilot had brought a thermos of something, and the sentry sat down happily on a little three-legged stool and turned his attention to it. The older military officer, whose face was tanned and tightened like the leather on an old pair of boots, unlocked the door to the shed with several different keys and a combination lock, and the men from the helicopter all went into the shed and closed the door behind them.

I looked to the owl, and he nodded his snowy head. This was my moment to try to find out how much time we had. I flew around the shed looking for a way in, and Benjamin followed me. Luckily the sentry was too preoccupied with his soup to notice us fluttering by. Finally I found a narrow gap between the wall and the roof and squeezed my body through with some difficulty, finding a spot to rest in the eaves. Benjamin's skylark body was too big to get through, but I could see him perched outside. I was glad he was there.

I couldn't see well inside the shed. It was dim, and one of the officers held a flashlight. On the floor in the center of the room was a long, horizontal cylinder with a coffinlike box lying alongside it. The box was about eight feet long, and dull gray. I had expected it to have a round nose and tail fins, like the bombs we had dropped on Japan, but they weren't dropping this one from a plane. It didn't even need to be mobile. It made no noise and had no markings, but it had an ominous, deadly aura. I didn't like being in the close space with it.

Sakharov placed his small metal box at one end of the bomb. The young helicopter pilot opened a toolbox for him reverently, as if assisting a famous surgeon. Sakharov chose a wrench.

Danby walked around the bomb, looking it over. "It's beautiful," he said. "It's the design I provided?" I could tell he was looking for praise, and he seemed as pathetic as someone in one of his Latin classes, bragging about having done extra credit. Sakharov said something in rapid Russian, under his breath.

"Don't call me a traitor!" Danby complained.

"I believe you fit the very *definition* of a traitor," Sakharov said, attaching a fitting on the little metal box to the bomb. "And if you understand Russian, why must we use English?"

"I'm a little rusty," Danby said. "I understand more than I speak."

"Somehow I doubt that."

"Please, comrades," the senior officer said. "We have important work here."

Sakharov tightened a small bolt, then straightened and stood. "The design is this," he said, with clear contempt for the traitor who wasn't a physicist and didn't speak Russian. "In the atomic bomb, we split the atom. This is called fission. In this new bomb, the hydrogen bomb, we also split the atom, and use the energy produced to combine the nuclei of two atoms. This is called fusion. Then we use the energy released to make a second fission reaction, which will be twenty times the size of the explosion that destroyed Hiroshima. So *yes*, my idea is similar to what the Americans have given to the English military. But it is not the design you stole from them—which was flawed, at any rate, in ways I don't believe you understood. It was not necessary for you to be here, as I have said. The Americans and I have come to similar conclusions. This is because there is only so much you can do with an atom. You can split, you can combine, or you can leave it alone." He handed the wrench back to the helicopter pilot.

I tried to sort out what Sakharov had said, and realized that if this bomb was so powerful, it might overpower the apothecary's antidotes. I was about to squeeze outside to warn him when I heard the Scar's gravelly voice, as if observing something about the weather, say, "There is a bird."

I felt a concussive blow of air and the room went dark. I was trapped inside some kind of tight, musty space, and couldn't move my wings. A crack of light appeared, and I saw a scarred human face peering in. I was inside the Scar's wool cap.

"It's the American robin," he said.

"Are you sure?" Danby asked.

"We should not have animals in here," the Russian officer said. "I'll make a note."

"This is not the point," the Scar said. "The bird is not native here. It is a spy."

There was a pause of amazement at this bizarre claim. The senior officer said, "It has a camera?"

"It's *human*," Danby said. "I mean, it's a human who became a bird."

The senior officer cleared his throat and spoke carefully, as if talking to dangerously crazy people. "The trigger mechanism is installed," he said. "We have twenty minutes. We must return to the ship."

"Wait!" Danby said. "We should search the island for other birds! They may be trying to stop the test!"

"We will go now," the senior officer said.

The Scar carried me out of the shed, inside the hat. I didn't know if Benjamin had heard everything, and I had no way of telling him that the bomb might be too powerful for Jin Lo's net. Then the rotors of the helicopter started up, and I knew that even my tiny robin's scream would be drowned out.

☙

I'd never been in a helicopter before, and riding blind inside a not-very-clean wool cap on the lap of a Stasi murderer, when you have information that your friends might desperately need, is not the way I'd recommend trying it. The hat smelled of sweat, and the noisy, rickety helicopter swung sickeningly through the air.

Finally we landed on what had to be the deck of the destroyer.

"We need a box, or a cage," Mr. Danby's voice said.

A hand grabbed me around the chest and pulled me out of the hat. Light flooded my eyes, and I looked around frantically. The ship was huge, nothing like the bathtub toy it had seemed from the air, but almost no one was on deck. I tried to wriggle free, and stabbed at the Scar's hand with my beak, but he only squeezed me harder, and I gasped. I thought he would crush my tiny bones.

The young pilot appeared and thrust a toolbox into Danby's hands. "We go belowdecks, below water level now," he said. He pointed toward Nova Zembla. "Bomb, yes? Much *radiatsii*."

"Yes, I'm aware of that," Danby snapped.

The boy hurried away, and Danby opened the metal toolbox, which was the size of a loaf of bread, and empty. They were going to put me in it. If I became human while inside it, I would be crushed as my bones grew. I would die painfully, I was sure—half bird, half human, too big for my prison. I shut my eyes and tried hard to imagine becoming human *now*, my heartbeat slowing, my wings becoming arms.

Nothing happened, and the Scar put me in the box. He seemed to be trying to figure out how to close the lid with his hand still in it, or to get his hand out without letting me go. I screeched in protest.

And then it began. I felt my heart slow, and my bones get heavier, and my skull thicken, and my feathers retract, and then I tumbled to the deck in my peacoat and boots. The toolbox clattered beside me, and the Scar was so surprised that he lost his hat, which blew across the deck of the destroyer. He ran after and snatched it from the air. I stood up, feeling awkward in my human limbs.

"I knew it!" Danby said, grabbing me by the shoulders. "Where's the apothecary? Is he on Nova Zembla?"

"He didn't make it," I lied. "He fell into the sea."

Danby searched my eyes to see if I was telling the truth.

"I'm the only one who got to the island," I said. "I couldn't save them." A tear rolled down my cheek—for I did really feel hopeless—and I let it stay on my face. I didn't know what to do except try to buy the apothecary time.

Then a loud alarm went off on the destroyer, and a Russian voice over a loudspeaker issued a command. I wondered if the ship was shielded in some way against the radiation, or whether the water alone would protect us, down below.

The Scar said, "We leave her on deck."

Fear seized me. "You can't! I'll be poisoned and die!"

"Then that will be one problem solved," the Scar said.

Danby smiled and let go of my shoulders. "That's true," he said. "I envy you for seeing what it really looks like, Janie. We have cameras, of course, but film is never the same. It should be very beautiful, so close."

"Why are you doing this, Mr. Danby?" I asked. "It can't be because you read *Anna Karenina* when you were fifteen."

Danby seemed surprised for a moment that I knew about his Tolstoy conversation, but then he considered the question. "What better reason could there be?" he said. "I want the nation that produced such a book to survive, and not to be annihilated by your naïve and vicious American government."

"But a *person* produced that book," I said. "Not a nation. That's—" I caught myself using the present tense. "That *was* the great thing about the apothecary. He wasn't working for a country. He was working to save people everywhere."

"As am I!" Danby said. "A Soviet nuclear force is the only way to keep the Americans in check and ensure that their weapons will never be used. The U.S. needs a deterrent. I'm sure your parents would agree. Now I really must go below."

"Don't leave me out here!" I said. The Latin words on his chalkboard came into my head. "*Decipimur specie—rectie!* We are deceived by the appearance of right! Remember? You think you're right, but this is wrong!"

Danby smiled at me. "You really were such a promising student, Miss Scott. I wish you all luck."

He followed the Scar toward the last open door, to go below. I thought about running after them and trying to fight my way down, but I knew I would never be strong enough.

I turned to the rail of the ship. I'd been acting as if I believed the bomb would go off because the apothecary wasn't around to stop it, but now I needed to believe that it wouldn't. I had to believe that the apothecary was strong enough to stop something twenty times more powerful than he expected. I was alone on the gray deck of the destroyer, in the vast silver sea, and I wanted to be brave. Snow had started to fall. I stood a little straighter and tried to have some of Benjamin's fire in my eyes.

Then I looked toward Nova Zembla and waited.

CHAPTER 34

The Bomb

For what seemed like a long time, I was alone on deck in the silence. I held my breath, standing at the rail and blinking at the island through the snow, hoping that Benjamin and his father had gone ahead with their plan—that Jin Lo's net would work, and the Quintessence would absorb the radiation. Imagining them working away on the island helped. They would carry on and succeed, and save themselves and the Samoyeds on the island, and the reindeer and the fish and the Norwegian children—and also me, exposed on the

deck of the destroyer. I didn't want to think about what would happen next, when they would have to leave Nova Zembla. They couldn't possibly rescue me from the Soviet Navy, and the idea left me feeling hollow and abandoned.

I tried to be selfless and hope only for Benjamin's safety, since he and his father were trying to save the world. But what I really wanted was for *all* of us to be safe, and out of this wretched place. I just couldn't see how that was going to happen.

As I strained my eyes at the horizon, it began to change. Something small grew out of the surface of Nova Zembla, blooming orange and red like a monstrous flower in the failing light. It rose slowly, ominously, into the air. Then there was the sound of the blast, bleeding into a long, diminishing roar, and the ship trembled on the surface of the water.

I thought of Benjamin in the lunchroom, saying, "We'll be incinerated. We'll turn to ash." The idea that all of them were gone, instantly—Jin Lo with her fierce competence and her hidden sorrow, the affable Count Vili, the kind and haunted apothecary, and *Benjamin*, my Benjamin—was too intolerable for my brain to handle. The fact that radiation would be drifting toward me in toxic waves was nothing compared to my friends vanishing.

The orange cloud was building and roiling in a way that looked agonizingly slow, and I seized the hope that Count Vili was freezing time on Nova Zembla. That would mean he was still alive—that they all were. I ignored the nagging thought that the slow rising was just the nature of the explosion, and allowed a little hope to rise in my heart.

The orange bloom spilled over into a second cloud rising above it, separating until the stacked clouds had only a thread of orange light between them. The two clouds didn't look intelligent in the way of the Dark Force, but they did look *alive*. They seethed with smoke and grew, expanding inexorably, unstoppably.

And then, instead of billowing ever upward, they stopped expanding. I thought of Jin Lo casting her shimmering net out over the sea, and hoped she had gotten it around the bomb. If she had, and it worked, then the polymer triggered by the radiation would contract and snare the explosion. I waited, holding my breath.

There was a moment of hesitating stillness, and then the topmost cloud rejoined the one below it with a kiss. They became one glowing shape again, and that shape, in turn, began slowly to contract. It looked like the newsreel of an atomic blast being played backward, in bright color.

The cloud collapsed in on itself, growing smaller and smaller, and then it was gone, like an orange sun slipping below the horizon. There was a strange hush on the empty deck: no seabirds, no splashing waves.

And then a smell came toward me on a gust of wind. It was the sweetest smell I have ever known, even in the many years since. It was sweeter than orange blossoms, sweeter than night-blooming jasmine. It smelled like life, somehow: like green grass and sunlight and birdsong, and the ache in your heart when you love someone deeply.

I knew it must be the Quintessence, distilled from the blossoms in the garden to absorb the radiation. I saw tiny particles winking in the last of the light, among the drifting snowflakes.

The mushroom cloud had collapsed, and I felt a burst of pride and relief. The blast, even contained as it was, had been enormous, and my friends might not have survived. And if they had, I didn't know how I was going to get back to them. But they had done it. I strained in vain for any sign of movement on the distant island, and saw nothing.

An hour must have passed before the hush on the destroyer ended. A few men ventured back on deck, speaking in Russian, moving as gingerly as people approaching a land mine that hadn't gone off. A young sailor wore earphones attached to a box that I recognized from newsreels as a Geiger counter, for measuring radiation. He listened, frowning in confusion, and then handed the earphones off to someone else to see if he was mistaken: There was no radiation.

I tried to look inconspicuous and boyish, in my peacoat and watch cap, like a smallish crew member, but someone grabbed my arm roughly and turned me around.

"What happened out there?" Danby demanded, his face close to mine. "We felt the blast, but then something happened. The photographs don't make any sense."

"It was amazing," I said. "It was beautiful. And you missed it, because you were afraid!"

Fury flashed in Danby's eyes. "Is the apothecary on the island?"

"I don't know," I said. "I'm *here*, remember?"

Danby dragged me toward the helicopter by the arm. The Scar followed.

"Where's Sakharov?" Danby demanded. "Where's that bloody pilot? Bring that Geiger counter. We're going back!"

CHAPTER 35

The Frozen Sea

The helicopter ride was no more pleasant now that I was human and could see out the windows. The rickety machine swung wildly with every gust of wind, and creaked and groaned as if it were ready to fall apart. It was too noisy for anyone aboard to bother speaking, and Sakharov and the Scar stared grimly down at the sea.

To keep myself from feeling sick and terrified, I tried to fix my eyes on something that wasn't moving, like I did when I was carsick. That's when I saw, out the window, a stationary black cloud. It was perfectly round and seemed to hold itself apart and aloof from the others. I thought of Count Vili's genii, and of the Dark Force that had drifted away from the jaival tree.

Then the helicopter lurched, and my stomach seemed to flip into my chest, and we started to descend. Nova Zembla was as barren and white as it had been before, but there was a great charred circle where the shed with the bomb had been. The Samoyed houses were tiny in the distance, and seemed undisturbed, and so did the island's spindly pine trees to the north. The helicopter avoided the burned patch and landed on the frozen ground a little distance away. The others climbed down, and Danby dragged me out into the snow.

The men walked with a dreadful tension toward the test site, staring at the cratered, blackened earth. The snow was melted even beyond the burned area, but there was nothing like the damage a nuclear bomb should have left. Danby gripped my arm so I wouldn't run, but where would I go? There was no sign of any of the others, and I tried to think that they had escaped, far away. The charred ground seemed a fitting place for the desolate hope that my friends had abandoned me for their own safety. My heart felt as flattened as the little shed.

The young helicopter pilot carried the gray metal Geiger counter to test the radiation. He shook his head, baffled. "*Chisto*," he said.

Sakharov grabbed the earphones from him and held them to his ear, listening, then dropped the headset. It swung from the cord in the young pilot's hand. The faint sweet smell of the Quintessence still hung in the air. Sakharov looked around the deserted point.

"How is this possible?" he demanded in English. "It is *not* possible!" His intelligent face was in torment. He had bent atoms to his will, and he wasn't used to being confronted by things he didn't understand.

"The girl knows," Danby said.

"The girl!" Sakharov said. "Where did the girl *come* from?"

"She was the bird," Danby said. "I *told* you we should have searched the island."

"She was the *bird*?"

"And she knows what happened."

"I don't," I said. "I wasn't here!"

"You are going to *rot* in a Soviet prison, Miss Scott, if you make it that far," Danby said. He shook me by the arm so hard that I bit my tongue and tasted the metallic tang of blood. "What did the apothecary do?"

"I don't know!"

Sakharov said, "I think I am not understanding this word, *apothecary*."

"He's not an ordinary apothecary," Danby said. "He's—a kind of alchemist. Or a magician."

"A *magician*?"

"No, he's a scientist," I said, because Sakharov seemed my only hope. "Just like you are. You'd like him. They wanted to meet you, and thought you'd understand what they're doing."

"They?" Sakharov said. "Who is *they*? And what is it they are doing, besides destroying my work and my reputation?"

Then we heard a cry that sounded not entirely human, and my heart froze. I couldn't tell where the sound was coming from, except that it was above us. It cried out again in terror, the voice nearly carried off by the wind. I looked up, over the sea, and saw a boy falling from the sky.

"Benjamin!" I screamed. I watched, horrified, as he plummeted into the waves.

"How fitting," Danby said. "The boy who flew too high."

"That was a *boy*?" Sakharov said.

I tried to pull my arm free of Danby's grip, but he dug his fingers in. "We have to go save him!" I cried.

"The fall will have killed him," Danby said. "Or if not, he'll drown instantly, in that cold."

"No!" I pounded Danby's chest with my free arm, and he grabbed that wrist, too. I felt helpless, faced with his total indifference. It wouldn't matter to him that I loved Benjamin, that he was fearless and clever and loyal and brave, and that he'd been trying to come back for me. I had to find a reason for Danby to *want* to save Benjamin, and the seconds were ticking away. "He knows all the secrets!" I said. "He knows *everything* about his father's work."

I saw a flicker of interest cross Danby's face. I turned to Sakharov.

"That was the apothecary's son who fell," I said, trying to make my voice steady. "His apprentice, his closest ally. He can explain what happened to the bomb—how it was contained, and why there's no radiation. You *have* to interrogate him! Don't you want to *know*?"

I knew that if they took Benjamin alive, they would force him to give up what he could of his father's secrets, or give up his father himself. That would be awful, but the alternative was worse. It was unthinkable that he might die right then, in that cold water. Danby and Sakharov looked at me. The pilot waited.

Finally Sakharov said, "Start the helicopter."

We all ran for the horrible machine. It took off shakily into the wind, and flew low toward the place where Benjamin had fallen.

"There he is!" I yelled, over the noise of the rotors. I could just see Benjamin's sandy hair, soaking wet, and his arm coming out of the water in a weakened crawl stroke, before a wave obscured him completely. My stomach felt as if it had been tied in a series of painful knots, and I willed Benjamin to stay afloat until we could get there.

The helicopter lowered a rope ladder, and the Scar climbed down it. The ladder whipped in the wind when he was halfway down, and he ducked his head and hung on. I never thought I'd be rooting for the Scar, but I desperately wanted him to keep going. He reached the bottom of the ladder, but he was still ten feet above Benjamin. Sakharov shouted something over his shoulder to the pilot. The helicopter dipped lower.

I'd lost sight of Benjamin in the flat light, with the surging waves and the ladder swinging below. I thought I saw him swimming away, as if he didn't *want* to be rescued.

"Benjamin!" I screamed. "Come back!"

The helicopter lurched, and the ladder was over him again, but Benjamin was fighting against being taken. The Scar struck Benjamin across the face, then nearly tumbled off the ladder as it swung. I held my breath, hoping Benjamin would give in and the Scar would stay strong.

"Just get him!" Danby shouted impatiently, but his voice was carried off in the wind.

Then the Scar was lifting something heavy under one arm. He swung Benjamin like a rolled-up rug over his shoulder and pulled himself up one rung of the ladder, then another. Benjamin's body was dead weight, and awkward, and I closed my eyes. I couldn't watch the climb, not with Benjamin looking so still and lifeless, and the Scar looking like he might drop him.

I thought about the apothecary, and wondered if he had some kind of healing power that could bring Benjamin back to life. I thought about the sweet smell of the Quintessence, how it smelled like life itself, and I wondered if there was still enough of it lingering in the air to do Benjamin any good.

The Scar reached the top of the ladder, and Danby and Sakharov helped drag Benjamin, in his heavy, waterlogged clothes, into the helicopter. Sakharov felt his neck for a pulse, and listened to see if he was breathing. Then he rolled him on his side and pressed his fists under Benjamin's sternum until seawater came up. Benjamin coughed, and threw up more water, and inhaled hoarsely, but his lips were purple with cold and he didn't seem to be awake.

The Scar, too, was freezing and gasping for breath, and the helicopter pilot swung us back toward the destroyer.

"We need vodka and blankets," Sakharov said.

I was pretty sure that vodka was *not* what Benjamin needed, and I knew there was nothing for us on the destroyer but pain and death. They had saved Benjamin so they could interrogate him, but now I couldn't let them hurt him, or force his father's secrets out of him.

In a pouch hanging on the back of a seat were the tools the pilot had taken out of his toolbox, including the heavy wrench Sakharov had used to tighten the trigger mechanism on the bomb. The Scar was exhausted, and Danby and Sakharov were distracted with trying to revive Benjamin. I slipped the wrench from the pouch, and no one noticed. Sakharov put his jacket over Benjamin, who was shivering uncontrollably. I didn't know what my next plan was, but if I could get rid of Danby, maybe I could persuade the pilot to land on Nova Zembla . . .

That was as far as I got before Danby turned to me. I saw suspicion cross his face, and I swung the wrench and hit his head with a sickening thud. He cried out in pain and surprise, and I caught his collar with my free hand. I tried to swing him toward the door, but he was heavy and immovable. He wrested the wrench away and held it furiously like a warrior with a club. His forehead was bleeding. I scrambled back and covered my head with my arm, waiting for the blow.

Then the pilot shouted something in Russian, and Danby turned.

I saw, out the windscreen, the dark cloud I had seen before, coming toward us. It was alone in the sky, and seemed to shift in the air, as if readying for something. Then it floated darkly around the windscreen, blotting out the light, and came through the open door. I felt a misty chill that wasn't like the blunt Arctic cold but more insidious, as if damp fingers of fog were clutching at my heart. The dark vapor enveloped the helicopter. It *wanted* to envelop us. It was attacking.

The pilot, blinded by the vapor over the windscreen, shouted something in Russian. Danby dropped the wrench as the helicopter pitched suddenly to one side, and we all grabbed for something to hold on to. I caught a seat belt in one hand and Benjamin in the other, with my arm across his cold chest and under his arm. The helicopter was heading fast toward the water.

The others were in chaos, shouting commands at each other. Benjamin started to slip from my arm, and I was going to lose him. He was too heavy, and the helicopter was tilting too sharply toward the waves below. Finally I had to make a choice: the seat belt or Benjamin. I let go and grabbed his other shoulder, and we slid toward the open door.

There was a sickening plunge, and then we hit the water and sank below the surface. It was like being immersed in icy slush. I kicked to the surface, my arms still tight around Benjamin's chest. When I got my head above water, I tried to breathe, but the muscles in my throat seemed to have seized up in the cold. I tried not to panic.

The swells were so big that I couldn't see where the

helicopter had crashed in the water, and I couldn't see the shore. I held Benjamin's head up and started to kick in the direction I thought the shore might be. I tried to remember how far from land we had been—a hundred yards? Two hundred? I had no idea. My throat relaxed enough to let a little air through, but my legs were so cold that they barely responded to my brain's commands. In junior lifesaving, back in Los Angeles, they had taught us to take off our heavy, wet clothes in a rescue, but that was in warm California, in summer—I didn't dare do it here. I'd need the clothes if we ever got to shore.

I kicked and pulled and sank, and fought my way up to the surface, where I caught a glimpse of the island, but it didn't seem to be drawing any closer.

Another wave came over both of us, dark and salty and freezing, and I kicked to the surface again. I heard Benjamin cough and sputter, regaining consciousness.

"So cold," he whispered.

"I know," I cried. "Kick! Help me!"

He seemed to grasp the situation, looking around at the waves as I struggled to tow him. "I can't," he said. "Let me go."

"No! Kick!"

"Let me go, Janie," he said. "Save yourself."

"Kick!" I screamed, drowning him out. But I knew he was right. I was going to have to make a decision. My hands and feet were completely numb. I might still be able to save myself, but if I kept trying to save him, we were both going to die.

The most important thing is not to become a victim yourself—the lifeguards had taught us that, on those giggling, sunny days at the beach, when the very idea seemed impossible.

"Please, Janie," Benjamin said, and then another wave came over the top of us.

It tumbled us down, filling my mouth with salt water, and we sank. The water was so dark and cold. I tried to kick toward the surface, but the surface didn't seem to be there. I felt myself drifting, still holding on to Benjamin's chest, feeling oddly calm. At least we would die together.

And then something caught me by the hair and pulled me up, and my face was above the surface again. I gasped, choking, as I was dragged backward across something hard. I tried to hold tight to Benjamin, but he was being dragged up, too—I didn't have his whole weight in my frozen arm anymore.

We were in a boat. It was narrow, and a man with a fur hood around his face had pulled us into it. He had a coat made of skins and a double-bladed paddle, and when he had stashed us both in the bow, he started to paddle hard toward the shore. My wet eyelashes froze in the wind, and I couldn't see clearly, so I closed my eyes, just for a second, to melt the ice.

Then I sank into a darkness far deeper than the cold ocean, and everything was gone.

CHAPTER 36

Escape

The voyage to Norway is, to this day, like a terrible dream, only partly remembered. I was in and out of consciousness, sometimes shaken awake by someone who wanted to feed me or to know that I was still alive. I was dimly aware of being in a smoky hut, wrapped in blankets and warmed by an enormous white dog lying on top of me. There was a round-faced woman who gave me soup. I saw Benjamin's face, unconscious and pale, cocooned under a second dog. Then I was in the bow of another boat that rode low on the water, hearing the sound of paddling behind me, and feeling rocked by the swells.

I woke when the sun rose, and saw that our rescuer was asleep sitting up, with his paddle resting across the gunwales. He had a round face like the woman who had fed me, although he was taller than she was, and he had dark skin with mottled marks across his cheekbones from frostbite or sunburn. His fur hood was tied tightly under his chin, and his mouth was set in determination, even as he slept. The boat was like a canoe, and one of the white dogs was in the stern behind the man. It lifted its head and whimpered when it saw I was awake, then settled its chin back on its folded paws.

Benjamin slept beside me in the bow, wrapped in blankets. The sea was vast and blue-gray in all directions, and I felt very small and insignificant. No one would notice if a wave swallowed up our little boat, and no one would know if Benjamin slipped away into his fever. He looked terrifyingly gray. I felt his forehead, which was cold, and he didn't respond to the touch. His eyes stayed closed.

Our rescuer woke up and said something in his language.

"I don't know what that means," I said. "Do you think he'll live?"

The man didn't understand what I'd said.

I pointed. "Benjamin," I said. For some reason it seemed important, if Benjamin was going to die with only two witnesses, that both of them knew his name.

"Benjamin," the man repeated. Then he put a hand on his chest. "Hirra," he said.

"Hirra," I said. I touched my coat the same way. "Janie."

"Janie," Hirra said. The *j*s in both of our names seemed to give him trouble. He reached forward to feel Benjamin's forehead, then made a longish statement. I decided he was saying something hopeful, even though his tone wasn't reassuring.

I pushed Benjamin's fever-damp hair inside his fur hood, curled up close to him, and slipped back into a hallucinatory sleep.

The next time Hirra shook me awake, I saw a boat towering above us, and voices were shouting from her rail. I struggled to sit up, thinking that the Soviet destroyer had found us, but then I realized that the boat was red, not gray. It was the still-disguised *Anniken*, and the apothecary and Count Vili were calling to us over her rail. I had a hazy memory of trying to describe the red icebreaker to the Samoyed woman who gave me soup, and trying to draw a map of Kirkenes on the floor, but I hadn't really thought we would get there. Some kind of hammocklike rig was lowered to the kayak, and I was put into it and lifted up into the boat, still wrapped tightly in blankets. I tried to tell the others that Hirra had saved our lives, and that Benjamin needed medicine, but people kept hushing me.

The last thing I remember was being carried below to my old cabin and put in my sleeping bag, and the apothecary measuring something out of a little bottle in the lamplight. The other bunk was bare.

"Where's Jin Lo?" I asked.

But the apothecary only gave me something bitter to drink, and then I was asleep.

When I woke, we were on a tiny airplane, and the apothecary was sitting beside me. He was grim-faced and remote, and he was writing in a notebook in a tiny, crabbed script that I recognized from the margins of the Pharmacopoeia. Benjamin was bundled in blankets, asleep on the other side of the narrow aisle. My mind felt clear for the first time since I'd fallen to the sea from the crashing helicopter.

"Will he be all right?" I asked.

"The fever has broken," the apothecary said, as if he had no faith in predictions, only in facts.

"Did you give him something to heal him?"

"I did," the apothecary said. "But it wasn't easy. He was very close to death."

Vili took up two seats in front of us, and he seemed to be asleep, too. Jin Lo wasn't on the plane, and I feared she had died on Nova Zembla and no one had told me in my vulnerable condition. I looked to the apothecary and he seemed to read my mind.

"She's fine," he said. "She's staying in Norway for now. It's safer for her there. She's too recognizable to the authorities in London."

I breathed again, relieved.

"You understand," he said, "that we stood no chance against a Soviet destroyer."

"I know," I said. "You made the right decision."

The apothecary shook his head. "Benjamin took the

extra avian elixir to go back for you. I should have known he would. I can never forgive myself. I made so many mistakes."

"But it all worked out."

The apothecary made a gesture that was both a shrug of assent and a head shake of dismissal. "I'll do better next time."

The idea of a *next time* made me feel tremendously tired. "Can I go sit with Benjamin?" I asked.

The apothecary nodded. I was amazed how weak my arms felt, pushing my body out of the seat.

"Janie," the apothecary said. "The police will be looking for us in London. Our forged papers identify us as a family. When we arrive at Heathrow, my son's name is James, and you're his sister, Victoria."

I smiled. "I'll see if we can work up some kind of spat."

"Good. Oh, and Victoria—"

"Yes?"

The apothecary's eyes were serious behind his spectacles. "I can never thank you enough for saving my son's life."

But I didn't need any thanks. I slid into the seat beside Benjamin's sleeping body and slipped my arm under his. After a few minutes, he stirred and interlaced his fingers through mine, and turned to look at me.

"Janie," he said hoarsely.

I was so happy to hear his voice that tears came to my eyes. "You're awake!"

He tried to sit up straighter, then winced as if moving hurt. "Ow," he said, reaching for his forehead.

"Don't move," I said. "Just sit."

He closed his eyes again. "You're here," he said. "My father didn't want to go back for you."

"He was trying to save you," I said. "But you did come back."

"I couldn't stay a bird. I tried, but I was falling."

"I know."

"I keep having dreams about it."

"Me too."

"But we're safe now?"

I nodded.

"And the others?"

"They're fine. Jin Lo's in Norway and Vili's asleep. Your father's here. He's so happy to have you back."

The apothecary handed me something across the aisle in a little brown bottle, for Benjamin to drink. After a few minutes, I could see the color coming back to his cheeks, and he was able to sit up straight without wincing. By the time the plane shuddered to a stop on the runway, he was able to walk off by himself.

We moved slowly through Heathrow Airport, and through customs, and my heart pounded as an official glanced at our forged papers. I hoped I wouldn't have to put on an English accent and say my name was Victoria. But the official asked us nothing. He stamped the papers and handed them back, looking bored.

As we left the terminal, we passed the portrait of the

young Queen Elizabeth II that my parents and I had seen on our arrival in London, only a month before. I remembered my father saying that things could be worse—I could be queen. But the queen looked very warm and dry and clean, and not wanted by the police. It didn't look so bad.

"What are we going to tell my parents?" I asked the apothecary.

"What do you want to tell them?"

"Everything," I said. "But I don't think they'll believe it."

He nodded. "We're all very tired," he said. "We'll take you home, and you can sleep. We'll meet tomorrow to tell them the whole story. Perhaps your friend Pip could come, too."

CHAPTER 37

The Wine of Lethe

We took a taxi to my parents' flat, and I went in alone. I expected them to be furious, but instead they caught me up in their arms, first my father, then my mother, crying and holding on to me as if they would never let go. I started crying, too, just because they were. They didn't seem to notice that my clothes smelled of seawater and reindeer fat. My father was so overwhelmed that he couldn't speak right away, a rarity for him.

"We were *sick* with worry, Janie," my mother said, wiping

tears from her face. "That ridiculous Mrs. Parrish said you were staying with someone named Sarah, but the Sarah we found at your school said you'd gone on a boat trip with someone's uncle. But whose uncle? What boat? The school knew nothing! How could you just go off like that?"

"Benjamin's father wants to meet tomorrow," I said. "So we can tell you everything."

"I'm going to wring that kid's neck," my father said.

"He saved my life," I said. "You'll understand when they tell you the whole story."

"When we went to the police, they said you'd been arrested," my mother said. "They said you'd been released to a teacher and then vanished, and they threatened us with deportation when we couldn't tell them where you were. But we were asking *them*! Janie, we've just been sick."

"I know, I'm sorry," I said. "But I'm so tired, I couldn't begin to tell it all. And I really, really want to take a bath."

They seemed to be afraid I might disappear again if they denied me anything, so they agreed. I understood, as I filled the tub, how truly luxurious it was to have a private bathroom in the flat. I was careful not to kick the drain lever, and I took my first bath—*alone*, in hot water, without Benjamin and Pip waiting for me to become invisible—in what seemed like a very long time.

When I was out and dry, my parents kissed me good night and said again how terrible it had been, and extracted promises of the *whole* story, no omissions, in the morning.

Then I climbed into bed. My diary was tucked beneath the mattress where I'd left it, and I brought it up to date, from sneaking Benjamin through my window a million years ago to the flight home. I fell asleep with the little red book still in my hand.

The next day was a Saturday, and I woke to yellow sunlight streaming through my window. I stretched my arms and legs, happy to be in a bed, in London, in my parents' flat: I almost thought the word *home*, which I never thought I'd use for any place except Los Angeles. My mother made scrambled eggs for breakfast, and they were the best things I'd ever eaten, hot and salty and delicious.

The telephone rang, and it was Benjamin. "My father and I will be in the newsreel cinema at Victoria Station in an hour," he said. "Can you and your parents come?" He sounded odd, but I couldn't put my finger on exactly how.

"Are you all right?"

"Just tired," he said. "We didn't get much sleep. Listen, you know that diary you keep?"

"Yes."

"Will you bring it? There are some things I want to check against my notebook."

I should have been suspicious right then. I should have been more wary all along. But I was so glad he was safe and healthy, and I wanted so much to see him and talk about everything we hadn't gone over yet, that I would have done anything he asked.

There were early daffodils blooming in window boxes as my parents and I walked to the Underground. The weather was brisk and cold, but it was balmy compared to the Arctic, and it was good to be outside on a beautiful day. My parents were eager to hear the apothecary's story, and were in surprisingly buoyant moods, as if he had already slipped them a potion that produced a happy complacency. They had even started speculating about what the nature of my absence might have been.

"You joined a traveling circus," my father guessed.

"You joined a band of wandering troubadours," my mother said.

"You were an elephant tamer?" my father said. "Or a tightrope walker. I can't decide."

"Just wait," I said. "It's much stranger than any of that."

At Victoria, we went into the darkened newsreel theater, and I spotted Benjamin and his father sitting with Pip in a back row, in the flickering light of a news story about fighting in Korea. Pip grinned and waved at me, from down the aisle.

"Were you followed?" Benjamin whispered.

"I don't think so," I said. My parents and I slid into the seats at the end of the row.

The first newsreel ended, and another began. It wasn't about a foiled nuclear test in Nova Zembla, but about new ladies' fashions. The models wore full skirts with tiny belted waists, like Maid Marian had worn when I'd first gone to Riverton Studios such a long time ago. The voice of the newscaster described the remarkable imagination that went into these new skirts and dresses. My parents were getting restless.

The apothecary must have been satisfied that there was nothing in the newsreels about us, because he stood. "Let's go to the refreshment counter," he whispered.

The theater was on a sort of mezzanine above the train station, and the tables were empty at that hour, and hidden from the crowds below.

"Thank you for helping us escape on the dock," I said to Pip.

"I shouldn't've—I missed ev'rything!"

"Did the policemen catch you?"

"Course not. Fat old coppers."

"This is our friend Pip," I told my parents. "Dad, you already know Mr. Burrows, the apothecary. And this is my mom, Marjorie Scott."

"I'm so pleased you've come," the apothecary said. "I owe you both an explanation."

"You bet you do," my father said.

"Please, sit down. Pip, will you fetch some glasses?"

We took a table, and my mother unwrapped her scarf, her face alert for lies. My father, too, surveyed the apothecary with skepticism and curiosity, deciding how trustworthy he was. I felt protective of him, and hoped he would live up to my parents' standards. Benjamin looked healthier than he had the day before. His freckles had gotten back some of their color.

"First, a toast," the apothecary said. He uncorked a bottle of champagne and poured the golden, fizzy liquid into the small glasses Pip brought. "I think it will be all right if the children have a sip today. We have so many reasons to be grateful."

He lifted his glass in a toast, and we all drank. The champagne was cold and tangy, and the bubbles tickled my nose.

The apothecary watched us. Finally, he said, in a deliberate tone, "We traveled by sea to an island in the archipelago of Nova Zembla."

"To *where*?" my father said.

"It's in Russia," I said.

"In *Russia*?"

"I have been concerned for some time," the apothecary said, "about our current race to develop catastrophic weapons. So I had been working on a way to contain an atomic bomb after it had been detonated. The Soviet Union was testing a new weapon in Nova Zembla, providing an ideal opportunity for our own test. I didn't know when we would have another chance."

I glanced at my parents, who looked like they were listening to someone speaking another language. I wasn't sure his meaning was sinking in. Or maybe they just thought he was insane. In a way, I thought he *was* insane, to tell them so much. It was a clear security risk. But I had told the apothecary that I wanted to tell them everything, and he seemed to have taken me at my word.

My father turned to me. "Is that really where you were, Janie?"

I nodded.

"Janie and Benjamin helped me escape capture in London," the apothecary said. "They wanted to go to Nova Zembla, but I refused to take them. In the end, they stowed away on the boat, over my objections. I have to say I was grateful for their help. But I can't imagine the anguish it must have caused you to have your daughter missing for so long. I offer my heartfelt apologies. Please, have some more champagne."

"Wait, back up," my father said, holding up his hands. "Did you say you wanted to contain an atomic bomb *after* it had been detonated?"

"To control its impact," the apothecary said. "Immediately after detonation."

"Are you working for the British government?" my mother asked.

The apothecary shook his head. "Our Security Service has a bit of a problem with spies, I'm afraid. And nations with atomic weapons, or with the intention to possess them, have their own interests in mind. Their power lies in the fear the bomb creates. If there were no fear, there would be no power. Those nations, including our own, would want to prevent the use and knowledge of any antidote to the bomb."

"So you're saying—it worked?" my father said.

"It did. And now that we've proven that it's possible, we can improve our methods, in league with scientists in other countries doing similar work. If a bomb is ever used, as the unimaginably destructive force that it is, we will try to be ready."

"Wait—wait," my father said. "I'm sorry to keep backtracking. But I'm trying to follow you. How did you get to Nova Zembla?"

"We took a boat until we reached Russian waters and were stopped by a Soviet patrol," the apothecary said. "Then we flew."

"In a plane?"

"As birds."

I cringed a little. I knew my parents weren't going to believe that.

"As *birds*?"

"Yes."

My father turned to me, expecting me to tell him the *actual* truth.

"It's spectacular," I said. "You'd love it. I was a robin."

My father blinked.

The apothecary said, "And now Benjamin and I are going away."

I whirled on him. "Wait—*what*?"

"It isn't safe for us here," he said. "We have a train in . . ." He checked his watch. "Four minutes."

"But you can't just leave!"

"Listen, Janie," Benjamin said. He sat forward in his chair and caught my hands, turning me to face him. "We have to go. If you thought about it, you'd know. None of us is safe. The thing you drank, that champagne, will take a little time, but it's going to make you forget everything that happened in the last three weeks."

"Forget?"

"You better be bloody joking," Pip said.

"You've *drugged* us?" my father said.

"Davis," my mother said. "Please."

"You'll still be able to get through your days," the apothecary said. "But everything about the last few weeks will be erased. My shop, Benjamin, the trip to Nova Zembla—all of that will be gone."

"He drugged us, Marjorie!" my father said. He stalked away from the table in a fury, the way he did when he needed to cool off, and my mother went after him, to calm him down.

I said, "Benjamin, you can't do this! Those memories are *mine*! I saved your life! More than once!"

"I did too!" Pip said.

"I know," Benjamin said. "But there's no other way. It would be best if you gave me your diary now."

I shook my head. "No. I promise not to show it to anyone."

"I'm trying to keep you safe."

"But I need to remember you!"

"Please, Janie."

His eyes were pleading, and I took the little book from my pocket and handed it over.

He looked at its red cover. "I hope it says that you fancy me," he said. "And that wasn't just the Smell of Truth talking."

I was too furious to answer—it was so *obvious* how I felt about him, and we had been through so much since the Smell of Truth. I felt my eyes fill with tears. "Where will you go? How do you know you'll be safe?"

"Whole cities could be wiped out if there's a war," he said. "We have a responsibility to protect them."

"So let me go with you!"

"You have to stay here with your parents." He took both my hands and looked down at them. "Listen, Janie, do you remember that night on the bow of *Anniken*?"

"Yes," I said. Tears were running down my face now, and I let them.

"I don't think any potion could erase that," he said. "Not for me. I hope you'll remember that part."

A loose strand of hair had fallen across my face, and Benjamin tucked it behind my ear. He smiled. "American hair," he said.

Then he leaned forward, and I could feel the warmth of his breath and smell his clean, soapy skin. I wondered where he had slept and bathed, but then his lips touched mine and I felt a steady current of electricity running through my whole body. I knew I would never forget that feeling, as long as I lived.

Then a vaguely familiar, silkily snide voice above us said, "Hello, Jane."

We both looked up, and it was Detective Montclair, the wispy-haired policeman who had arrested us at school. He was standing on the other side of the low iron railing that ran around the refreshment counter's tables. His partner O'Nan stood beside him.

The apothecary stood to greet them, extending a glass across the railing. "Gentlemen," he said. "Will you join us for some champagne? I'll open another bottle."

I remembered how Detective Montclair had reminded me of a cobra, swaying slightly, waiting to strike. "You're under arrest for treason, Mr. Burrows," he said. "I'd advise you to come quietly. Mr. and Mrs. Scott, I'm afraid you'll have to come with me, too."

"Why?" my father said. "What for?"

"Colluding with traitors?" the detective said. "Falsely reporting your daughter missing? Criminal mischief? The question is whether to send you back to the United States to face questions about your Communist friends, or to lock you up here."

"I can explain everything," the apothecary said. "Officer, please join us for a drink."

Officer O'Nan shook his head, but I thought he looked longingly at the bottle.

A train was announced over the loudspeaker. While everyone paused to listen, Benjamin sprang from his seat and vaulted over the low metal railing, running for the stairs that led down from the mezzanine. The policemen ran after him. The apothecary dashed away through the other tables.

Pip and I looked at each other. My memory of the exact connection we had to the apothecary was starting to grow hazy.

"What's going *on*?" my mother said.

"We have to help them get away," Pip said.

My mind cleared again, and I remembered that Benjamin had been saying good-bye. Everything in me protested, but I knew Pip was right. We left my parents and sprinted down the stairs, taking them three at a time.

When we reached the tracks, I saw Benjamin pulling his father up into the door of a train that was starting to move. The two policemen were gaining on them. Pip ran ahead and darted between the policemen's legs, grabbing their ankles, and they all went down in a sprawl.

I dodged around the fallen men and leaped onto the car behind Benjamin's as the train started to pick up speed. My foot slipped and I clung to the door handle, my feet hanging free over the platform for a few long, dizzy-making seconds. Then I recovered and pulled myself up.

I looked back and saw the policemen on the platform struggling up after their collision with Pip, but then my mother buttonholed them, brushing off their coats, asking if they were all right. She had a hand on Officer O'Nan's chest, and I could tell she was keeping him from getting up, while pretending to help him. Through my gathering fog I thought how brave and smart she was. Pip was still tangled in the policemen's legs and loudly complaining. My father leaped onto the train beside me.

The train was full of passengers stowing their bags and finding their seats, and my father and I made our way through them, dodging bodies. When I reached the passageway between our car and the next, Benjamin was crouched on the other side, pouring a liquid out of a vial. There was a strange smoke coming up from the rattling floor, over the couplings between the two train cars, but it wasn't the orange smoke Jin Lo had used to get us out of the bunker. It was pale gray, with wisps of yellow, and had a sulfurous smell.

"Benjamin!" I said.

He looked up, and his eyes were sad. He stood and pocketed the vial. "We can't get arrested, Janie," he said. "You understand, right?"

"Pip stopped the police," I said. "They aren't on the train!"

"We can't take the chance."

"Just let me go with you!" I was about to step over the gray-yellow smoke, but my father caught my arm and I looked down. The floor was dissolving between our car and Benjamin's as the metal corroded and started to fall away. The sulfur smell became stronger, and the smoke thicker in the air. I could see the exposed coupling between the two trains, until that started to crumble, too.

"Wait!" I said, not knowing if I was talking to Benjamin or to the floor. It was impossible to take my eyes off the melting of everything that kept the two cars attached. Soon a single cable was all that was left, and finally it corroded and snapped. The front of the train seemed to leap free of its burden, and Benjamin was racing away.

"No!" I said, reaching out, in an agony of regret. My father put his arm around me.

"I'm sorry I put Janie in danger, Mr. Scott!" Benjamin called. "But she won't be, now. She'll be safe!"

Then the disappearing train was swallowed up in a pea-soup fog, which had settled over the city out of nowhere. The last I saw of Benjamin was a flash of his sandy hair in the doorway of the car.

Our part of the train had come to a noisy stop, engine-less and helpless. My father and I climbed down and pushed past the confused people milling about on the platform. Someone said the engineer had stopped the train on the tracks ahead, but I knew that Benjamin and his father would have vanished already into the suspiciously sudden fog. There was no point going after them. We walked back almost a mile along the tracks, through the confused crowds and over the awkward stones between the ties.

The strange champagne we had drunk was making its stealthy way to our brains, carried by its innocent-seeming bubbles—as I would later discover all champagne does—and our memories were fading fast. My father seemed to grasp at the questions that occurred to him in flashes. "Did that boy's father say you became *birds*?"

"I think so," I said.

"What did he mean by that?"

"I'm not sure. I remember flying, sort of. And there was a skylark." I thought hard about the skylark. "That seems important. But everything around it is too hard to remember."

When we got back to the station, my mother was waiting for us on the platform.

"I feel so strange," she said. "And I know I should know *why* I feel so strange, but it keeps escaping me."

We found Pip sitting at the bottom of the staircase that led up to the newsreel theater, with Detective Montclair and Officer O'Nan. The apothecary's two bottles of champagne were on the step between his feet. I had just enough of my memory left to recognize them.

"I'm just having a drink with these two ducks an' geese," Pip said. "Seemed a good idea at the time, but now I haven't got the foggiest *why*."

The three of them had polished off the second bottle, and the detective, all his snakelike cunning and his threats of deportation vanished, stood to shake my father's hand.

"How do you do," he said. "I'm Detective Charles Montclair of Scotland Yard. I don't believe we've met."

CHAPTER 38

The Guardians of Peace

My life, as it began in Victoria Station that day, was very strange. The memory loss of those of us who drank the champagne was precise and focused: The last three weeks were simply gone. My parents and I were able to make it back to our flat on St. George's Street—my father seemed to know that we needed to get there quickly, and he pulled my mother and me through the streets by the hand—but we had to rebuild our lives from the clues that we found there.

My parents still knew that they had a job working for Olivia Wolff, and they could find Riverton Studios, but they had completely lost the thread of the storyline they'd been working on, and had to face Olivia's bafflement and impatience with no explanation. Olivia thought the trauma of my disappearance had made them black out the memories. But they weren't traumatized, because they didn't remember that I'd disappeared, and neither did I. Our landlady, Mrs. Parrish, was sheepish and apologetic around my parents, and sharply disapproving of me, for no apparent reason.

I had a uniform and books from St. Beden's, so I went to school there and followed the written class schedule I found tucked in my notebook. The pretty blond girl who sat in front of me in Latin asked how the boat trip had gone. I looked around to the empty desk behind me, thinking she was talking to someone else.

"With Benjamin," she prompted.

"Who's that?"

Sarah stared at me. "Oh, *no!*" she said. "It happened to you, too!"

"What did?"

"You and Pip, you both forgot everything."

"Who's Pip?" I asked.

The awkward young Latin teacher, Miss Walsh, asked us please to stop talking unless we had something to say to the whole class. Sarah rolled her eyes and passed me back a note: *I miss Mr. Danby!*

Who's Mr. Danby? I wrote.

Sarah read the note and I watched her braid swing as she shook her head slightly. There was something about that braid, and about the slope of her neck beneath it, that seemed important, but I couldn't think why. She scribbled a response and passed it back. *You have to come to lunch with me.*

Sarah's friends made room for me at their table, which took the anxiety off going to a lunchroom I'd never seen before. The girls were silly, but I liked Sarah's boyfriend, Pip, at once. He was shorter than Sarah, with wide eyes like some animal I couldn't think of, and a quick smile. He was new to St. Beden's, too, having transferred from the East End.

"I showed up at my old school," he said, "and they said I had some kind of scholarship here. It's like I got hit over the head or something, and three weeks is gone."

"Three weeks *are* gone," Sarah said.

Pip grinned. "She wants me to talk all posh," he said. "But you'll like it here. I'm in chess club, which I learned when this bloke Timothy comes up and gives me half a crown out o' the blue. You should join."

"I'm not very good at chess."

"Perfect!" Pip said. "Then we'll play for money."

Again I felt a little electrical charge in my brain, as if my synapses were trying to tell me something, but I didn't know what it was.

"There was this Russian bloke who was president of the chess club, they say," Pip went on. "But he moved to America, so now I'm president. I think I'll move to America one day. You're from there, right? Is it grand?"

I said it was—but that London was, too.

When Sarah found out my parents were writing a TV show about Robin Hood, she wanted to go see the studio, so I took Pip and her to Riverton after school, on the train. My parents were just happy to see I was making friends—any friends—but Olivia Wolff fell in love with Pip, with his enormous eyes and his acrobat's grace. "Where did you *find* him?" she said.

Olivia took a cab that night to the East End to see Pip's parents, who didn't have a telephone, so she could cast him as the youngest member of the Merry Men. Pip loved the job and the money and the attention. When the show aired, people started recognizing him in the street, and I thought it must have been the first time in Sarah's life that she didn't get all the attention of people walking by, just for being beautiful. I guessed it would be good for her, if she could stand it.

I joined chess club, and Pip was a patient teacher. He showed me how to think three or four moves ahead instead of leaping headlong into the moment. Slowly I became a passable opponent.

Sergei Shiskin, the club's ex-president, sent a short letter from Sarasota, Florida, with a blurry photograph of a man with a beard and a woman in a headscarf standing on a pretty beach with two teenage children: a tall, solidly built boy and a pale, fragile-looking girl. It was hard to see their faces, but they seemed to be smiling, squinting in the Florida sunlight. The letter said Sergei was fine and liked his new school. At the end, it said, *PS Tell Janie and Benjamin I said thank you, please. I don't have the address.*

"Does he mean me?" I asked Timothy, the spotty boy who had given me the letter to read.

"Sure," Timothy said. "You're Janie."

"But I don't know him."

"Course you do! You were on the science team together!"

"What science team? There is no science team."

Eventually our friends got used to the irritating amnesia. It was just a thing about Pip and me, like the fact that I was from California and Pip was from the East End: We'd both lost the same three weeks of our lives.

Some British agents in suits came to question my family, but we had nothing to tell them. They asked about Mr. Danby, and I said I thought he'd been the Latin teacher at my school, but I had never met him, and now we had Miss Walsh. They also asked about an apothecary named Marcus Burrows and his son, Benjamin, who was my age. We knew there was a boarded-up apothecary shop around the corner, but that was all.

The Cold War carried on, and the Americans and the Soviets kept working on their nuclear weapons. There were rumors that England was about to stage a test in Australia. We still had bomb drills at school, but when the loud alarm bell went off and people started climbing under tables and desks, I didn't feel afraid—though of course I didn't know why.

🜋

Exactly a year after I returned to St. Beden's, I got a package in the mail, with no return address and with a strange postmark that I didn't recognize. I took it into my room and tore off the brown paper. Inside was a small red diary.

I opened the book and recognized my own handwriting, but I didn't remember writing the words. I flipped through the pages, reading a February entry about how furious I was at my stupid parents for dragging me to London. Then I read one about my miserable first day at St. Beden's, and how the only good part was meeting a boy named Benjamin Burrows who wanted to be a spy. One entry was interrupted when Benjamin climbed the tree outside my bedroom, because his father was missing and he had nowhere else to go.

Memories started coming back in bits and pieces. Something made me stop reading and flip to the blank pages at the end.

There was a note on one of those pages, and it wasn't in my handwriting. It seemed to have been written carefully, with thought, and it said:

Dear Janie,

It should be safe now for you to have this. I've read it every day. I

hope you don't mind. I don't think
you would have minded, before.
Reading it is how I kept you with
me. I'm sending it back now to help
you understand why we had to go
away, and to tell you that I'll come
back. It might be another year, it
might be more, I don't know. But
start working on your chess. I'll
expect a good opening.

Love, B.

It was a rare sunny day at the beginning of spring, and
the tree that Benjamin had climbed to get to my window was
bursting with green buds. I *had* a good chess opening, and I
sat with the diary on my lap, feeling like I might spill over
with a helpless, giddy laughter, and with a sad and serious ache
underneath. I hadn't understood the strange feelings I'd been
having all year, but now I did. And I knew without question
that Benjamin was out there somewhere with his father, looking out for us, risking his life to keep the world safe.

And that I would see him again.

Acknowledgments

I'm indebted to my friends Jennifer Flackett and Mark Levin for the existence of this book, for bringing Janie and Benjamin and the mysterious apothecary to me, and for trusting me with the beginnings of a story they cared deeply about. They described what they had imagined as a movie, let me run with it, and talked through the convolutions with me as it changed. In the process I discovered two new worlds: wintry Cold War London, and the incredibly welcoming world of Penguin children's publishing, and it's been a life-changing adventure.

In writing the book, I drew on David Kynaston's *Austerity Britain 1945-1951*, the exhibition *The Children's War* at The Imperial War Museum in London, and Lyn Smith's *Young Voices: British Children Remember the Second World War*.

The Adventures of Robin Hood was an early television program produced by Hannah Weinstein, who moved to London in the early 1950s and hired blacklisted U.S. writers to write scripts under pseudonyms. I have taken liberties with the real details of the show, as I have with the historical figure of the physicist Andrei Sakharov.

The real Chelsea Physic Garden in London is, in fact, a magical place, growing medicinal plants from all over the world. There really is a mulberry tree in the center with draping branches under which you can hide. Whether the garden grows herbs that can make you tell the truth or become a bird, I'm not sure, but I think it's important to allow for the possibilities.

MAILE MELOY is the award-winning author of the short-story collections *Both Ways Is the Only Way I Want It* and *Half in Love* and the novels *Liars and Saints* and *A Family Daughter*. This is her first novel for young readers.

www.mailemeloy.com

www.theapothecarybook.com